IMMORTAL

SUFFERING

I0603449

BOOK 2

SHANA J. CALDWELL

First Edition

ISBN 9780646814414 (paperback)

Editing by Tara Routley
Cover Front Design by Salome Totladze
Cover Back Design and Wrap by Cover Design by Covers by Combs

This is
for all the ones who struggle to find hope in their darkest nights. Without the darkness, stars can't shine.

ACKNOWLEDGMENTS

Well, here I find myself again at the end of another novel. Another piece of Ali's story has been told, and if it wasn't for my supporters and my readers I don't think I would have continued Ali's story.

First off I'd like to start this by thanking my amazing editor, Tara Routley. Without her eye for detail and passion for these characters and this series I wouldn't have been able to produce the best version of this novel.

Secondly, I can't explain the gratitude I have for Salome Totladze. She's one of the best artists out there and I'm so proud to have her artwork as my cover!

Thanks to the continuous supporters in my life, without their constant courage and reassurance I'm not sure there would have been a book two.

Thanks to the writing community on Instagram and Facebook, I've made so many valuable friends through my writing and I can't be more grateful.

I'll make this short and sweet, but thank you from the bottom of my heart. I can't wait to finish Ali's story in Immortal Reckoning, I'll see you all there.

PROLOGUE

Clouds clustered in the sky, hiding the full moon. The two shadows walked along, moving at an inhuman pace as they searched the low valley for a specific creature. A creature that could turn the tides if a war was to come between vampires and humans. They'd been gone for weeks now, determined to bring some sort of information to their King.

They turn into a patch of moonlight; the glow illuminates their identical features, their Asian heritage is dominant in the moonlight. One twin's hair touches their shoulders while the other's hair is spiked.

Down the valley, beneath a darkened cliff face they hear a low screech. If it wasn't for their inhuman hearing they would have missed it.

Deep in the valley a beast awakens, unlike any other beast the world has faced. The shadows move like liquid motion as they manoeuvre to the sound; this is the break they'd been waiting for. The break they needed.

As they approach the creature's lair they ready themselves, for these creatures are their own sort entirely. It's been a long time since they'd ruled by the vampire's side, it had been so long since the twins had seen one so free in the wild.

They enter a large cave, water droplets echo throughout the large, open space. Their steps are as soft as a feather as they go deeper, their vampire vision aiding them.

At the end of the cave they are greeted with darkness. Hundreds of golden eyes open and focus on the twins. A high screech envelopes them. The twins grin at each other before facing the creatures.

It was time for a new world.

1

Allison

Wind whistles through the cracked-open window of the sitting room as a storm begins to brew in the night sky. Lightning dances in the darkness, listening to a song my ears can't hear as it journeys closer to the castle. Lightning flashes in the sky, while a rumble vibrates the sitting room; lighting up the city of Dafria. Between us and the city is a huge thicket of forest that protects us from lurking eyes. What I hope will protect us.

I curl my legs beneath myself on the red Victorian sofa, pulling the black fur blanket over my legs. I'd been sitting out here in the darkness for a long time now, listening to the storm. I'd been here for less than a week and I already wanted to go home. I wanted to crawl into my own bed and forget all of this.

Unfortunately that wasn't how it worked. Did I even have a home anymore?

My small town was long behind me now; my old life was now a mere memory. After the small battle, Kalabhiti had insisted I stay with him in this ridiculously huge castle until he saw fit that I was safe to be in the city.

Which would be never. Because although I'm part vampire; I'm also part human. A lot of vampires wouldn't take to me strolling the city streets lightly. Although Kalabhiti has a responsibility to me, he also has a responsibility to his people, his kind. I knew he would want to put their needs first; which put me on a tight leash. I didn't like being held captive. I hadn't seen Nardia since the river although I could vaguely sense her down our bond every now and then. The morning after the battle, all vampires I'd seen in the castle had vanished. On strict orders I assume to not go near me.

I was an abomination. A monster. My identity wasn't my own anymore, and I couldn't come to terms with that. *Wouldn't.*

I get up and walk over to the window, while I was consumed by my thoughts heavy rain began to pour down, blowing wild droplets onto the cobblestone floor beneath the window. I pull the window shut and lock it. I press my hand briefly to the cold glass and a sense of longing drowns me. Freedom seems so close but so far away.

I don't want to be here.

I keep my footsteps light as I make my way through the sitting room; a huge bookcase hugs either wall beside the wooden door. I lower my eyes and keep walking. I didn't deserve books. I shut the wooden door behind me and steadily walk down the open hallway. A thin run of red carpet runs to the next opening before ending, helping keep my footsteps unheard.

To my left are six candles hanging from the wall, a knight's armour sits silently in the middle. A shiver racks my body as I look away, I never understood having empty armour for display; it had scared me more times than I'd like to admit.

To my right are six, large windows looking out into the forest. Thunder booms in the sky, rumbling the ground beneath me again. The knight's armour clangs lightly. I pick up my pace, wanting to be out of this hallway and in the safety of my temporary room.

Lightning strikes somewhere deep in the forest; the force blows the candles out. I look out the closest window in amazement and freeze. My throat closes up as my eyes widen.

Outside, in the middle of the thunderstorm a creature crawls. Its pale skin illuminated by the lightning; its bald head is focusing on something on the damp ground. I put my hand over my mouth, afraid it might hear my small intake of breath.

Its head comes up again as it leans on its back legs, opening its black mouth in what I assume is a scream. I turn and flee from the hallway, not caring if Kal hears me. My heartbeat is loud in my ears as I round the corner left, running down a similar hallway to the last. The room I'd been staying in was at the far end of the castle; it overlooks the garden below.

The hallway comes to an end as I open the wooden door to my right. Both sides open up to other hallways; wooden doors spot the dark walls. In front of me is a small staircase that shapes in an L, I take the steps two at a time; turning and running up the last few. I run down the hallway, at the very end on a cement post a gargoyle sits; snarling angrily at me. I come to a slow stop. It blinks.

It blinks.

I shake my head, it's a cement decoration. They couldn't come to life. I walk closer to the right wall; the end wooden door is the key to my safety. I move swiftly as I reach the door, slamming it behind me.

I breathe heavy against its frame, taking a moment to regulate my breathing. What on earth was that thing? I'm sure Kalabhiti would have warned me if he had creatures lurking in the forest as guards. I flick on the light as I look around my small room; opposite me my window sits open. Rain has drenched the curtains and a small puddle has formed. I take slow steps towards my bed, its brown wooden frame sturdy. I lean a hand on the white doona as I glimpse under the bed. Nothing.

I stand back and do a circle of the room. I only had the bed suite, which consisted of the bed, the two bedside tables, a chest of drawers and a small wardrobe. I owned nothing, I had no idea who owned the clothes in the wardrobe or drawers before me but they fit fairly well.

Apart from feeling like a trapped animal I was grateful for everything, having a roof over my head was the main one. Since the dead Queen was a part of me, Kalabhiti didn't have a choice but to treat me any less than well. After all, I had the blood of a woman he once loved running through my veins.

I walk over to the draws and I pull out a white towel from the bottom drawer; laying it over the small puddle. I shut the window tightly cutting off the cold breeze, the garden dark beneath the window. I'd have to take the curtains off tomorrow and hang them out in the sun.

Oh that's right; there is no sun in this place.
I should have known. The vampires had advanced so much they'd managed to form a protection spell around their city; every day was lived in darkness. My days would be lived in darkness. I didn't know how long I would last before going crazy.

I turn the light off, crawling into the cool sheets. I lay back and stare at the ceiling in the darkness. My physical injuries had healed, I was functioning perfectly normal. My mind was scattered, I had never felt so isolated and lonely in my life. It was like a slap in the face knowing I had no one; the one solid friendship I'd made with Xavier had been broken.

I'd done that willingly, and I'd never see him again. I didn't want to know what he would think of me, after seeing what power I possessed, seeing what damage I could do. I had so many questions, but I refused to confide in Kalabhiti. I certainly didn't trust him, I know now everyone has their own motives. I had mine, but they were simple.

I wanted to escape, I wanted to be free of this curse I'd been given. It was no blessing in my eyes, I wanted to be normal. I'd avoided looking in the bathroom mirror, I couldn't know how much my eyes had changed, how much my vampire part was overtaking. I'd pushed my power deep down inside myself, locked it away in a vault and thrown it into a black hole. I never wanted to use it again.

A soft knock comes from the door; a hesitant knock. I lay still in the darkness; I don't think the creature I'd seen would be able to knock so it ruled it down to one person who could be on the other side of the door. The knock comes again.

"Yes?" I say, sitting up in the dark. The door opens with a creak; Kalabhiti steps into the room and shuts the door behind him. I can barely make him out but his presence seems to fill the space around me.

"What's up?" I ask, my hands clenching and unclenching the bed sheet. I'd tried my hardest to avoid any conversation with him with no one else around.

"I heard you running through the castle." his voice is soft as he stands in the darkness; I vaguely make out his shadow as he walks towards the window. He gently grabs the curtains; examining their drenched state.

"Oh, um yeah. Got a spook I guess." I say lightly. If I saw the creature again I would let him know, until then it wasn't my problem.

"A spook?" he asks, he pulling back the curtains and looking down at the garden, which is still in darkness.

"Yeah you know? Like I got scared and spooked myself out." I explain, lying back on my side to watch him. I curl my hands under my head.

"I can't say in all my years I've ever heard that terminology. Why were you scared?" he lets the curtain go and faces towards me, leaning against the window.

"You'd think you would have, considering you're a mummy. I don't know, thought I saw something. It was just the trees though. I'm not a huge fan of these storms." I say quietly. I nibble my lip as I watch him. My eyes are adjusting to the darkness and I'm able to see more of him, he's wearing a loose black shirt and a pair of loose, white long pants. He must have been sleeping, if he ever sleeps.

"I am most definitely not a mummy, the opposite if anything. But alright then, if you say so. We only have the storms once a month, just to keep the wildlife and plants flourished."

"Don't they need sun?" I ask. As he crosses his muscular arms over his chest, my heart picks up its pace. I hate myself for it; the last thing I wanted was to be attracted to him.

My heart got the better of me last time and I did not want that to happen again.

"Not the ones here, the animals adjust easily whereas the plants are a new species we've created to only live in the darkness. If there was light they would all die."

"Well that's morbid." I roll onto my back, the sheet slipping down to my waist. I rest my hands on top of my belly and stare at the ceiling.

"They're immortal, only the sun can kill them. Everything dies eventually and turns to dust, even I will one day." his voice is soft as he says this. I would die too and I knew this, it wasn't what scared me.

What scares me most is that if I fully turn into a vampire where did that leave me? I would be dead, and not just physically. I didn't want to live for hundreds of years, that isn't in the cards for me. It hadn't even been a thought that'd crossed my mind.

"That's true. Maybe then you won't be such a pain in my ass." I say lightly, trying to lighten the mood. I didn't want to think about me being vampire. I look towards him, he's smirking at me. A small dimple on his left cheek catches my attention.

"You really think I'm that bad?" he asks; I roll my eyes at him. Yes. No. Maybe? I didn't know.

"You act like it isn't obvious." I look back to the ceiling and twiddle my fingers together.

"Why are you so nervous around me?" he asks. I frown at the question. My fingers stop moving.

"I wouldn't say I'm nervous. More like cautious." I say slowly. Why would he think I'm nervous?

"Why would you be cautious? Is it because I'm a vampire?"

"Yes and no. You're the vampire king; of course I'd be a little nervous around you. But I need to be cautious because I won't let myself fall back into the same thing that happened last time." I say, looking back towards him. I don't hold the eye contact for long, I look down and focus on his lips.

Which really do nothing to help me.

"It's just strange to me. Although I'm a king I also saved your life… I remember seeing you in a dream while I was in the city. You seemed comfortable around me then, so why now is the wall going up?" My cheeks burn at the mention of that…dream.

"I don't see how it's strange. I'm sure there are plenty of people who are nervous around you, not just me. So why do you care?" I ask, avoiding his last question. He takes a deep breath and looks away from me, back to the door. I pick at my fingernails.

"I just thought you would be accustomed to being around vampires, considering your bond with Nardia." I sit up on my elbows and watch him. My hair falls over my chest and shoulders with the movement; the silver strands seem to glow in the darkness.

"That doesn't answer my question. What Nardia and I have is completely different. It's a friendship and well, we're bonded as well." I suck my bottom lip, I didn't think there was a way to erase the bond we had, I wasn't sure I ever wanted to. He sighs and looks at me, his eyes never leaving mine.

"It isn't important why I care or not, I just want you to be comfortable and feel comfortable here. Cassidar was much better at this than I ever was, but I'm trying." his jaw tightens at the mention of his dead queen. I sit up and look away from him, studying my hands in my lap. I could see everything in the room, as if there was a dull light on behind my eyes that could show me everything.

"How am I meant to feel comfortable here? I've been taken from one messed up situation and put into another. What even happened to those other vampires?" I ask, meeting his eyes. I had to know if some lived, I had to know it wasn't all for nothing.

"We managed to get half out."

"What happened to the other half?" I whisper, my stomach tightens. I think I already knew.

"We were too late. They'd already been ashed. The survivors we have are in recovery, I'm sure they'd be more than grateful for your help." he says softly. I look away. I'd been responsible for killing half of those vampires, and the countless humans that would have been casualties. I hope the children were okay.

"Ali, you did better than anyone expected." he takes a step closer and I focus on him. He stills, seeming like he wants to come closer but thinks better of it.

"It wasn't good enough. They all should have been saved." my hands shake in my lap at the memory of them cramped in those small cages, fangs ripped out. I search his face, not knowing what I needed to make me feel better.

"It gets easier. I promise. Casualties on both sides will always be something we can't avoid. Once you're more settled in I will take you to see the vampires we managed to rescue. It's hard, but it's worth it. You can't pick and choose with war, you just have to take it in your stride and adapt."

Easy for him to say, he's had hundreds of years to practice and adjust and overcome. I didn't. I try and push the guilt down, not wanting to show it to him. I didn't need him more worried about me.

"Okay. Thanks." I lie back down and shut my eyes. I was done with this conversation. It was all too much for one night. He takes the hint, his footsteps are light as he heads to the door; I feel him pause, then the door opens and shuts behind him. I quickly walk over and lock the door before collapsing back into bed.

Tears escape and land on my pillow softly. I swipe at my eyes, only causing the tears to fall more. I roll onto my side and sob into my pillow as I look out the window. Lightning briefly lights up the room. I felt the rage of the storm inside of my heart, a never ending battle between the light and the darkness.

What if darkness is all there is to me?

Allison

"Allison, it's nearly mid-day. You can't hide in your room forever." Kalabhiti's deep voice rumbles through my closed door. I stay facing the open window; I had been doing just that before he'd interrupted. Hiding in my room forever. I didn't plan to leave anytime soon.

"You've missed breakfast and you're going to miss lunch. This has been going on for a week now." I growl under my breath. I wanted to be left alone. I didn't want to get out of bed or get food. I hear the door knob turn, but catch on the lock. I'd only just begun locking it; he had a tendency to sneak in and leave breakfast on the bed side table and I didn't like intruders. I didn't know to handle him being so nice.

"Allison." he sighs heavily against the door, a small part of me feels guilty. I knew I couldn't hide away from everything forever, but I wanted to try to as long as I could. He has no idea what is going on in my head.

"I'll come out for lunch. But that's it, nothing else." I say weakly, I was stubborn I knew that. I was also raised with manners and knew it would be ungrateful for me to be a brat. I hear his footsteps walk away. I roll out of bed and turn the light on. I shrug off the overly large tee shirt I'd been sleeping in which I'd stolen from Kal's dirty laundry basket in the bathroom and slip on a loose pair of white silk tracksuits with tight cuffs at the ankles. I pull on the long sleeved loose crop top to match. I walk slowly to the door, listening. Silence.

I unlock the door and leave. I follow the path to the sitting room; I walk past the open hallway ignoring the knight in armour. I continue down the current hallway. The house is lit up, each candle and light bulb on. There was always darkness with light; I could see it in the places the light couldn't reach.

Two potted plants sit on each side of the open archway to my left. I walk through into the kitchen. It took my breath away the first time I entered; it seemed to be as large as my house. The high rise roof was sculpted telling the story of vampires at war, fighting with tooth and nail against human warriors clad in steel armour.

The spotless stainless steel benches ran against the back wall, with an island strip in the middle. Over it pots of all shapes hung, to my left was the ovens and stoves. To the far right end of the kitchen was another archway. I walk through to find Kalabhiti sitting at the end of the long wooden table, a cup of blood resting between his folded hands.

My shoulders sag slightly, this wasn't just breakfast; I was going to get a talking to. He sits deathly still, not acknowledging my entrance. The space beside him has a plate full of freshly cut up fruit; waiting patiently for me. His long black hair is pulled tightly into a low pony tail; his black skin tight armour bulging against his muscular chest. I look away, not wanting to let my mind even think of him that way. I don't think I could ever trust someone the way I did with Xavier. I take a hesitant seat beside him, keeping my eyes on the full plate. I clasp my hands tightly together under the table.

"You're going to eat all of it before you leave this room." his voice is calm; in the corner of my eye he takes a sip from his cup. My mouth tightens in distaste. I don't want to eat. *I wonder what human blood tastes like.*

"I will sit here as long as it takes for you to finish the fruit. No ifs or buts. You've barely eaten this whole time you've been here. I won't sit around and do nothing while I watch you starve." I can feel his eyes burning the side of my face. The power of his shadows brush against my right leg, tickling it slightly.

"I'm just not hungry." I say quietly. He places his glass firmly on the table.

"Look at me." I keep my head down.

"*Allison look at me.*" under the force of his words I break my gaze with the fruit and am immediately ensnared in his deep, lightless eyes. The vampire part of me adored his eyes, wanted to do everything for him in the beat of a heart. My human part wanted to be stubborn and make everything harder than it had to be. Unfortunately I was currently more vampire than human.

"Please *eat the fruit.*" without breaking eye contact my right hand automatically closes around the silver fork and pierces a piece of strawberry. My mouth opens robotically, the strawberry falls onto my tongue. I take a bite.

My mouth explodes with flavour, the sweetness awakening the hunger I'd been ignoring. I break eye contact and look back at the fruit, piece by colourful piece I begin to devour it. Once I've finished the last piece of banana I place the fork on the table. The trance he held over me now broken. A part of me feels violated, forced against my free will. A small part of me is thankful; I'd begun to enjoy the fruit towards the end. I wouldn't tell him that. We sit in silence, my breathing is the only thing my ears can pick up.

I stand and move the chair back into place.

"Don't you *ever* do that to me again." I turn and leave the room without glancing back. I need fresh air. I need to breathe somewhere that isn't so quiet. I go down the hall back towards the sitting room and through the end door on the right. Instead of going up the stairs I turn left; humming softly to myself as I walk along. I am doing something I hadn't attempted to do while I was here. Through the door on the right, I am greeted by a well-lit smaller sitting room, the walls on the left are glass panels; exposing the exotic garden before me. My breathing falters as I look out before me, I hadn't bothered taking much notice of it through my window; caught up in my self -loathing. Plants and flowers of all different shapes and sizes sit in small clusters; a clear dirt path twisting through. Large mushrooms stand tall, glowing a radiant light that lights up the whole garden. On the outskirts of the garden large trees twist together to form a wall, their dark leaves concealing the glow.

I open the glass door and take a tentative step outside, the creature from the night before flashing briefly into my mind. The sunlight couldn't drive something like that away if there's no sunlight to begin with. The soft dirt is cold beneath my bare feet.

I leave the glass door open behind me. I walk the small distance towards the garden, as I grow closer the smaller flowers clustered around the path begin to glow a light pink. I take a step into the garden and my feet sink slightly in the dirt. I scrunch my toes up, savouring the damp feeling. I walk slowly, taking my time to admire the beauty and life this small area holds.

More plants and flowers begin to glow, and before I know it I'm surrounded by a rainbow of soft hues, illuminating my skin; seeming to make me shine. I brush my fingertips against the edge of a large yellow hue mushroom, the surface smooth to the touch.

Left over droplets from the rain fall onto the plants below. I continue walking along the dirt path, humming softly.

The plants thrive off the darkness; creating and becoming their own source of light. If only I could just learn to do the same. I'd like to think I'd glow bright and strong, I'd find my place to belong.

The plants sooth my nerves, if only I could keep one in my room at night to chase away the nightmares and thoughts that keep me awake. I thought I was strong, but each passing day makes me feel weaker than the last. I knew I had the essentials I needed to survive; I know I could leave this place and make it. Maybe even returning to my old prison I called home and old bed.

I didn't want to fulfil whatever purpose Kalabhiti had for me, I wasn't going to be some war weapon to turn the tides. I was not going to be used as a pawn in a game I knew nothing about. The sooner he realised that the better but there's no way I'd be able to get it across to him.

The path smooths out as the garden stops; in front of me is the open archway towards the thick forest that protects the back of the castle. A chill so strong it causes me to step back shakes my bones, that creature could be out there.

I walk closer, edging myself bit by bit as my courage grows and then falters. Kalabhiti would hear my scream if it came to that. I rest my hand on the right side of the twisted tree; the branches woven underneath are a tight knitted braid. I peer into the darkness, my vampire senses only allowing me to see the first defence of tree line, the rest is pitch black. I stare intently, unsure if I am hoping to see something or to calm my fears.

I take a relieving breath and turn away; the garden greets me warmly as I trudge through it; my feet dragging. As I reach the glass door I shake as much of the dirt off as I can. I shut the door firmly and look back at the garden; all that remains glowing is the large mushrooms.

I wander around the castle aimlessly, most of the wooden doors are locked; the ones that aren't don't contain anything exciting. When I first started my trek around the house I'd left full dirt marks behind; now the remaining dirt had crusted on the outside of my toes and feet.

I'd need a shower, I knew Kalabhiti was somewhere in the castle; attending to his own affairs as he liked to call them. I go back to my room and grab a fresh towel, along with tight dark green pants and a loose fitting white singlet. The bathing chambers were on the opposite side of the castle, towards Kalabhiti's sleeping chambers. I hadn't allowed myself to even look in the direction of where he sleeps every night, that would only lead me to trouble.

Getting there was easy enough, I'd gotten lost a handful of times already; my aimless wandering was actually coming in handy. I step into the hallway that leads to the bathing chambers. The large hallway stretches out long and wide before me. The first door to my left was the bathing area; the large red wooden door that enveloped the ending of the hallway was Kalabhiti's room. I keep my eyes low as I step lightly to the bathing door. I rest my hand on the cold metal handle.

Kalabhiti's door opens at the end, the door swinging outwards with ease. I glance up in curiosity, despite my earlier stubbornness. He's flicking through papers as he stands there, his eyebrows furrowed in a frown. He'd traded his black fitting suit for a more casual attire, the dark blue suit pants low on his hips; his loose white long sleeved shirt is rolled up to the elbows, the first four buttons undone exposing his open chest. My eyes fixate on the papers in his hands, what could he be reading that is so bad?

He seems to notice my eyes and looks up, catching my gaze. His eyes look over me lazily, casually. I can feel my cheeks heating; I know I'm not ravishing or something out of a fairy tale; especially with crusted dirt around my feet and a bird's nest for hair. I hold my head high as our eyes connect once more, I won't allow him to see the effect he has on me. He walks towards me, I know I should escape into the bathroom; he had more decency than to follow me in there. But I don't. I stay put and wait for him to come.

He stops a metre in front of me, facing the papers away.

"Ah, I see Zuriel told you I can read." I say, gesturing towards the papers. The corner of his mouth rises slightly. I should be hostile, not trying to start a conversation with him. God.

"Indeed he did. The library in the sitting room is open to you at any time; you can read as much or as little as you want. Words are knowledge and knowledge is power in a place like this." he watches me with a hint of amusement.

"Thank you. I haven't attempted to look at anything yet. I seem to be side tracked more often than not." I say softly, not wanting to delve deeper into my feelings with him than I had. The worst part is I know he would listen, he would drop it all and listen and try and make me feel better.

"It happens to the best of us. They're there when you need them." he glances down at my bare feet. "I see you've explored the garden."

"It's beautiful out there; I've never seen anything like it before." the garden is my favourite part of this whole castle, it expected nothing from me.

"It is isn't it? It thrives in the darkness; they're the only plants that last long enough here." it saddens me, I would have loved a day here in the sun; but I couldn't destroy those beautiful plants, no matter how much I craved those warm rays.

"What are you up to for the rest of the day?" he asks.

"I'm not sure yet. Explore some more maybe." I say, holding his eye contact.

"You should begin to train again." I cringe inwardly at the

thought, training would only remind me of Xavier and cleave open my still mending heart again.

"I...can't. I'm not ready." I say quietly as I look away, knowing his vampire ears would pick anything up. I didn't know if I'd ever be ready again.

"Ali..." his voice is soft, "I know it's scary. I know it's hard going through what you are, but you are so strong. Don't let it put out the fire in your heart that I know is there."

My mouth twists, but I don't reply.

What could I say?

I nod once before dismissing myself into the bathroom, locking the door behind me. My feet are cold on the white tiles as I pad over to the open glass shower in front of me that runs along the back wall; the back wall is cobblestoned with vines and moss growing in the cracks. It was nice to see nature incorporated, and it was far fancier than the one I had back at home.

To my right is a full length mirror that runs from the roof to the floor, opposite it is a small bench, a toilet and a basin. I undress and leave my dirty clothes on the bench. I push the button above the basin; water begins to pour from the ceiling like rain.

I shut the glass door behind me, taking a seat on the ground and lean against the wall; letting the water wash me away.

I lounge on the couch in the sitting room, not doing anything in particular. Kal has come and gone a few times, checking up to see if I was hungry or thirsty. I assured him I wasn't, and that I was capable of getting something myself if need be. He'd still been frowning over the papers from this morning and a large part of me is curious to read them; to see what was so flustering.

I'd contemplated sneaking into his room, but that seemed like it was more trouble than it was worth. I knew his patience with me would wear thin soon enough and I'd see the warrior wrath he possesses.

I sit up and look around the sitting room, the window is open; revealing the distant sparkle of the city lights. I wish I could go back to the city, to explore everything it had to offer.

"Ali, are you busy?" Kal asks, entering the room. I raise an eyebrow at him.

"No. Why?" I say.

"How would you like to help me with something?" he raises an eyebrow in challenge.

"Depends what it is. I'm rather comfortable doing nothing." I say coolly, running a hand over the top of the couch.

"It's rather important, otherwise I wouldn't be asking." his eyebrows narrow in irritation. The King wasn't accustomed to others not obeying his orders right away. I stand up and walk towards him.

"Alright, what is it?" I say, giving in. He grins before turning; I hurry to keep up with him. We head towards his side of the castle, growing closer to his room.

"Thank you. I know you'd rather be doing nothing and feeling sorry for yourself but I have too much on my hands to do this. I trust you'll do it with the best of your abilities?" he eyes me as I walk beside him, I frown at him.

"Clearly it depends what it is. You can't expect too much from me." I say, keeping my head high as we continue along the first floor of the castle. We walk down a narrow hallway, the air growing denser.

"Where are we going?" I say, the hallway seeming too small for Kal's large build.

"To the dungeons." he says simply, like it was obvious. A laugh escapes me before I can hold it in. He turns and grins at me; I narrow my eyes at him. We stop in front of a metal door and he opens it slowly. A staircase spirals below, torches lighting the path. I follow him down; the entrance disappears as we go deeper below the castle.

I should have known he'd have a dungeon. What he had down here though was another mystery. Our footsteps were the only noise my ears could pick up on, no hint of life dwelled below these levels. We come to a short hallway, a large wooden door with a large skull shaped lock waits patiently for us.

"Now I need you to be very calm… No matter what sort of instinct you have do not scream or run or do anything stupid. This is no game, I will show you what you must do and then leave you to it." he pauses; I stare hesitantly at the door. He unlocks the large door with a skeleton key, tucking it safely back into his pocket.

The door opens with a groan, the room before it is in utter darkness; my vampire sight not helping. Kal walks in and suddenly the room is lit with the soft glow of torches. In the middle of the large room a creature is chained, facing away from me.

The creatures muscular arms were twice the size of its body with three clawed fingers digging into the stone. Above each wrist and reaching up to its elbow are folded leathery wings on both sides, bound closed by three sets of metal shackles. Dark brown skin covered in tiny brown hairs, it is hunched over on thick small legs; two large toes supporting all of its weight. The creature's large chest heaves up and down in an uneven rhythm; the middle of its back is covered in thick, coarse black hair. Its head shoots up as I step into the room.

It turns towards me and my eyes widen.
Small beady golden eyes narrow on me, the nose is ribbed and leaf shaped in the centre of its face. Large ears twitch slightly. The muscles on its thick throat strain, with narrow cheek bones a dark red; two sides of its mouth are folded over, the two large yellow bottom teeth meeting in the centre.

"This is a very special friend." Kal emerges from the darkness in the corner of the room to my right. He stands beside me. The creature's metal shackles on each leg, two more on its wrists.

It turns around and stands tall, nearly touching the ceiling of the dungeon.

"What on earth..." I mutter; its mouth splits open, revealing more razor sharp yellow teeth, letting out an ear piercing screech; slamming two fists into the stone. Kal looks at it steadily.

"You expect me to look after this thing? You're out of your mind!" I exclaim, taking a step back. I was not being left alone with this creature.

"Yes I do. For today anyway. All you have to do is groom him, feed him and refill his blood trough." my eyes go to the large rectangular cement trough sitting against the left wall. Kal looks at me, amused.

"It's fairly easy, behind us on the wall a brush is hanging. And over there," he gestures towards a small metal door in the wall, "All you have to do is open it, the food will fall in and he'll dig in. Just be careful not to get in his way as he's very protective of his food." My eyes are the size of saucers by now.

"He has no hair to brush though?!" I gesture towards it.

"It's like a horse; he won't harm you in any way. I'll stay with you until you're comfortable." Kal turns back and shuts the door, enclosing us in the room. The metallic stench of blood is strong in the air. Kal gestures towards the trough.

"Turn the nozzle on this side of the tub; turn it back off once it's full." my feet are like lead as I shuffle towards the tub, the creature watches every movement I make. The nozzle is caked in old blood and I hold in a gag as I wrench it open. A piece of the stone wall opens, thick red blood flows into the trough. The creature approaches the tub cautiously, eyeing me before eyeing the blood. I step back as it saunters closer; leaning its large bat head into the path of the flowing blood. It gulps it down, one large clawed hand digging in the stone wall.

I turn the nozzle off, the creature steps back, blood drips between the cracks in its mouth onto the floor. It looks at me with curious golden eyes. I walk back to Kal, my hands coated in dry blood speckles. He grins as I scowl at him, moving towards the feeding area. I pull the lever; the metal door swings open. Dead carcasses spill out and onto the floor, some I've never seen before. The large creature bounds over; digging hungrily into its meal. I shut the lever off; the metal door swinging shut.

"There's no way you're getting me to brush this thing." I say, walking back to where Kal is standing. His arms are folded over his chest.

"Yes you are missy. You can't get yourself out of this one. He's rather stubborn as well, so you both have something in common." I elbow him in the side, not caring that it hurts my elbow more than it hurts him. We watch the creature.

"What is it?" I ask.

"It's a mighty beast from the first war. The last of his kind, we've looked in nearly every continent across the earth for more. If there's any left they've gone deep into hiding. We call them Were-bats, we used them to fight in the first war, and they can fly and destroy anything in their path. This is Dominic, he is mine. If we can find more of his kind, we can use them once again." I look back to Dominic, his back is covered in thin white lines; what I can only assume are scars.

"Dominic." Kal calls, he looks up; head tipping to one side; a deer head slips out of his mouth. Kal grins.

"Ali here will be doing your grooming. Take it easy on her, she's new but stubborn. Call me if she gives you any grief." I growl at Kal. Dominic grunts and goes back to the remainders of his meal.

"There you go, you're all set. He won't touch a hair on your body. Respect him and he will respect you." Kal turns, opening the door. I reach towards him, snagging the back of his shirt. He looks back, raising an eyebrow. I immediately let go of his shirt.

"You're not locking me down here are you?"

"Of course not, here is the key for this door. Lock it once you've finished and blow out the torches please." he chucks me the key; I snatch it hastily; stuffing it into my pocket. He shuts the door quietly behind me.

"Well Dominic…looks like it's just you and me."

3

Allison

Laughter echoes off the hallway wall as I prowl to the sitting room. I am covered in blood and I am pissed.

Kal managed to leave out that Dominic was also a little shit and liked to play with his food while he ate it.

I round the corner into the sitting room and freeze. Cassidy is laying on the couch, Zeke leans against the fire pit dressed all in black; Kal is standing in the middle. Cassidy looks over to me, grinning wickedly.

"Well well, look what the cat dragged in. Or should I say bat?" she sits up and eyes me, scrunching up her nose as she sniffs the air. She is wearing a red blouse with a black corset, exposing more cleavage than necessary. Zeke watches me intensely; his hair has grown, now resting against his shoulders in a wavy mess. Kal looks over to me, I scowl at him.

"Oh Kal this is too good, you actually managed to get her to brush that beast of yours?" she smirks at him, her high tight blonde pony tails swings with the movement.

"Yes I did, I'm sure Dominic would have enjoyed himself." his eyes are light as he watches me. I feel like the laughing stock of the room, did he only get me to brush the stupid beast so I could entertain them?

"I've definitely enjoyed myself. I haven't seen something so amusing in such a long time." Cassidy says; Zeke looks away towards the open window of the city. I wrap my arms around myself, suddenly feeling very self-conscious. All the anger I'd felt shrivels up, leaving tiny footprints of sadness.

"If only I could take a photo. That look really suits you Ali, it reminds me of your home." I stare blankly at her. She arches a plucked eyebrow and moves her hand around to emphasise her next words.

"The slums? You know; that filthy pit you crawled out from?" she leans her head to the side, I'm gobsmacked. She looks at Kal. Is that how they really saw Penrith? Is that how they saw all human cities?

"Did you remove what little brain power she had left as well?" Kal narrows his eyes at Cassidy, he opens his mouth to say something but I beat him to it.

"I was just letting you know I was finished. Here's your stupid key." I growl, throwing the key towards him. It bounces to the ground near his feet, he frowns at the key and then up at me.

"And I'm also telling you I'm never doing that again. You can god damn do it yourself. I'm not your slave." I spit the words at him, watching him flinch. Zeke catches my eye; I turn and storm out of the room. Cassidy snickers behind me, I wipe furious tears away as I storm towards the bathing chambers. I was not being made a laughing stock. He wonders why I didn't want to leave the room, why I was beginning to hate it here.

I don't notice the footsteps behind me until it's too late. A cold hand wraps lightly around my right elbow, turning me towards them. I roll my eyes.

"Kal—" I'm cut short to see Zeke standing in front of me, his eyebrows crunched in concern. I sigh a breath of relief.

"Ali, I don't even know where to begin. I'm sorry about her, she's very..." he trails off, trying to find the right word.

"She's a bitch." I say, hoping she heard me. Zeke gives me a weak smile. I'll never understand why she doesn't like me, if she'd give me a chance like everyone else I'm sure we'd have some common interests.

"Yes, that suits her well. Look, I have so much I want to apologise for. I'm sorry I dragged you into this; I didn't think you were Cassidar's descendent right away but Zuriel was sure of it. That's why I returned the second time, to find out for myself." I stay still as I listen to him, his hand still holding my elbow. I wasn't expecting the conversation to take a turn like this. Why hadn't Zuriel come back as well? He was just as important as Zeke.

"I didn't really have any idea what I was doing, I just needed to talk to you but make it seem worth it so you'd agree to talk to me as well."

"Why didn't you just tell the truth? Why go to such lengths for it?" I ask, confused.

"Because we did have vampires going missing, I could have finished the mission myself but I knew you'd do it for me. I knew you'd want to help in any way you could. I also had to show Kal that you were Cassidar's descendant. I am sorry I used you, but I'm glad because it brought you out of your shell. It showed you that you're not as weak as you think you are." his eyes blaze with intensity. I knew I couldn't trust him, I couldn't trust anyone here. I wasn't making the same mistakes again. No matter how much I wanted to believe him. I used to feel so much for him, but now that too had shrivelled away.

"You acted like you hated me that entire time." I say, gritting my teeth. Zeke lets go of my arm, running a hand through his hair. I wrap my arms around my body again.

"It was hard...I wasn't accustomed to seeing a human as a companion. I wasn't accustomed to... feeling things for a human. I'd always seen them as a source of food, not someone I could... learn to like." my eyebrows shoot up as I look at him; I take a small step back in disbelief. Did he just say... he felt something for me?

"Look I know I shouldn't be dropping this on you. I know it's been rough for you, I've heard about what happened at the camp. I just needed to tell you. I needed you to know I'm so sorry and if I could go back and redo it I would."

"What, so you can feel better about yourself? What would you change? Would you just kidnap me and bring me here as some experiment?" I ask, stepping back again. I want to put an ocean between us. His eyes widen and my heart beats rapidly in my chest.

"Ali, that's not—" I put my hand up, cutting him off. All the emotion from the past few weeks had been bubbling up and he was here. I had to let some steam out, I didn't care who got caught in that process.

"Yes. It is. You have no *idea* what I had to go through. Words can't erase the damage I've caused and the damage I've done to myself. I wish they could, so we can both leave this conversation feeling better about ourselves. You don't have nightmares of the innocent man you killed plaguing each second of sleep you have. You don't carry the burden of all the people that will now be killed because of me, the guilt. I have to."

"Ali you didn't—" I step back again, a chasm opens up before us and I finally feel the bridge between us burning.

"I did. I'm the reason he is dead now, that they'll all be dead. He was so *nice*. He didn't deserve that. None of them did." my throat begins to close in on itself. I swallow hard, needing someone to hear what I was going through, even if it was Zeke.

"I *liked* you. I *believed* in you. And you threw it in my face, I was innocent and you've stained me. I can't escape that feeling." I pull the necklace out from underneath my shirt, unclipping his pendant. The golden charm feels warm in my hand. I grab his hand and curl his fingers around it.

"Did you just think once I was here you could just waltz back into my life with no consequences? That I would fall to my knees for you? What I felt for you is *dead.*

Thank you for apologising. But *please* leave me alone. I don't want your help and I don't want to hear anything about you feeling anything for me. You've burnt that bridge to the ground." tears swim down my cheeks, but my vision stays clear.

"Ali please I want to make it up to you, let me help you. I'm begging you." I drop his hands, wiping my eyes. His face falls and I see his walls go back up.

"Just go back to seeing me as a food source; it'll be easier for both of us." I turn and walk away. He doesn't follow.

I turn the corner and run the rest of the way to the bathing chambers, sobs racking my body; my vision blurry.

Everything hurts. I just want it all to stop.
Was that too much to ask for?

My mending heart is now broken again.

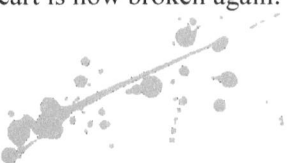

I stare out into the garden from inside the small sitting room. I bite my lip to stop any more tears from falling. I'd avoided Kal for the last three days. I hadn't eaten, I'd barely slept. Each time I close my eyes to welcome darkness, Cassius's face is there to haunt me, taunt me and remind me of the monster I'd become.

Everything felt like too much, I didn't have enough of me to fight the battle I felt inside of me. My eyes were nearly all red now, a sliver of my human side intact.

And maybe that was why I was feeling the way I did, maybe that was why I was alienating myself. Vampire me wasn't a good version of me, but the dark and unforgiving version. Maybe she was the parts of myself I tried to bury, the parts that hurt too much to think or talk about.

I don't want to find out.

The mushrooms outside are the only source of light, this room is the only room that is keeping me intact. Keeping me sane; human even. I can only hope their light will help chase out my dark. The small couch was only big enough for one; I have my legs curled underneath me as I sit there.

The door opens and someone enters the room. I don't bother looking up, I know it's Kal. His footsteps are light as he approaches; hesitant. I was no threat or danger, I don't know why he had to tip toe around me.

"You don't have to treat me like a ticking time bomb. I'm not going to explode at any given moment." I say quietly, not taking my eyes from the garden. I feel his presence to my left.

"I know, I just didn't want to startle you." his voice is soft, careful. I stay quiet.

"I heard the conversation you had with Zeke. I want to apologise for how Cassidy acted and to apologise for using you." I turn towards him, my eyes narrow on him. He has his hands clasped behind his back as he watches me, on guard. Because I am unpredictable. A threat.

"Why does everyone apologise? They're just words. They change nothing. Actions speak louder than words and so far everyone's doing a pretty shitty job of showing me that." he frowns. His shadows encase his feet and the darkness behind him, his long hair is damp and swims around his chest.

"If you weren't so receded into yourself you'd see I have been trying in every way. It's hard… when you close yourself off. I thought bonding with Dominic would help bring you out of the dark place you've found yourself in." he comes closer, looking out to the garden. I study him, my jaw clenched. His back muscle ripples underneath his white shirt.

"It would have if I didn't end up the laughing stock of the room. Was that your plan? I was humiliated." I say with venom in my words. He scoffs, turning back to me.

"Of course it wasn't. I'm embarrassed you'd think that low of me Allison. I hadn't intended for their visit. They were updating me on the rescue of the vampires you found."

"And?" I ask, I needed to know and find some sort of closure from it. Kal sighs, his shoulders falling. He rubs his face, thinking about how to tell me.

"Most were killed by the time the first rescue team arrived, burnt alive. You already know that though. They scouted the human camp; double protection is being used now. They've implanted silver bombs along the outside of their base. We lost two of the rescue team to an explosion." My heart falters in my chest. Another two dead because of me.

"I'm sorry." I whisper, looking back to the mushrooms. The guilt is suffocating, crushing my chest and taking my breath away. I dig my nails into my palm as I try to slow my breathing.

"What for? If it wasn't for you we wouldn't have been able to save the ones we did. And Nardia, I'm sure she's more than thankful for the sacrifice you made." he looks down at me, his eyes swimming with worry. This is the first time we've spoken about what had happened, a wound I wasn't ready to face but was being forced to.

"I know she would be. I'm glad she lived. I should have saved them all; I should have gone back for them. I had the power to just knock the humans out and rescue the other vampires but I ran. I fled with Nardia and left the rest to die. That is why I'm sorry. My main mission was to rescue the vampires and I failed." tears swim in my eyes, I try to push them away and hold them in.

I wouldn't cry in front of him, my tears were only for my pillow.

"Ali you couldn't have known. You saved Nardia and others, I'm sure they'll thank you if they ever get the chance to meet you. You succeeded in my eyes, you saved vampires." a tear slips down my cheek.

"I couldn't save myself. Now I'm stuck in this huge mess and I have no idea what to do. What happens to me now? What of that?" I ask, my hands shake in my lap. I didn't want to think about it but I needed answers.

"That's up to you. I can't make that choice for you. You still have the option to be human, or you have the option to be vampire. You won't change fully unless you drink human blood, and by that I mean you would have to drain the life force of a human and take their soul. No matter what you choose you're not the evil monster you portray yourself to be, we're all good and bad. Even I am, but we constantly learn and grow. You can't have bright days without darkness." his words haunt me; I can't ever see myself killing a human by drinking their blood. I don't want to acknowledge the good and bad he's mentioned.

"Do I even have fangs?" I ask as I reach up and touch my canines; they felt human to me. He gives me a weak smile.

"I'm sure you would, it wouldn't be easy to summon them I don't think. It would be very painful as well, nothing near pleasant."

"What triggers them?" I was still touching where they should be. He kneels down in front of me, eyeing me intensely.

"Deep emotion; it's usually anger or the urge to protect but each person is different. Especially for you, since you're still part human. I'm not sure what would trigger them. Once you've been vampire for a while you can call them whenever you need. Why is that?" he slowly pulls my hand away from my mouth, I don't breathe. He doesn't let go of it, his coolness seeps into me; comforting me.

"Curious." I breathe out; if I had fangs I wanted to know. If I did, I had to find a way that could get rid of them. He searches my face for any other hints; I keep myself calm and collected.

"Can I see yours?" A part of me felt like I was in a trance. I knew he wasn't encouraging me or influencing me silently, I feel like the old me. The curious me, the confident me. He frowns slightly but opens his mouth, his white teeth glow in the darkness. Slowly his fangs ease through his gums over his canines, they are large and white; indenting his lower lip. A chill runs through me, I'd hate to be at the receiving end of those fangs.

"Can I touch them?" I whisper. He doesn't move as I scoot closer to him, my legs dropping to the ground. I lean in, our faces inches apart. Slowly I reach up and tenderly touch the tip of his left one; it is very sharp. I press it slightly harder and hiss as it breaks the skin on my finger tip. I frown as I pull my finger away, a small bubble of blood had formed; a drop on his fang. The metallic smell fills the room and I can feel something change in him as he stays deathly still. I suck on my finger before feeling his fang again. It still bleeds lightly, leaving small traces of blood as I feel the hardness of it where it connects to the gum. I look into his eyes; they are solely focused on me. A blush creeps into my cheeks. Satisfied I sit back, shoving my finger back into my mouth; putting some space between us.

He slowly retracts his fangs, his tongue running over them roughly; catching the drops of my blood. A low moan comes from his throat as it dissolves in his mouth; I force myself to look away. He probably thinks I taste like the slums I come from. We sit in silence; he slowly stands, still watching me. I wasn't sure what came over me.

"Are you leaving?" I ask; my voice soft, kind.

"Do you need me to stay?" his voice is thick. I look away, back to the garden. I need to be alone; I have to think about what just came over me. God I was stupid. I let my guard down.

"No. I'll see you at dinner." I don't watch as he walks away;

shutting the door softly behind him. I sag down in the chair, warmth spreading in my lower stomach. I growl at myself, I would not let myself be attracted to him.

I stay silent as I watch the mushrooms, trying to dissolve the uncomfortable feeling of something similar to happiness that Kal left me with.

4

Kalabhiti

My mind swarms with darkness as I leave Ali to her own thoughts. I wanted to stay; not leave her side. A growl rips out of my throat; I could kill Cassidy for making her feel that way. A part of me suspects they'd had a run in with each other before. Cassidy reveled in Allison's sadness, she enjoyed seeing her miserable.

I felt responsible for her feeling that way, before I'd met her I saw her as another human; another food source. I couldn't believe she was Cassidar's descendant. Neither of them were similar; no inch of Ali was the same as my sweet Cassidar. Allison was rough all around; she didn't have the luxury Cassidar did of this world.

She was brave above all, when I first met her, those eyes shone with such raw power that I don't think she even knows she has. And I knew; I knew she was the one I've been waiting for. It pains me to see her so broken, moving around my home as a ghost. Barely conscious of her surroundings. I never imagined she would give in so easily to the sadness.

Her once plump face is now all angles, still as beautiful as ever though. She carries the guilt heavily on her shoulders; although she is very good at hiding it. But she is also human, and humans are vulnerable and easy to read.

Her blood though—
God her *blood*.

It was the sweetest thing I have ever tasted; I can still feel the traces of it in my mouth. It had made me uncomfortably turned on; the shift in me was all I could sense in the room as she sucked her finger delicately; not taking her eyes away from me.

I growl again, I can never put her in that situation. I will never give in to the urges that would force me to my knees in front of her. I am a King, I have to be strong. I think back to the conversation Zeke had with her, I'd heard the entire thing but I had acted like I didn't. He'd returned to the room in a foul mood. Cassidy had used that to her advantage, stirred him up even more.

I should have said something; I should have shut Cassidy up. I shouldn't have let Ali walk away upset.

I walk into my chambers, frustrated with myself. I have to bring Allison back, I have to guide her out of that darkness that has warped itself around her; she will be coming to dinner tonight. I should try to get her to open up more, I have to chip the wall away.

These things took time. I had to remind myself that. If she chooses to stay human, I will be there to support her. I'd always linger for her human years, making sure she was okay and safe. Where was this protectiveness coming from?

My mind lingers back to when she asked about her fangs, if she had them; what would she do with them? I cringe at the thought of ever having my fangs tampered with or broken, the pain would be unbearable. Surely she wasn't foolish enough to do anything to harm herself, she was still human.

I devour documents from the other vampire cities that are closer, they've heard of the vampire Queen's descendent. I haven't told Ali yet, I won't burden her with that. I have to keep things light.

They want to meet her, to see if the rumours are true. I growl at the thought of the other vampires looking at her like a science experiment, like a piece of flesh. I can't trust their motives, a vampire Queen rising would make my city the most powerful one. I was currently a threat that needed to be dealt with.

5

Allison

I enter the dining room with light feet; I have chosen to wear something less moody and sad and something more wild. I don't know how my mood had flipped after seeing Kal but here I was, almost humming to myself like a stupid love sick teen.

I was in a pale blue silk gown; it barely hid my body underneath and reminded me of the vampire females I'd seen when I first arrived. I've pulled the front strands of my hair back and clipped them to the sides. The gown split at the sides of my thighs and exposed my legs as I walked; I'd tied a silk piece around my waist to act as a belt. My back was exposed, the front piece coming up and covering my breasts and tying around my throat. I'd stood staring at myself for the last half an hour, working up the courage.

Now that I'm in the empty room I immediately have regrets, what was I thinking? I should have just worn long pants and a shirt, something casual. The table is overflowing with a roast pig and vegetables, the aroma in the air makes my stomach growl. I still had time to change, I wasn't sure where Kal was or what he'd gotten up to after our moment. I wasn't actively looking for him but he was nowhere to be seen. I keep my head down as I turn, the dress swimming around me; exposing my left leg. Someone clears their throat and I look up, mortified. Kal stands there in his usual black warrior suit, his eyes fixated on the exposed skin.

"Um. Hi." I say, trying to calm my nerves. A blush has stained my cheeks. I clamp my hands together behind my back, his eyes find mine.

"You look lovely." he says; his voice warm. I fight off a smile. Wasn't that the point of wearing this though? I wanted him to compliment me, didn't I?

"Thank you, I guess we should eat?" I gesture towards the table; his eyes follow the length of my arm. He is making me extremely nervous. I feel like we're on a date, I've never been on one before but I had no doubt it felt like this.

"Of course." He walks over to me, I stay still. He brushes past me, pulling out a chair. I take it politely; he pushes it in gently for me. He takes the seat across from me, I frown.

"You're not eating at the head of the table? That's not very kingly of you." As I begin to fill my plate with slices of pork and cooked potatoes, Kal pours himself a blood drink.

"I don't eat darling, I drink. I thought I'd give my King duties a rest tonight." he sips it gingerly, studying me. I roll my eyes at him.

"Well *darling*, you should try it some time. It's exquisite." I emphasise my point as I fill my mouth with pork. It's warm and falls apart as I chew. He grins at me, rolling his eyes once.

"Did you have a good day?" He asks. I begin to cut apart a

potato. Dear God how I'd missed this food.

"It was... interesting. Yourself?" I eat a few pieces of potato, watching him from my peripheral vision. He sips his drink again. I am beginning to feel full; my hunger strike had shrunk my appetite.

"I could very well say the same." we both feel the immediate tension in the air, he's tasted my blood. I hadn't had a moment that intimate with anyone since Xavier. I near choke at the thought of him. I couldn't think about him. Not now.

"Where did you go?" I ask, looking back to him.

"Did someone miss me?" he asks cheekily, a gleam in his eyes as he grins at me. I cough once, the potato piece going down too fast.

"You could only dream I'd ever miss you." I say sassily, I was beginning to slowly feel like myself again. I couldn't let myself become too familiar, but I could have fun. Right? For one night I'd love to forget about the mess I'm in and just enjoy myself. He swirls the blood around in his drink.

"I think that's what they call nightmares love." I open my mouth, shocked. He is being so cheeky!

"Well... well, I'm lucky I don't get scared easy then." I huff; slightly flustered. He takes another mouthful, draining the rest of its content. I wonder if vampires can drink alcohol or if blood was like that to them.

"If you can survive the presence of Dominic you can very well survive anything I'd say." My mind flashes back to the white creature I'd seen. I hadn't seen it since, I debate telling him. I hadn't seen any sign of it again, and I was beginning to think maybe I'd imagined it. If I saw it again he'd be the first to know.

"Ha. Very funny, Dominic is the least of my worries in this place." I say slowly, focusing my eyes on my food; I'd already eaten half the plate's worth I'd piled on. I can feel Kal watching me.

"What do you mean?" I look back to him, my mouth twisted.

He seems genuinely curious. How could I tell him? Not only was he one of the worries but I was myself.

"I just have bigger things to worry about, like the vampire king and myself and whatever thing I have inside of me that is uncontrollable" I say quietly. He pours himself another drink, my eyes fixate on the red thickness as it pools in the glass. A part of me wanted to taste it, *needed* to taste it.

"I can safely say the vampire king isn't something to worry about, he's rather harmless. But Ali, if you're worried about yourself and that power, I really encourage you to take up my offer of training. I know it will be hard the first few times, it might not stop being hard, but I believe it would be good for you. It's not far of a walk either."

"What do you mean it's not far of a walk?" I place my fork and knife down, satisfied I'd eaten enough. I was curious as to where the training area would be, and who I'd be training with.

"The training area isn't in the castle, we do have a small one but it's nowhere near as good. It's behind the castle, a short walk through the forest in a large cement building." I debate this, I'd never be able to walk alone because of that creature; I was far too vulnerable for that.

"And who trains? Who would train me?" I sit back and rest my hands on my stomach, drumming my right hand over my left one. His eyes flicker to them before resting back on my face.

"Zuriel, Zeke, Cassidy, Nardia and a few others you haven't had the chance of meeting just yet. Who would you like to train you to start with? Usually they all train together but since you're just a beginner you'll get a personal trainer until you're ready to merge with their group." my stomach drops as he says Cassidy, I could handle Zeke but I wasn't sure I could be strong enough to handle Cassidy.

"Oh okay. Would you train me?" the last part comes out as a squeak; I know he's probably up to his knees with king stuff to do but I'm sure he'd let up some time for me. I don't think he really has a choice. He leans back in his chair, a smile tugging at his lips.

"No not every vampire; the city has their own gyms. They're my elite team, my strongest and most loyal and trusted warriors. They've been by my side for many centuries now. Although Nardia only has one eye she's still as sharp as ever." I wince at the comment, I was glad I wasn't there when they did that to her. He continues, "You want me to train you?" he asks, amused. I frown at him.

"It only seems logical; you're the most powerful vampire in the city. I don't want to be half assed trained and left not knowing how to actually fight. I know you'd show me everything and you could maybe even... teach me more about that thing I have?" I wouldn't say power out loud; I couldn't identify it as a part of me just yet.

"You have a good point. You'd be in safe hands. Yes, I can do that if you wish." I let a sigh out, relieved.

"Thank you. What will the schedule be then? Like is it every day or what?"

"We'll start with small sessions every day, an hour at max. We don't want to put too much strain on your body straight up. There will be others when we train, are you okay with that?" he asks, leaning his elbows on that table. I gulp; I didn't want Cassidy to see how weak and clumsy I was.

"Uh, I guess I have to be." I whisper. He drains his glass quickly, he stands up and offers me his hand. I raise an eyebrow at it.

"Let's go have a look at it now, get you somewhat familiar with it before your first session tomorrow." I take his hand politely as I stand up but let go to push my chair in. He gives me an amused smile; I give him a pointed look.

"Lead the way." I follow him through the castle; we walk through the small strip of garden and out through the tree arch and head towards the forest. I stay closer than usual to him; I was not becoming a human kebab for anyone tonight.

Kal was right about one thing, the walk is short. A worn down path had been created between the trees, once we emerge on the other side my breath is taken away by the large stone building; it is surrounded by the trees, vines have made their homes in the cracks of the stones. Dim light shines through the cracks of the wooden door, the building has no windows.

Before reaching the steps that led to the door I can hear others inside, talking and laughing amongst themselves. Kal gives me an encouraging smile as he opens the door and the room goes silent as I follow him inside. To my distaste Cassidy is here. The large rectangular room is padded with black mats, at the end a portion is sectioned off by two stripes of large red rope.

Both walls were covered in weapons ranging from knives to clubs; I didn't know what half of them were. Beside the door are six treadmills, a boxing bag sat beside one. The roof reaches high above me; covered in hundreds of little golden circle lights.

"Wow, you managed to drag her out of the castle." Cassidy says as she saunters over to us. Zeke avoids my eyes and stays holding the two knives. Zuriel is a blur as he runs to me; wrapping me in a hug and twirling me around. I'm more than aware of how much my dress just displayed. I giggle as he goes around, he was the only one that seemed like they were going to treat me the same. Once he puts me down my cheeks are flushed and I have a huge grin on my face. Kal is frowning slightly.

"Oh how I've missed you my sweet little ally cat." his hair is still trimmed on the sides with the top creating a curtain that falls and covers the right side of his face. He was still the same Zuriel.

"I've missed you too." I say, smiling like an idiot. I was so glad Kal persuaded me to train; I couldn't wait to train beside Zuriel.

"I'm surprised the King hasn't made a meal of you yet." he winks at Kal as he flexes his arms, the muscles rippling against his pale skin. Kal rolls his eyes.

"If anything, I'd be the one ending up as a meal. She's quiet vicious when she wants to be." he says, grinning. I smirk at him; at least he'd been paying attention. I cross my arms over my chest; I could see why this room was only for his most trusted group, to work alongside one another while fighting in such a small space would require trust and precision. I was worried about how I would go with my... thing I had deep down.

"Ali has decided she wants to begin training, so I'll have the pleasure of preparing her until she's ready to be handed over to you animals." Kal grins as he says this, his gaze going to each one of them. I didn't realise how much of a bond he had with them, and no doubt Nardia. Cassidy stares at me, her scarlet red lips are the only thing colourful about her; sweat glistens on her forehead. She was wearing a pair of black combat pants and a tight black singlet that exposed her slim but muscular body.

"Why would you train her here with us? Why not take her into the city's gym with the others. It's not like she's joining our team." She says pointedly, raising an eyebrow. I bite the inside of my cheek, Kal looks to her.

"And how would you know that?" He asks, his voice is on the edge of dominating. She doesn't break eye contact, her eyes blazing.

"She's a *human*. We all know that's what she's going to choose at the end of the day. You can't just pretend she's a vampire and try and make her fit in. Because she won't. I refuse to put my life and trust into a human girl who doesn't even know how to fight. What side is she fighting for in all of this?" She throws her hands in the air, pointing at me.

"Regardless of what she chooses, she still deserves respect and the chance to learn. I don't want to hear anything about this again Cassidy." I take a step back; the vampire part of me wincing.

"You've got to be kidding!" She exclaims. In a blur he has his hand wrapped around her throat. He snarls at her, his fangs ripping through the gums.

"I said I didn't want to hear any more of it." his shadows begin to sweep around them; shackling themselves to her ankles. She stays silent.

"Is that clear?" he threatens, I can't look away. I'd never seen Kal so... angry before. She looks at me before diverting her eyes to the ground, a burning hatred in them.

"Yes." her voice is muffled by his hand. He lets go and steps back, his shadows swim around his feet.

"I am your King; you have a tendency to forget that." he says, his voice calm and clear. She stays silent. I had the tendency to forget that as well, I was a guest in his home. He had no idea what sort of person I was and nor did I. Zuriel leans down to me, his breath tickles my cheek.

"Don't worry about her. I'll keep you safe if she becomes too much."

"Thank you, I might need it," I whisper back. My eyes trail over to Zeke, he was now watching Kal and avoiding me. I couldn't blame him, a part of me was still angry at him. I guess I should be angry at Zuriel as well; he was also a large influence in what happened. I zone back into the conversation. Cassidy walks back to Zeke's side and takes a knife, they head towards the sectioned off area. Kal walks over to Zuriel and I.

"Well that could have gone better." Zuriel murmurs, looking towards Cassidy and Zeke. They begin to fight, their weapons blurring with their speed. I had no hope of fighting against a full vampire, not when they were so fast and strong.

"You're telling me. I knew she wasn't going to like this." Kal says, rubbing his face. Zuriel clasps him on the shoulder.

"You have nothing to worry about. I'll take care of Ali and I'm positive Nardia will as well. You'll have to introduce her to the twins; they might enjoy her company more than you know."

"Twins?" I ask, looking between them. Zuriel grins.

"They're the other two of the elite team, brother and sister.

They're identical apart from their hair; otherwise you'd constantly be calling them the wrong names." Zuriel smiles at me, hopefully I had nothing to worry about. I needed more friends than enemies in this place. So far I wasn't coming out on top.

"Vampires from a shadow clan, some of the most skilled fighters I've ever seen. I came across them when I was searching for more of Dominic's kind. They were ensnared by him, he was the main reason they came back with me. Their home is across the continent," Kal says, turning to me. They sounded interesting, and dangerous. I couldn't make them my enemies.

"They sound nice." I say simply.

"Just don't get on their bad side, they're absolute psychos." Zuriel was so casual about everything; he didn't seem to have a worry in the world. He gives Kal a quick handshake before ruffling my hair.

"Alright, I'm off love birds, I have to go show those two who's still boss in this team." Zuriel walks over to them before I can deny that we're in fact not love birds. I grumble as Kal leads us back outside.

"What did you think?" He asks, walking in step with me.

"Uh let me think. I have to trust my life with a vampire who wants to kill me. So yeah, great. It went great." I say, exaggerating my point. I couldn't ever trust Cassidy, not when she held so much resentment for me.

"Why does she hate me so much? Is it because I'm still human? She'd damn well still hate me if I was a vampire!" I exclaim, frustrated. Kal stares ahead.

"I'm sorry Ali. It's from a long, long time ago. Cassidy and I were intimate once, nothing too serious. It was something to distract us and help pass the time. I wasn't in the right frame of mind at that point of my life, I was still mourning Cassidar. I wasn't in love with Cassidy; she never voiced how she felt. She might have wanted something more serious but I think she knew

I wasn't ready. She's loyal as anything and one of my strongest fighters, I couldn't let the fact we'd been together interfere with business. So we're civil. After I went into hibernation it ended whatever we had, I think once I was awoken she thought there was a chance.

"When they came to me with the news Cassidar's descendent lived I could have cried. Cassidy tried many advances and was rejected each time. I wasn't interested and I'm still not. I think with you living here it's just a reminder to her. It has nothing to do with you but with how I went about things. I hope you're not angry." I stay silent as I think about what he said.

Cassidy loved him, I imagine she always would. I couldn't really be mad at her for that. I didn't ask to be Cassidar's descendent. I didn't ask for any of this and surely she had to realise that. She couldn't stay mad at me for simply being me.

"I guess that makes sense. I didn't ask for any of this you know. I don't want it. I was fine just being a human living a simple life." I say quietly, I wish more than anything I could go back to normal and be normal.

"Ali, if there's one thing you and Cassidar have in common it's that you both want peace and equality for humans and vampires. That's what she stood for, she loved the humans more than herself and I know if she could go back she would do the same thing. She was too good for this world." we break the tree line. The castle looms over us as we grow closer to the garden.

"I'm not her though, I'll never be her. Of course I want equality but I'm not the key to it. Humans and vampires can be cruel things, some things I witnessed other humans do to their own kind makes me want to curl into a ball. Both races destroyed this world and now they have to live with the consequences. I'm no Queen Kal, you need to realise that." I stop walking and study him; I need him to understand this. He turns back to me, his face flawless in the moonlight.

"I know you're not her. I'm not asking you to be her, I'm

asking you to be the hope for humans and vampires. Yes, there is evil in this world but it doesn't outweigh how much good the world has. They need someone to fight for that, I believe that's you. I'm not asking you to be my queen, but I am asking you to be something they can look up too," he says, taking a step towards me.

"Look at me Kal; I'm a broken human and vampire girl who was experimented on in that camp. Who knows what I'm going to turn into. I'm not stable and I don't know if I'll ever be. I want to be their hope, I want salvation but I can't give it to anyone. If I can't help myself how can I help others?" I search his face. His eyebrows furrow, his eyes sadden. I felt relief; I'd finally voiced how I really felt about this.

"Let me help you. I don't expect anything from you, Ali." I take a step back and look away.

"You can't save me Kal, it won't bring back Cassidar." I brush past him and head into the castle, he doesn't follow. Tears fall into the garden and my vision blurs as I continue walking; not knowing where my destination is but I can't stand still any longer.

6

Kalabhiti

I sit in my private study, sipping a glass of human blood. I needed to taste it again; the deer blood was becoming overwhelming. The conversation with Ali is still replaying in my mind; I would never lie to her and always tell her the truth. I believe she is the key to save races, human and vampire. I am not the same man I was when Cassidar was murdered; peace now seems to be the only way to go about this entire mess.

Vampires need humans to survive; there is only so much animal blood to go around. With numbers growing in other cities it is getting hard to keep up with the demand, more and more transfers are being made. I sigh as I look down at the opened documents in front of me. The three highest ranking vampires from the three cities over where coming to meet Ali in two weeks, regardless if I wanted them to or not. I cannot deny them;

if I do it will only raise more questions. They insist they need to see if Ali is as real as the rumours.

I have to tell her.

"Kalius, can you escort Allison to me please?" I call through the wooden door; Kalius is a trusted male, always quiet. I don't think I'd heard him say more than three words in the last century. Which is a good thing, I know he can hear the conversations that happen in this room.

Ali walks in cautiously, her hair is pulled into a high bun; loose silver strands sit against her bare neck. She'd taken off her necklace. Her red silk skirt brushes against the floor, a matching red silk crop top exposes the flesh of her stomach. I force myself to meet her eyes. The wooden door shuts behind her and I watch as she studies the room. She is completely different today, as if the care free Ali was gone again to be replaced by the Ali that was always on guard.

It isn't a large room by any means, my desk sits in the middle covered in paperwork. The walls are a dark red; the glow of one light is dim and leaves room for many shadows. The wall behind me has a self-portrait of me with a crown on my head. I have a bookcase that runs along one wall, opposite that I have a glass bench that holds a fridge with blood. It was enough to do business.

"We need to talk," I say and her eyes sharpen on me. We'd barely spoken after last night. I gesture towards the black leather chair across from me; she takes it reluctantly, folding her hands in her lap. I have trouble understanding how we've managed to take a step backwards.

"What?" she asks.

"We've got… visitors coming. Very important visitors. To see you." I pass her the letter they'd sent me; I had two weeks to prepare her for them. She reads it quickly, nibbling her bottom lip.

"So this is what you've been hiding from me?" she says matter of fact as she puts the papers back on the desk.

"As well as other things that don't concern you. But this does, they want to meet you." I choose my words carefully; I don't want her to feel cornered or trapped. Not after what she shared with me.

"They think I'm a vampire, don't they?" her ruby eyes blaze. I take a long sip of my drink; I wasn't sure what they thought she was.

"They've heard the rumours about you and have come to make their own conclusion of the whole thing. Nonetheless, they will be coming. I need you to be prepared." she straightens in her chair.

"What if I say no?"

"Is there any way I can persuade you?" I ask. I knew she wouldn't make this easy. I hadn't expected her too. She debates my offer.

"I want to live in the city," she says, eyeing me evenly. My hand tightens on the glass.

"You're not ready, you've shown me that." I sit back and try to calm myself; the vampires in the city respected me, but a human girl walking around unclaimed? Chaos.

"That's my offer. Give me an apartment in the city and I'll be whoever you want me to be for the night." She taps her fingers gently on the chair, my jaw tightens. My shadows grow restless around me and I have to restrain them. They don't like defiance. She knows exactly how to push my buttons.

"The city is a dangerous place." She looks away and studies the room, her jaw set in place. Stubborn, absolutely stubborn.

"So? You're training me. I'll learn to protect myself."

"That will help, yes. But you're unclaimed. It'd be an open invitation to a buffet. Humans can't enter unless they're claimed and or, chipped. They know of your circumstances and I'm sure there's a few prowling around wanting to taste it for themselves." The thought of anyone tasting her blood makes my own blood boil. There was so much more to it than she could imagine. She looks back at me and narrows those gorgeous ruby eyes on me.

"I'm part vampire, remember? So technically I'm not a walking appetiser," she hisses, hating she's had to admit it out loud. I rub my forehead.

"I'll give you a week to prove you're serious about training and learning to control and harness your power. If you show me anything less the answer is no and I'll find a way around the meeting." I straighten and clasp my hands together on the desk, she watches me suspiciously. Reluctantly she gives in.

"Okay, fine. You've got a deal. Who do you need me to be when they come?" She asks, leaning in slightly. I take a deep breath, I didn't need to breath but I liked the novelty of it. I figured it would help Ali feel more comfortable around me. I knew she wasn't going to like the answer, I'm not sure I did myself.

"My Queen."

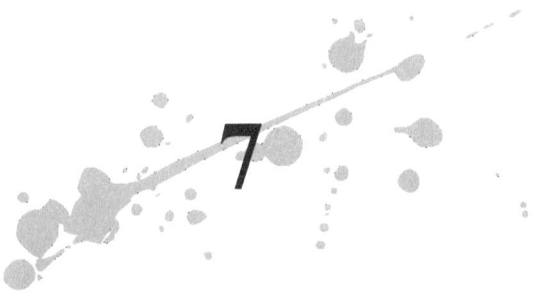

Allison

M y Queen.

"You want me to be your queen?" I ask, baffled. How would I even begin to act like a queen? I was a girl from the slums; I didn't know the first thing about being royalty.

"I know it's not ideal. This is what they're expecting and I have to give it to them, I need to deflect their suspicions on you." Kal leans back, his eyes never leaving mine. I flinch under the intensity of his gaze.

"I don't know one thing about acting like a queen." I cross my arm over my chest and fiddle with the silk material of my shirt.

"I'm sure you're capable of having manners and respecting others. You won't have to do much, just polite conversation. I will try to do most of the talking." he finishes off the contents in his glass, licking a stray drop from his lip. I watch as his tongue trails over it, frowning slightly with how soft his lips look.

"I guess I can do that. Is that all you wanted? May I leave now?" I ask, standing up. I keep a firm grip on the chair as I wait for his answer. His eyes do a quick sweep of my body before settling on my face.

"Yes you may. Training starts tomorrow, early. I will come and get you when it's time." he looks away and begins to shuffle through the pages on his desk. Like that, I'm dismissed. I turn and leave the room as gracefully as I can, feeling his eyes burning into my back.

Kalius nods once as I walk past him, then takes up his position of standing directly in the door way.

Well, what was I to do now?

I aimlessly walk around the castle, exploring rooms I hadn't dared enter when I first arrived. If I was meant to be a queen for a night I suppose it was fair that I knew the layout of the castle. Especially if things were to go wrong.

My feet carry me to the metal door that leads down to Dominic. I open it without thinking and begin the descent downwards. The torch light flickers on the wall as I go deeper, the air growing thicker.

I hold my shirt over my mouth and nose and try to filter out the horrible stench that was growing the closer I was getting to Dominic.

The stairs open to the small hallway, everything still looks the same. Nothing out of place. I walk up to the locked door and lean my head against the wood.

A scuffling sound can just be heard through the thick wood. I frown.

"Dominic? You okay in there little buddy?" I ask, tapping my hand against the door. My shirt falls from my face and I gag as the stench of decay and death fill my lungs.

I splutter and cough as I step away, covering the lower half of my face again. Tears sting my eyes as I take another step away from the door.

Something was wrong.

A low screech comes through the door, along with more scuffling. A sharp yelp and snapping.

"Dominic I'm coming!" I turn and flee up the stairs; pushing myself to the very limit of my vampire powers. The stairs blur beneath me as my heart races wildly in my chest. My legs strain against the speed, my body not use to using my full potential.

I don't care at this point what I am, Dominic needs my help. I explode from the door and flee to Kal's study. Everything blurs around me as I pinpoint him within the castle, I let my feet and instincts guide me to him through the invisible tug I feel.

My view sharpens as I get closer, time almost seems to slow down as I enter the hall and spot Kalius.

"MOVE!" I screech, not slowing down. Kalius looks at me with wide eyes as he steps out of the way, I fly through the study doors and pull myself to a stop.

Papers fly around as I stop. Kal looks up at me, surprised. He'd spilt his fresh drink over his shirt. He looks from the spill to me and frowns. I gasp as I try to catch my breath.

"What on—"

"No time, give me key to dungeon. Dominic in trouble." I manage to form a coherent sentence. Deep within the dungeon I feel Dominic shudder, his life force weakens. Without thinking I jump over the table and snatch the key from Kal's side. I'm out the door as quick as I had entered.

Vaguely I can hear Kal's footsteps behind me, nearly keeping pace. My only focus is on Dominic.

We fly down the stairs; I don't bother covering my face as we reach the dungeon door. Kal gags and coughs at the smell. My hands shake wildly as I try to unlock the door.

More mangled noises come from behind the door; I shove the

key into the lock and tear it open.

Kal and I freeze as we enter. Surrounding Dominic is eight of these creatures I had seen the other night. Dominic is covered in cuts and bites; dark blood is creating a puddle beneath him. Three of their kind lay unmoving around him.

Up this close I can make out more of their features. Their milky eyes are blind to us; two large oval splits between their eyes act as their nose, opening and closing as they sense us.

It's like they are vampires gone wrong, their naked bodies had no hair; only shiny white skin.

The smell in the room has intensified a hundred times, my eyes water as I cover my mouth to stop myself from spilling up the contents of my stomach.

He bellows once he sees us. All the creatures turn to us, the one closest to us opens its black mouth and shrieks; revealing yellow sharp teeth. Its shriek is high enough to pierce our eardrums; luckily Kal doesn't give the creature a chance.

In a blur he's behind the creature, his hands gripping its jaw as he rips it open. Black blood sprays from its mouth as he rips its lower jaw off and throws it to the ground. The other creatures are on him in an instant.

My legs kick into gear as I dive into the fight.
I make contact with the one that's clinging to his back; I grab it by the shoulders and throw it back. It quickly regains its posture before hurtling back towards me.

I have no weapons.
You are a weapon.

I'm ready for the creature; I duck and kick it hard in the stomach. Before it can get back up I'm on top of it. I straddle its chest and grip both of its wrists; black claws try and find their way into the soft skin of my arms.

I do the only thing I really know how to do. Destroy.
I lift the creature up and smash it back into the stone floor, it shrieks as its head cracks back. I repeat the move, smashing it

with vampire force. I try not to listen to the crunch as the back of its skulls caves in. I tune into my other sense.

Dominic is whimpering.

I let go of the creature's arms, grab its head and smash it four times back in a blur, black blood splattering onto my skirt. Its arms fall to its side; it doesn't stir again.

Three of the creatures are on Kal, while the other remaining two are attacking Dominic. Kal would be okay, I had to help Dominic.

I rush over and rip the one from his back; if I could just get his shackles off he would be able to defend himself. They focus on me as they circle to the front of Dominic. I crouch down and snarl at them, Dominic's breath is warm against my back as he watches me.

They all come at me, full force. Without thinking I dive deep inside of myself; to that power I said I wouldn't touch again.

I dive deeper, screaming out to it. It comes willingly, happy to have contact with me again. I can't deny it, I am happy as well.

I scream and rip my arms open and let the power explode from me in a blur of blue vines and light. My body gives way as I fall to my knees. In an instant the two creatures are wrapped in my blue shackles. They screech in defiance.

I dive the power through their mouths; snuffing out their shrieks. My body is alive and on fire all at once, I feel my power tunnel through every cell in the creatures. Destroying everything it touches. The two life forces begin to flicker out.

I grip my fists together; all I had to do was want it.

Kill them.

One by one the creature's heads explode, their bodies sagging against their blue prison. Already my power is searching for its next victim, it grabs onto the one behind Kal. There were only two left.

I snap my eyes to one, snuffing out its existence as I squeeze the blue tendrils tight around its body. Black blood and white flesh ooze to the ground from the bottom of the tendrils. They fall to the floor and swim towards the last one, before they reach it Kal finishes it off with one swift movement, ripping its head from its body.

Kal turns to me; the blue tendrils grow closer to him; curious. His shadows seep out of him and mix with my own, calming the call for blood. Slowly his shadows push them back towards me, into me. My mind is exhausted; I don't have much pull over them.

Kal takes slow steps towards me, his shadows coaxing and relaxing me. A foot away from me he gives a final push and the blue tendrils spiral back into me, filling me up once again. They sit under the surface of my skin, swimming around. My arms fall in front of me as I cough and heave and vomit up every morsel of food I can manage.

I wipe my mouth with a shaky hand and look up to Kal, my hair had fallen out of its bun during the fight and is hanging around me like a damp curtain.

Without hesitation he helps me stand, allowing me to lean against him as I turn to see Dominic.

The bleeding has stopped but he is still covered in cuts of all sizes. I wobble out of Kals reach as I collapse against his side, stroking the coarse hair along his neck.

"It is okay boy, we're here now." I whisper, shutting my eyes. He takes a deep breath and supports my weight, shuddering against me. The fog in my mind is slowly clearing; I can now control my own body. I am not strong enough to push my power any deeper so I let it enjoy its time on the surface. I open my eyes, my arms are covered in thin blue moving veins; swimming under my skin. I imagine all of my body currently looks like that.

"I don't even know what the fuck just happened." I say, looking back to Kal. He's watching me with a closed expression, not giving anything away.

"First thing we need to do is get someone down here to tend to

Dominic's wounds, the second thing we need to do is figure out what these creatures are and how they managed to get down here." He pauses and looks towards my mouth. I frown, now wasn't the time to think about kissing.

"What?" I step away from Dominic and towards Kal.

"You might want to feel your mouth." He says softly, nothing but kindness in his eyes. I reach up hesitantly, on each side where my human canines should have been are two long fangs, indenting my bottom lip.

I gasp as I drop my hand away, running my tongue over them; their sharpness nearly drawing blood.

"How do I get rid of them?" My voice is shrill as I stand there, afraid to move. Kal comes closer and takes my face gently in his soft hands. He tips my face towards him; I hold my mouth open as he looks at them.

"You need to relax."

"Sorry it's kind of hard after what just happened," I growl, narrowing my eyes at him.

"Take a few deep breaths; you need to call them back into you. It won't work if you're not relaxed." Relaxing seems impossible at this point but it is the only option I have.

I take a few deep shaky breaths as I focus on my fangs. Distantly I'm well aware of how close my body is to Kal's, I'm more than aware of it as my pulse picks up at the thought of it. I push those dangerous thoughts from my mind.

"Now just ask them to recede." His voice is soft, his breath hits my cheek. He was far closer now than he was before.

Come back to me.

Slowly and very painfully my fangs begin to retract, finding their home hidden in my gums once again. Once they've finished, my mouth aches from the force of them, it was like getting a sore tooth pulled out.

I open my eyes and shut my mouth, quickly running my tongue over my teeth to make sure they are back to normal again. Kal is still holding onto my face.

"Thank you," I whisper. He blinks slowly as his eyes study my face; much to my dismay slowly heat begins to rise to my cheeks.

He clears his throat and steps back, the moment lost.

"Go and get cleaned up, Dominic will be okay. We'll discuss this later." I walk past him, willing my leaden legs to move. I struggle up the stairs, leaving Kal alone.

Now I wouldn't have a choice in learning to control my power, not after what Kal had just witnessed.

Allison

I pull on a pair of black tights and a black singlet, Kal would be here any minute to drag me to training. I had prayed to every God I could think of last night before bed that Cassidy wouldn't be there.

I shove my feet into a pair of black sneakers and open my door. May as well meet him half way. I reach the hallway that leads to the sitting room and kitchen, Kal has just turned from the sitting room and is striding towards me.

His figure is wrapped in his black fighting uniform, his long raven hair tied back in a high ponytail. I'd managed to pull my hair back into a low bun; I wasn't phased with my appearance. I had no one to impress here. Kal pauses once he sees me, his eyes quickly check over me.

I struggle to hide my scowl; the blue veins had long faded. So had the power I felt with them, I'd pushed it down once again. I was horrified with myself; I couldn't even begin to fathom what I had done.

"It's good to see you're ready." He says evenly. I cast my eyes down as he walks past me. I fall into step behind him and follow.

"Well, I didn't have a choice," I say quietly. I had one focus and that was to get my own apartment. I was sick of being on house arrest.

"Good observation. How are you feeling?" Pine and vanilla waft off him and smother my senses, I crinkle my nose up. Why did he have to smell so damn good all the time?

"I feel fine." I pick up the pace and fall into step beside him; he towers over me, his ponytail swinging across his shoulders with ease.

"Good."

"Will it just be us in there?" I ask, watching him out of the corner of my eye. We'd just finished walking through the garden; I was not ready for whatever he had in mind for me.

"Mmm. I'm not sure; they come and go as they please most times." He looks down at me, raising an eyebrow. "Why, does it bother you if someone else is here?"

I make eye contact, raising my chin sightly.

"No. Just wouldn't want to embarrass you with my strength and all." He grins wickedly, amused.

"Now that's the girl I know." He strides ahead of me, I watch him. He didn't know me. I didn't want to know him. Why did he have to be so nice? Why couldn't he have chained me in a dungeon?

He holds open the door for me. The training room is empty, perfect. No one would see me embarrass myself.

"It's good to see you're still a gentleman." I call, walking over to the wall of weapons. I hear the door shut, trapping us in.

"Oh please, I'm still a lot of things." His voice is warm and a lot closer than I anticipate. The mats mute our footsteps. I turn and catch myself. His obsidian eyes gaze down at me, his body mere centimetres away. I suck on the bottom of my lip; it's suddenly too warm in here. I take a step back.

"Didn't your mother ever teach you not to sneak up on strangers?" I growl, collecting myself. He shrugs vaguely.

"Here and there. Are you ready to begin?" I eye him warily but nod. He walks back into the centre of the room.

"Okay, the first thing you need to learn is how to defend yourself. We'll go through the first basic steps." My body locks up; Xavier had taught me to defend myself and taught me how to fight. I already knew what to do.

"I...I already know." I mumble, I cross my arms over my chest. He raises an eyebrow at me.

"Well come and show me then." He doesn't back down. I slowly approach him, doing this would mean remembering Xavier.

It would mean remembering the friendship we had, that I broke.

That I ruined.

"Okay let's begin, I'll attack and you defend." As soon as the words leave his lips he's upon me, gentle and slow to begin with. My limbs are slow and choppy, earning me a soft blow to the stomach. I grunt and spin out of the way of his next hit.

"Xavier, is this really necessary?" I ask, crossing my arms over my chest. He puffs his chest out at me, his loose hair sticking to his neck from the sweat of our ongoing session.

"Yes it is Ali, now I'm going to defend and you attack." He gestures towards himself and grins, I roll my eyes and get into position; ignoring the way my legs burn in protest.

I lunge and throw my weight at him, he easily side steps and wraps his arms around my torso. He swings me through the air, laughter bubbles from my lips and soon his chest erupts as he joins in.

He lowers me to the ground and I look over my shoulder at him, the warmth in his eyes knocks the breath from me—

I spiral back to the present, I'm lying on my back staring at the high ceiling and the golden lights above me. I wasn't sure how I got here.

"Ali, you need to try better than that. You didn't even defend the hit." Kal swarms my vision as he looks down at me, frowning and puffing his lips out. I growl as I pull myself up, my stomach throbs slightly. I turn and face him, not quite ready for more memories to surface. If I could just push it down a little longer.

He comes towards me again, his movements a blur. He wants

me to use my vampire abilities. I twirl out of his way effortlessly; my body is finally remembering the moves Xavier had shown me. How to dance around your opponent and dance with them. It was a beautiful thing, being in sync with your competitor.

After taking a graze to my arm I let my body take over, it dances around Kal happily; avoiding each fist and swing and kick he sends my way. We move around the open space, it's a lucky thing no one else is here otherwise they'd be caught in the carnage.

Slowly my limbs begin to burn; I wasn't sure how long we'd been going at it. It was time to show Kal I wasn't as helpless as he thought. As we had danced, I realised he had a pattern; an attack strategy.

I counter the swing from his right fist and move into it instead of away. I slam my back into his solid chest and wrap my hands around his neck; in a swift movement I swing him and myself forward. His surprise is apparent as we roll through the air before connecting with the ground.

He cushions the collision, his breath *whooshing* out of him. Before I have a chance to claim victory he rolls us over; every part of him presses against my backside. His breath is hot and heavy in my right ear as my cheek is squished against the ground, my breathing is just as unchecked. I keep my eyes trained on the door in the distance; not daring to meet his eyes. My heart slams wildly in my chest.

"That was a cheap shot," he growls softly, the vibrations send a chill through me; the good kind. I bite down on my bottom lip, hard. I won't let him have that power over me. I know he is attractive, he knows it too.

"Don't be so predictable next time," I hiss. His body is a solid and heavy weight. If I could just…

"I'm far from predictable." I see the moment of vulnerability and take it, I anchor my body to the left and slam my right shoulder back; rolling him off me. With a blur I'm straddling him, gripping his wrists above his head. His eyes darken as they wander over my body.

Sweat clings to my skin, filling the air with a hint of salt. My chest heaves and my limbs shake, I still don't give up.

"Everyone is predictable if you pay enough attention." My voice is low and comes out softer than intended. I swallow the lump in my throat. My face is only inches away from his, my chest nearly pressing against his. Yet he makes no move to dismantle me.

Beads of sweat pool on his forehead, at least I know I'd given him a work out. Stray bits of black hair cling to his cheeks and neck, his lips are parted and moist as he takes voluntary breaths. His skin is flawless, apart from the thin white scar that runs along his right jaw.

I divert my eyes back to his, and am taken back by the intensity of them. I should move. I should let him go, climb off. I was too close.

As if the universe is answering my silent prayer the door swings open and black night pools in. My senses tingle as I pick up their scents, sandalwood and cherry. I didn't need to turn my head to know Cassidy and Zeke just walked in.

Kal gives me a lazy smile, as if this was his plan all along. A feminine growl echoes around the large space. I snarl as I'm pulled out of whatever trance I'd trapped myself in. I stand swiftly and brush myself off. I keep my eyes down cast as I stalk out of the training area, earning a more threatening growl as I pass Cassidy.

My cheeks burn with embarrassment. Foolish. I was a God's damned fool. What on earth happened back there? What was he trying to play at?

I storm my way through the castle, I needed fresh air. Screw waiting a week, I was going to Dafria.

I'm in and out of the shower as quick as my vampire speed allows me; I dress nicely, opting for the same red skirt and crop top I'd worn yesterday. It didn't take long to wash the blood out of it, leaving the faint hint of lavender. I let my wet silver hair swirl around me; it'd grown down to my belly button now. I think it was time for a change.

I knew in a matter of time Kal would be back in the castle, I hurry to my room and slip on a pair of black flats. In a blur I'm out the front of the castle and rushing towards and through the forest that was keeping me from freedom.

The cool breeze kisses my bare skin as I run along with ease, I manoeuvre through the forest easily enough; my vampire sight clearer than it was yesterday. My hair whips at my back, slowly beginning to dry.

Animals in the forest scuttle and bound away as they hear my approach; vaguely in the distance I can sense a larger animal than the others.

What I can only hope is an animal.

I push myself forward more, not wanting to dwell in this forest any longer. My steps are too loud, my movements not swift enough. The large animal begins to hurtle towards me, its large body crashes through the forest behind me; a growl rips through the night.

I will not be afraid. I will not be afraid.

Fear will only get me killed.

With each step I take, the creature takes two. It will be upon me before I reach the forest edge. I can't let that happen. I won't.

My fear turns to adrenaline as the city lights begin to ebb into the forest, I am nearly safe. Nearly free of its grasp.

The hot breath of the creature seems to be right at the back of my neck, a scream begins to bubble in my throat.

No. No. No. No—

In an explosion of leaves I leap from the forest and into the path of an oncoming tuk-tuk. I slam my hands into the ground to stop myself from falling over; the tuk-tuk driver slams his breaks on. The ground beneath my hands cracks.

"Are you stupid!" he yells. His black hair is shaggy and hangs limply around his face. A few weeks' worth of stubble shadows his narrow jaw. His crooked nose draws attention to his angry eyes. I push myself off the ground and step out of his way.

"I'm sorry!" I yell as he continues past me, which causes him to scowl at me. I move off the road and onto the crowded footpath. The city looms hauntingly over me, its bright lights a sore sight to my sensitive eyes. I hadn't seen anything as bright since I first arrived.

The vampires on the street make a point of glaring at me, some with hate in their eyes and the others with amazement. They move out of my way as I walk down the path, the cobblestone footpath is spotless. Kal must really like to keep his city in check.

The overcrowded streets teem with chatter and laughter, a faint hint of blood is hanging in the air like an invisible veil, so faint my vampire senses nearly miss it. Tuk-tuk taxis move up and down the streets, I figure I'm on a main street because of the traffic build up. I wonder where Nardia lives, which tall building she calls her home.

I try and tug on our bond, letting her know I am close. I don't receive anything back, maybe she's just busy. I brush the thought off and cross a main intersection.

I stop and peer into one of the many hair salons, a female vampire with dark skin and pastel pink braided hair is working away at another female in the seat. She moves with ease and grace, and a part of me believes she would be able to do this in her sleep.

Her loose white crop top swirls around her, her high waisted blue denim jeans are covered in little black skulls.

I like her.

Two other female vampires work away at their clients; I don't pay them much attention. I want *her* to do my hair.

I hesitantly walk into the shop; the bell chimes on the door and makes my presence known. Hairspray and lavender waft towards me, shrouding me in a cloak. She looks towards me but continues to work, her hands never pausing.

She grins a wide, white dazzling smile. Her golden nose ring glints from the light.

"Well, hello sweets. How may I be of service to you?" Her kindness takes me back, I smile shyly.

"I was … um wanting something different." I tug at the ends of my hair and shrug. She sucks her bottom lip as her eyes wander about my hair.

"Mmm, yes I can work with that. Anything in particular?" the vampire female she's working watches me warily. She must know who I am. What my purpose being in this city is.

"I'm not sure, whatever would suit me." I say softly. She nods once and looks back to her client. She'd styled her hair in black waves, with slivers of bright blue running through it.

"You're done love! What do you think?" She beams, proud of her work. The female touches it and smiles.

"I love it; you always do an incredible job." She rises from the chair, her black dress swirling around her. She passes the hairdresser a small vial of blue liquid before disappearing out onto the street.

She tucks it into her back pocket and beckons me into the chair. I sit hesitantly and stare at my reflection. I cringe inwardly, my round ruby eyes look out of place on my narrow face. Long gone are my soft plump cheeks I had worked hard for in my time at the camp. She runs her fingers through my hair.

"I'm Aliya, how would you feel about a cut and some colour to really bring those eyes out? Gorgeous eyes by the way." She hums to herself as she waits patiently for my reply.

"I'm Allison. And yes okay, surprise me," I say softly, not wanting to accept the compliment. She shrugs her thin shoulders and pulls my hair back, grabbing a bronze pair of scissors from her tray.

"Wait, can we cover the mirror?" I truly want it to be a surprise. She smiles and slips a black towel over it.

"Wait, I don't have any money." I say quickly. She pulls my hair back and sprays it with rose water.

"We don't use money here sweetheart, we accept gifts or debts. All kinds of gifts, no matter what they may be." I relax in the chair and close my eyes as the scissors make their first cut.

I drift away as she transforms me, not paying any attention to the process. Only slightly scrunching my nose at the bleach she uses, and the other chemical smells I couldn't place.

In a matter of hours, or longer, she claps her hands together.

"Are you ready? Oh my gosh. I'm so happy with it." She squeals; I open my eyes as she pulls the towel away. My eyes bulge as I take in my new hair. She was truly an artist.

My hair now only grazes my breasts; the silver roots melt down half way blending with velvet red tips.

I barely recognise myself. I run my fingers through the curled hair.

"What do you think?" She asks, admiring it through the mirror.

"I love it." I say softly, this was exactly what I needed. A new me deserved a new appearance.

"It's everything I've ever wanted," I say, my voice raw with emotion. She rests her small hands on my shoulders.

"This is why I love my job, I'm so happy you enjoy it. Oh do please come back again." I nod in the mirror; it really does bring out my ruby eyes.

"Own them girl, they're beautiful on you." She whispers before dropping her hands.

I stand and turn to her.

"I don't have a gift, will you accept a debt?" I ask, clasping my hands together. She nods and smiles.

"Of course sweetie. I'll call for you when the time is right. Now go, explore what the city has to offer you." I turn away and walk onto the street, somehow feeling lighter than ever before.

9

Allison

The deeper I venture into the city, the less civilised the
vampires become and the more vampire drunk humans I
see. I cringe as I pass them, their necks covered in bite marks. I
try to walk straight, but I find myself veering down different
streets. There are no signs here to tell me where I am; I have to
hope someone will point me in the right direction of Kal's castle.

The street I'm currently in is much darker than the other streets
I had ventured down, a handful of vampires lean against the
building to my right; hiding in the shadows.

I continue walking, hoping for an exit down a brighter street.
No tuk-tuk taxi would be able to fit down here; the buildings
were too close together and only seem to grow closer the deeper
I go down the street. The buildings tower over me, blocking out

most of the light from the other streets. My stomach churns, my skin crawls.

I need to leave this street. I stop and turn, my skirt flying around me with the sudden movement. Something is wrong. I take a step forward and freeze, the group of vampires I'd walked past had lined themselves up; blocking my escape. I gulp.

The six of them are all dressed in black; the paleness of their face is the only exposed skin. I take a step back, clenching my shaking fists.

"You look a little lost, dumpling," one of the males calls. They all grin, fangs flashing from the distance. *Oh god, oh god, oh god.*

"Cat got your tongue?" a female purrs; one of the males chuckles as they take a step forward. I don't take my eyes off of them. I could try and out run them; I could try and run through them. I had to do something.

"No, it doesn't," I call, my voice shaking slightly. In a blur they surround me, blocking me in. I turn in a violent circle, the taste of copper in my mouth. My heart beats wildly as my skin becomes clammy. Deep down my power stirs, feeling the threat.

"You look absolutely delicious. When we heard the king had brought you into the city, I had to see for myself." one of the males to my left says, to my right someone tugs on my hair. I stay still.

"But, then we noticed the king wasn't with you. So of course we had to keep an eye on you. There are some nasty vampires in this city that would do *anything* to have a taste of you." I wish I had just listened to Kal, oh god I was going to die here.

"You don't belong to anyone, so it's free for the taking." a female says in front of me. In the dark they all look the same; pale skin, black eyes with hoods covering their other features.

"I'm nothing special," I mumble; I loosen my hands beside me. My power flickers and comes to my silent calling. I feel its pressure building in the palm of my hands beneath the skin, waiting for the order.

"Oh but you're very special. No wonder the king wouldn't let you leave his side. Greedy of him to keep you to himself." I have to stop the bubble of laughter from slipping through my lips. Ha, if only they knew what Kal and my relationship was really like.

"I'm not his," I growl, unable to help myself and my stupid ego. I was no one's. A vampire to my right steps forward, running a gloved hand down my cheek. They watch me with wide, fascinated eyes. I sniff, old blood coats their glove. I bite down the inside of my cheek.

"I'm going to taste you." He grabs my arm, I try and yank it from them; the other vampires came forward and grab at me, holding me in place. I struggle and cry out as he brings my arm closer to his exposed fangs. This couldn't happen. No. No. *God please if you're there save me.*

Save me.

He licks his lips and runs his tongue over my forearm; I cringe and scrunch my face up. My breath comes in short gasps as they graze their fangs over my skin. My vision sways slightly.

Once he starts, I know he won't stop.

"Make sure you save some for us," a voice to my left growls. The hands holding me begin to squeeze, as if they're ready to rip me away if this vampire decides to become greedy. Oh god, I'm an open buffet. How ironic. I could almost laugh.

"I'm part vampire." I say, in the hope that would deter them.

"You think we don't know that?" One growls; pulling at my skirt.

"Wouldn't that make you sick?" I ask, frowning. The vampire had taken his mouth away from my arm. My distraction is working.

"You're mostly human sweetie," a female says.

"But… my eyes? I'm mostly vampire?" I say, confused. Why would my eyes be almost all red if I was still mainly human?

One of the vampires snorts while the others snicker.

"You really don't know much do you? Well, I will enlighten you. They're going to change to all red regardless of whether you stay human or vampire, the Queen's blood is a part of you. They always would have turned red; the vampire's blood you drank just helped speed up the process." I couldn't tell if they were lying or not but I felt so much relief I could have cried out in joy. I was still mostly human.

One sniffs my skin, frowning.

"What else runs through your blood?" It asks, confused. I raise my eyebrows.

"Nothing," I say, not wanting to remember the camp. The things I had to go through, I couldn't think of that. Not now.

"I smell it too, what is that?" one asks, pulling away.

"Grobbler blood," the vampire that was originally going to bite me says. Dread fills me head to toe. I thought by now whatever Luke pumped into me would be gone, cleaned out. I was mistaken.

"How did you get grobbler blood in you?" One asks, pulling my hair back to expose my throat. I could feel my pulse beating wildly.

"It was injected, I didn't want it." I say quietly. I shut my eyes and bite my lip.

"Why on earth would anyone do that?" They stay silent, trying to figure it out.

"So you're part human, vampire *and* Grobbler. What are they trying to turn you into in that castle?" The girl vampire asks.

"It wasn't at the castle. It was a human," I say. I don't know why I was letting them know so much. I figure if these are my last words they may as well be true words.

"So humans are trying to mutate themselves?" The original vampire asks, yanking my face towards him as he comes closer. His rancid breath forces me to hold in my gag.

"I don't know," I say, holding my breath as much as I can.

"*Lies,*" one hisses and they rip a few pieces of my hair out. I

71

hiss. The male vampire still hasn't moved his face away.

"Could that be why?" He asks, his eyes flicker to my mouth; looking for signs of a lie.

"Yes, but they never told me anything. I only fought once with a man that had it in his system; he matched my strength and I was half vampire at that time. If I refused the needles it wouldn't end well so I just let them do what they wanted." I am trying to calm myself down. He blinks slowly.

"She's telling the truth." By now I've figured he's the leader of their little group. If I could convince him I wasn't worth it, they might let me go.

"Well this is certainly valuable information. Have you told the king yet?" He asks.

I stay silent. A small seed of guilt plants itself; if I wanted equality for both races I would have told Kal already, right?

"Well aren't you a naughty girl, hmm?" He purrs, pulling away from me. He brings my arm back to his mouth. I begin to panic again, his fangs press against my skin.

"Let her go." A familiar male voice growls from the entrance of the street, they all turn and snarl towards him. I try and look around the bodies, but can only see his shadow.

"We found her first." One of them snarls; the others join in.

"She's mine," he snarls back, beginning to come towards us with ease. I try and place his voice, I know him. Relief fills me to the point I could almost cry.

"She isn't marked," a female voice calls. Nails dig into the flesh of my left arm; nearly drawing blood. If they went deeper nothing would be able to stop them.

"We were doing it today, I had foolishly left her to grab us refreshments and when I returned she'd wondered off. I've been looking for her this entire time. So I thank you for finding her, but get your hands the *fuck* off of her." He steps into a sliver of light. *Zeke.* Zeke was here to save me. They hesitate. My power was nearly bursting from my hands; I'd forgotten it was there. If

Zeke saw what I was capable of he'd never look at me the same, not that he does now anyway.

"No." That simple word makes the nails break the skin, my blood begins to trickle down my arm. In an instant all their heads snap towards it. With the second of vulnerability I unleash my power in an explosion. Blue light blinds me, before seeking out its threat.

They scream as the blue tendrils begin to wrap around each of their throats. I don't look at Zeke. All six of them are trying to claw at the tendrils, but their hands go straight through.

The hunger begins to overtake, want and need to kill is building. Their life essence surrounds me, pulsing warmth deep inside of me.

If I let it loose I won't be able to rein it back in.

Kill them. They were going to kill you.

No, I can't. I won't be able to stop.

The six of them begin to rise in the air as I hold my hands out. Zeke hasn't moved. The tendrils tighten; their life forces begin to blink out. I take a deep breath, and look at Zeke.

He stands there frozen, his eyes wide as he watches me. I make eye contact.

"Thank you again, it means a lot. I don't think I'd like to spend my last night here alone." He nods in understanding, his hair falling over his face. As I go to step past him my bad ankle gives way. Before I hit the ground, strong arms catch me. I wiggle around in his arms to look at him. His face is barely centimetres from mine, the corners of his mouth turned up slightly.

"Would you look at that, already saving your life?" I swat his chest softly and grin at him.

"Get used to it, because I have a feeling you'll have to do it a fair bit from now on." He chuckles softly, his chest rumbling against mine.

I gasp as the memory fades, my power snaps back into me as I choke. Tears swim in my eyes as I continue to stare at him.

The vampires drop to the ground and cough and splutter, Zeke is by my side in an instant. He takes my cheeks in his hands and his eyes roam my face.

"Are you okay?" He whispers. I nod once; holding back the well of emotions the memory has brought back. In a swift movement he's cradling me in his arms and we're strolling out of the dark street, leaving the vampires. I rest my head on his chest, his cold body bringing me back to earth.

"Where are you taking me?" I ask weakly. I look at my hands. They are a faint blue, cutting off just after my wrists. Why was my power changing my body in the process?

"To my home, I think we need to talk."

10

Allison

Zeke puts me down once we reach the main city street, from where I originally started. He stays close to me as we walk down the street, away from the direction of the forest. A few vampires give us glances before looking away.

In the distance I see the platform that releases us to the human world; the sunlight is so close but so far from my grasp. I would do anything to feel its warmth on my skin again.

As we walk along my legs begin to tire, the muscles burn with each step I take; my morning training session with Kal catching up with me.

We reach a tall, dazzling building. Its glass walls reflect the light from the street, giving each room its privacy. Zeke opens the glass door for me, I step in and look around. The white tiles are spotless; no other vampire is in here. A few fake plants are spread around the room, a gold elevator awaits us. He follows me in, shutting the door behind him. It blocks out the noise from the street. I follow him into the elevator.

He presses the glowing button for level thirty. The elevator kicks into gear and begins to take us up. I stay silent as I watch Zeke.

His jaw is locked, the muscle twitches. He isn't happy. He's wearing his usual get up, black jeans, black tight shirt with black boots. His hair is pulled up in a messy bun, with loose strands flying around.

He still smelt the same, smoke mixed with sandalwood. I look away and focus on the elevator doors; I still meant every word I had spoken to him at the castle. My being here wasn't going to change that.

The elevator dings as the doors open to a long, red carpeted hallway. Six dark oak doors line the walls on each side. I follow him to the last one on our right, he opens it and lets me in first. I walk down the short hallway, the white tiles sparkle underneath my feet.

It opens to my left, revealing a small, black and gold kitchen. A black frame of metal roses and vines work as a wall to my right between the kitchen and what I assume is the lounge room. I run my hand along the black marble island bench then I turn to the right and into the lounge room. It was larger than the kitchen, to my left is another small hallway, exposing a large bed with messy sheets. I turn away, a small white leather couch sits facing the open glass wall with a small round glass coffee table in front of it, overlooking the city below.

I walk over to the wall and look out; the city takes my breath away. Every vampire below is a small moving speck, as well as the tuk-tuk taxis. The building across from us is similar height, but has balconies you could walk out onto. I turn to see Zeke standing beside the metal roses, arms crossed over his chest.

"I like your apartment." I say softly. He raises his eyebrows, his jaw ticks. I sigh as my shoulders sag.

"Thank you for saving my life."

"Does Kalabhiti know you're in the city?" he asks; his voice neutral. I swallow hard, the last he'd seen I was all over Kal.

"No," I whisper. Zeke shakes his head and looks past me, out the window.

"Why did you come here? What on earth were you thinking coming here without someone to look out for you? Are you out of your mind?" his voice is beginning to rise; he still doesn't look back to me. I cross my arms over my chest.

"I was going crazy in that castle, Kal won't let me leave. I don't like feeling trapped." his eyes snap back to me.

"He's trying to protect you, because he knows not all vampires are going to be friendly with you and like you. Everything he's done has been in your best interest," he growls. I look away from him and stare at the white carpet; I should have taken my shoes off.

"Yeah right. Best interest, I'm sure." I sit on the couch and stare out. He moves and stands in front of me, looking out as well.

"Do you understand how hard it is for him to have you here? He can't let you roam free because these are his people as well; he needs to protect them from you as well." his words sting, I suck on my lower lip.

I hadn't thought of it like that, I hadn't seen myself as a threat to the vampires. I knew I was a monster, yes. But I hadn't realised that I could be the biggest one in this city.

Zeke turns to me and his eyes soften.

"I know it isn't easy Allison. I know what this city is like. I'm lucky I found you when I did." I meet his eyes.

"How did you find me?" I ask, curious.

"I was with Nardia; she was fine one minute and the next on the ground with her head in her hands, screaming your name over and over. That's how I knew you were in the city; I found your scent easily enough and followed it." I perk up at the mention of Nardia, I miss her so much.

"Is she okay? How is she?" I ask, leaning forward and gripping my skirt in my hands. His eyes flicker to them.

"She'll be fine, I think once I found you it would have stopped whatever was happening. In general she's recovering. She has a lot of… things to work through from that camp." he whispers the last bit, I understood what he meant. Her poor eye.

"I must have been screaming down the bond," I whisper, thinking back to when I was panicking. It must have reached her, which was odd because I hadn't felt her down the bond recently.

"Most likely. I'll visit her after I take you back to the castle. You'll have fun facing Kalabhiti." He raises his eyebrows and I frown at him.

"Why can't I come and see her yet?" I ask, crossing my arms. He sighs and rubs a hand over his mouth.

"Because you're nowhere near stable enough. You need to control that power of yours before you come back to the city. It's frowned upon to use your powers on others in the city." I stand up.

"They attacked me first!" I throw my hands in the air, it was self-defence.

"Ali, you didn't see it from where I did. You were literally something supernatural and the power was throwing itself off you in waves. What snapped you out of it?" he asks, taking a step closer.

"A memory." I say simply, not telling him that he was the reason. I didn't want to deal with the repercussions or feelings that would come if I did. He doesn't press it.

"Now I want an honest answer. How have you been?" he asks, his eyes roaming my body. I raise my chin, I knew I was skinner. Nearly as skinny when he first met me.

"I'm doing okay," I say, avoiding his eyes.

"No, you're not," he says softly. I bite my inner cheek and look away.

"I'm getting there. It isn't easy, but I'm managing. Kal wants me to pretend I'm his Queen in a week for some important vampires, and we made a deal. If I can show him I'm serious about training he'll let me get an apartment in the city in exchange. I'll act how he needs me to. I can't stay cooped up in that castle, it's driving me crazy." He snorts.

"You're going to act like a queen?" I look at him and frown, he was fighting a smile; and failing miserably.

"Yes, I am. I'm sure it can't be hard. I'll just have to talk proper and whatever else. I already wear pretty enough clothes." I gesture towards my skirt and shirt. He rolls his eyes.

"You'll be dressing in clothes much nicer than what you're wearing now. Your hair looks nice by the way. It brings your eyes out." I raise my eyebrows at his compliment; I can feel my guard slipping. I curse myself for being so forgiving.

"Thank you. Everything around me is changing so I figured I needed a change as well. I love it." I run my fingers through the curls, loving the silver and red. He moves closer, stopping in front of me. I freeze as he runs his fingers through the ends.

"Soft as well," he murmurs; he doesn't take his hand out of my hair. My heart picks up, this is where I step away and tell him to not worry about taking me back, that I'd find my own way.

"Mmm, thank you," I whisper, dropping my hand back to my side. His lips twitch as he steps away.

"You're welcome. Have you begun to learn about your power?" He walks into the kitchen. I follow him.

"No, today was our first training session. It was just defence techniques." I lean against the island bench as he opens the white fridge, pulling out a large glass bottle of blood.

"I saw that. Drink?" he opens the cupboard beside the stove and pulls out two champagne glasses.

"Water, please." he turns the tap on and fills the glass up, and then he fills his up with blood. I take the water from him and take a sip. He places the bottle back in the fridge.

"Nardia will probably be the one to teach you more about it, considering it's her power. Kalabhiti would be able to teach you how to control it, which is in your best interest." he takes a sip of blood, licking his lips. I swirl the water around in my cup.

"Yeah I don't know when that will be though. I think he wants to focus on my fighting skills first." Zeke leans back against the kitchen counter; watching me.

"He's not a bad man, as much as you may think differently. He really does... care for you." the words sound bitter in his mouth, but I doubt Kal cared much at all.

"You're wrong; he's only doing what he has to because I'm Cassidar's descendent. I've been thrown into his lap and he's just expected to look after me." I finish the water and sit the glass down; Zeke finishes the blood in a gulp.

"No, you're the one that is wrong. I'm sure time will show that though, much to my displeasure." he places our glasses in the sink, before turning back to me. "I'm taking you back to the castle." He begins to leave.

"Wait, those vampires said something that's sort of stuck." I say, Zeke turns and looks at me. I take a deep breath.

"While I was at the camp I was injected with green liquid every day after I was chosen or some bullshit, but those vampires could smell it. Why couldn't you or Kal?" I say gesturing to myself; Zeke rolls his eyes and comes over to me. He takes my right arm in his hands and brings it up to his nose. He takes a deep breath, breathing me in.

"There is something, it's faint though. I wouldn't have noticed if I wasn't looking for it." he lets my arm go. I fold them over my chest and follow him as we leave the apartment.

"It might be worth telling Kalabhiti though, in case it is something we need to be worried about." I nod as we step into the elevator. I was going to be in so much trouble.

"You'll be fine; he's got a soft spot for you. I'm sure he'll be relieved you came home in one piece over everything else. Just please, don't pull a stunt like this again?"

"Noted." I mumble, suddenly feeling utterly alone. That dark feeling I was running away from has crawled back under my skin, making its home there. Maybe I couldn't out run it.

"Do you think I'm a monster?" I whisper, not really expecting an answer. I don't know why I needed his opinion, or even wanted it. He stays silent, debating.

"We're all monsters here Allison, just make sure you're the biggest one in this city. The last thing you want to be is a deer in a home of carnivorous wolves."

Allison

Zeke opens the castle door for me and I reluctantly enter. He shuts the door behind us before heading to the sitting room. I was not eager to see Kal and explain myself. Our footsteps echo off the stone floor. Dread builds up in my stomach. We turn down the hall that leads to the sitting room; I close my eyes and send out my energy. Kal is indeed in there.

Zeke opens the sitting room door, gesturing for me to go first. I take a deep breath and stride through. I get halfway before Kal's eyes pin me in place. His eyes hold a fury I've never seen before and I can't look away. He is still in his leathers. His hair flows around him with his rage.

He stands in the middle of the room, in front of the couch. Zeke shuts the door, his presence still behind me. I keep my chin high, I wasn't a deer. I was a wolf.

"Zeke, thank you for bringing her back safely," he says,

deathly calm.

"That's okay. I found her at one of the clothes shops." I keep my expression neutral. He is covering for me, so I won't get in trouble. I send a silent thank you out.

"You're dismissed." Zeke leaves immediately. Once the door shuts the room is silent. I nibble on my bottom lip.

"Well… care to explain yourself?" his jaw twitches.

"I wanted some fresh air and I wanted to change my hair," I say simply, I wasn't sure what else he was expecting me to say.

"So you risked your life to get your hair done?" I suck at my teeth. When he put it like that…

"That's correct to an extent, I mainly just wanted to explore and get away from the castle for a little bit," I say clearly. I'm not lying. Maybe I should be.

"Allison, you can't just run off like that without letting someone know."

"Right, because if I told you, you really would have let me go in." Sarcasm drips off of my words. He walks forward and stands in front of me. His shadows swirl around my ankles, gently caressing my calves.

"I would have accompanied you or had someone else go with you," he growls. The situation was beginning to heat up. I wasn't just going to back down and beg for forgiveness.

"I forgot I'm on house arrest." I growl back, crossing my arms over my chest. His eyes flicker over my face. He steps closer, my arms just brushing against his torso.

"You're not on house arrest," he grits out. I throw my hands in the air.

"*Yes, I am.*" How could he not see it? "You take me from my world, bring me here to this stupid castle and lock me up! I'm not some princess waiting for her prince to come and save her!" I shout; the last strand of my patience snaps.

"I am trapped here with a fate I never wanted. Everything you do is only to benefit you. What about me? Have you ever considered how I feel in all of this? Or am I just a pawn to you and your stupid vampire followers?" My voice continues to rise. I take a deep breath and something snaps in him.

"You came to me! You begged me to save you and I did! I didn't trap you here; you're not a caged animal so stop acting like one. Everything I do is in your best interest. You have no idea what I have to go through to keep you safe here. Do you really think I'm the only vampire that wants you?" His hands gesture around us angrily.

"You're part vampire. The sooner you accept that the better, stop being a victim to your circumstances. I know you're stronger than that, I see it in your face every day. You show me every day."

"I don't want to be part vampire!" I scream, my hands shaking violently by my side. My whole body is on fire with the emotions coursing through me.

"Well too fucking bad. You made that choice. That's on you. When Nardia bit you it sped up the process. Regardless of whether you want it or not, you were always going to have it," he growls. I snarl at him.

"I can't even look at you." I spit out. I turn to leave, wanting to hide in my room for eternity. A cold hand wraps around my arm, gently. I turn back and look at him with wild eyes; tears threaten to stain my cheeks. I can't admit he's right.

I knew exactly what I was getting into when Nardia bit me; I just never thought it would be this hard.

"Ali, please. Calm down," he says gently. His eyes hold no hint of the rage that was in them moments ago.

"I-I can't." I choke out, my body still shaking. He pulls me in and hugs me. His strong arms wrap around me, one arm sits tightly around my waist while the other strokes my hair. I wrap my arms around his waist and cry into his chest, welcoming the coolness of his touch.

I scream and cry and sob. His hand doesn't stop stroking my hair.

"It's going to be okay, Ali," he whispers into my hair and I let the tears fall. I wasn't strong, I had no idea how I could let myself get this broken.

This isn't me.

Surviving isn't living.

"I just want the pain to stop," I whisper. I sob against him as my body shudders. I hold onto him tight, afraid to let him go.

"It will; I'm here for you. I'll be there every step of the way. You need to learn to trust me."

"I don't know if I can. I can't lose any more people. It's not worth it," I whisper. I'm still grieving losing Xavier. I can't imagine getting that close to someone else again only to go through the same thing.

"I know, trust me I know," he whispers back. I lean back and look into his eyes. Their sadness crushes me even more. He was still mending, just like I was.

"I'm not her Kal, I never will be," I say softly. He shakes his head.

"I don't want you to be anyone else but *you*." He licks his lips. I watch as his tongue moistens them and inhale a sharp breath. I am a crying mess and all I can think about is kissing him? God, what is wrong with me?

"Go have a shower and relax, dinner will be ready soon. You look beautiful by the way, I love your hair." He presses a cold kiss to my forehead before stepping out of my grip, surprising me. My arms fall to my side as a blush creeps into my cheeks. I nod and suck on my bottom lip.

I numbly walk to the bathing chambers. I strip out of my top and skirt, running the warm water. I sit on the bottom and let the water beat down on my back. I cry for the last time, I have to be stronger than this. If not for myself, for Kal. I didn't come this far to only come this far.

I walk into the dining room, my hair a wavy mess around me. I am wearing an oversized white shirt with a pair of black shorts. I am past the point of dressing up to impress. Kal sits at the head of the table, glass of blood in hand. He must be on the same page as me, with back loose pants and a black V neck loose shirt.

To his left at the empty chair, a full plate sits. Some sort of meat with a colourful salad awaits me. I take a seat and tuck my hair behind my ears, not missing the length of it.

"Thank you," I say as I begin to cut into the meat.

"That's okay. But we do need to discuss those creatures that were in with Dominic," Kal says, sipping his drink.

"Is he okay?" I ask, looking at Kal. I fill my mouth with the salad, savouring the exotic flavours. He arches an eyebrow at me.

"Yes, he is fine. Our medicines are much more advanced than the humans; most of his cuts are healed now. We think they somehow managed to get into his area through the feeding door."

"But that would mean someone let them in?" He stays silent.

"Oh my god, do you suspect foul play?" I whisper, afraid whoever it is might be listening. He sighs and sits his cup down, half the contents gone. He puts his head in his hands and massages his temples.

"It's too soon to come to a conclusion, but it is a possibility." I sit back and think about this. Who would want to harm Dominic? Who else would be able to get into his area?

"Who has access to him?" I ask, happy for a distraction and happy to try and help.

"Me and you. I'm the only one with a key," he says and the weight of his words settle in.

"Well it wasn't me!" I squeak, my voice high. He sighs again, his shoulders sagging.

"I know it wasn't, you don't need to worry your pretty little head about that." He sits back and looks at me. I suck at my bottom lip.

"There is something I need to tell you though." I muster up the courage, he raises his eyebrows. "Well, a few things." I take a steadying breath. He waits silently.

"In the first week I was here, I was in the sitting room listening to the storm. As I was heading to my room a flash of lighting startled me, I looked outside and I saw one of those creatures. That's what had scared me when you asked that night, I only saw one and I promised myself I would tell you if I saw one again.

"Um, also when I was going through the forest today I felt something following me, like chasing me almost. I can't really describe what it was, I never saw it but I could feel it and hear it all around me." He opens his mouth to reply but I hold up a hand to silence him.

"Also, when I was in the human camp they were… injecting

86

me with this green liquid. I've come to the conclusion it has something to do with the grobblers. I can't be sure what they were planning to do with it but I think they're trying to modify humans to match vampires in strength." I take a deep breath and sit back. As the silence ticks on, my courage slips and is replaced with nervousness.

"Thank you for telling me." He sits back and sips his drink.

"You're not angry?" I ask, leaning forward. He leans forward in turn and runs a hand lazily down my cheek. His hand holds my chin gently and his eyes flicker over my face. I nibble the inside of my cheek, the distance between us closing slowly.

"I've been angry enough for one day. I will consider what you tell me tomorrow."

"Okay, are we training tomorrow?" I ask; my voice soft. He swallows hard, his Adams apple bobs. The tension in the air picks up like static and everything in the room dissolves around me. Kal is my only focus.

"In the morning again. I'll defend tomorrow, you can attack." His voice is rough, I find myself getting lost in his eyes.

"Are you sure? I sort of kicked your ass this morning," I whisper, teasing. I lick my lips and watch as his eyes trail my tongue.

"That's only because I let you. Tomorrow it will be a lot…" He pauses, I lean forward more. Needing him to finish his sentence.

Anticipating it.

"Harder." The word is soft but rattles every nerve in my body as his breath hits my face. I never felt this much energy when I was around Zeke or Xavier. Blood fills my senses, which only makes me want him more. I squeeze my legs together and try to ignore the warmth that is spreading between them.

"I'm sure I can help with that." I murmur, biting my bottom lip hard. His thumb trails over my cheek and jawline, skimming my wet lips. I suck in a breath at his touch, the coolness of it sending electricity through me.

"I'll have to show you the right position." His voice is deeper and rougher and drives me over the edge. I might be mistaking the hunger in his eyes but I can't deny myself anymore. I stand up slowly and close the distance between us. He sits back and looks up at me, his arms resting on the chair's arms.

"Like this?" I ask, breathless. I rest my hands on his arms as I move in front of him. I straddle him, my knees resting between his body and the chair. I'm not entirely sure what I'm doing but he doesn't stop me. He sucks in a sharp breath as I sit on his lap, I run my hands along his arms; only stopping once I reach the back of his neck.

His hands hover over my hips, I ache for him to touch me.

"You're not very good at defending." I whisper as I undo his hair. Running my hands through the length of it, his eyes don't leave my face as I smooth out his hair. I'm amazed at how silky it is. I return my hands to the back of his neck, clasping them together against his cold skin.

All of me is on fire and is thirsting to be put out.

"I wouldn't call this attacking; I was more thinking this…" In a flash he has me on the table, his glass of blood tips over. He pushes himself between my legs as I sit there hanging onto him. I wrap my legs around his waist, relishing in the hardness of him.

"Now who's the attacker?" He asks, his voice a purr. It rumbles through my entire body. I pull him closer to me, our faces mere centimetres apart. His eyes are wild and untamed as he takes me in. I bite my bottom lip.

"If you do that again, I will be biting it for you," he growls, his eyes latch on my lip. I take a deep breath. It was time to leave my comfort zone.

"I dare you," I say, breathless. I take my bottom lip in my teeth, biting gently. A noise deep in his chest catches in his throat as his lips meet mine.

I kiss him hungrily and savagely, his lips are velvet against mine; moving in perfect sync. I pull myself closer to him, wanting to feel all of him.

Kal. Kal. Kal. His name a mantra in my mind.

He bites my bottom lip gently, the feeling ecstasy. I moan as he lets my lip go, his lips are upon mine again; hungrier this time. He pushes me gently down onto the table. My back dampens with the spilt blood, all my common sense flies out the window as he climbs onto the table with me, holding his weight above me.

I claw at his back as the kiss deepens, our tongues intertwine.

I welcome the taste of blood, wanting more of it. I grind my hips against his, pulling him down to me.

He moans against me, causing my body to arch into his.

"Oh Kal…" I whisper against his lips. He pulls back a fraction; his eyes wild as he watches me. I whimper at the distance. He smiles at me.

"You're beautiful Ali, so beautiful." he whispers but his eyes flash briefly with sadness. My breath is ragged in my chest as I watch him; my body is wound up tight. His lips meet mine again, gentle this time.

We kiss slowly; I wrap my arms around his neck and lose myself in his touch. He tugs at my lip gently as he pulls back again. I frown at the distance.

Someone clears their throat. I widen my eyes in horror as I watch Kal. He smiles lazily at me before looking up. He doesn't get up, his erection still hard and pressing against me.

"Yes?" He asks, casually. I close my eyes and try to hide my mortification. Oh god. All of the warmth leaves my body.

"Zuriel has gathered important information about the incident, we need to speak privately." Cassidy's voice is tight and I groan internally. If this wasn't more of a reason to hate me I don't know what would be.

"No worries. I'll meet you in my study shortly. You're dismissed." I wait for the footsteps to leave before I open my eyes, only to see him peering down at me; trying to supress his smile.

"Oh god," I groan, letting a hand fall to my face.

"If you could only see how red your face is right now. It almost matches the tips of your hair," he says; his voice playful. I look at him between the cracks in my finger.

"Can you blame me?" I ask. I pull my hand away and rest it against his chest.

"Well, important business calls. I will have to ask for a rain check," he says, bringing his lips to my neck. I roll my head to the side as he peppers the skin with gentle kisses. My body begins to heat up again.

"If you're lucky enough," I smirk as he pulls back. He climbs off the table, helping me sit up. The back of my shirt clings to me from the blood. I'd need another shower regardless.

He pushes himself against me as he stands there. I wrap my legs around his waist. I cup his face in mine and bring it closer.

"Your luck won't run out anytime soon," I whisper. I press a gentle kiss to his lips. I pull back and let my legs fall. I push against his chest gently.

"Go, before you give her more of a reason to hate me." I smile up at him.

"Have a good night, Ali. Don't worry about the mess, just clean yourself up." He kisses my forehead gently before forcing himself to step back. He pulls his hair up and corrects his shirt and his pants. To my fascination, the large bulge and length of him has me heating up all over again. His lips are swollen, as I can feel mine are.

He smirks before he strides out of the room. I let out a deep breath and lay back down in the blood. My body shakes as I lay there looking up at the ceiling. I either just made a huge mistake, or the best decision of my life. Something has changed between us, and I can only hope it is for the better.

12

Allison

I finally decide to give in to my needs and go to the sitting room. I look at it with new eyes, hundreds of books line the back wall. I skim my hand over the bookcase shelf, drawing my hand back and rubbing my fingers together, not a single trace of dust covers the books.

I run my eyes over the multiple titles, nothing in particular stands out to me. Finally I settle on a dark red leather bound book. Reaching up to pull the small volume down, I rub my hand over the front cover, it was a diary.

Cassidar Lonthropy.

Interesting. I go over to the couch and get comfortable, pulling a blanket over my bare legs. Crackles from the fire hearth are the only noise to be heard apart from my breathing. I have no idea when Kal will be back or even where he's gone.

I open the book to see a rough sketch of a female vampire, who I can only assume is Cassidar. The thin dark yellow pages are fragile, worn over the years from people constantly reading it. The thin black cursive words are hard to decipher at first, but I find myself getting lost in it.

All stories start somewhere, so mine shall too. For when I pass on and leave this earth, there needs to be some recollection of how we came to be. A retelling of sorts, by yours truly.
The first vampire to roam this earth was Edgar Polan, created from the darkest shards of magic and carved from the sharpest blade by a human hand. He emerged bloodthirsty and a new line of creature. A new evolution for humans to follow. Other vampires began to emerge, joining Edgar. Once, this world was dominated by humans. Vampires came in the late 1600's. Their traits were noticeable, speed, strength, pale skin, fangs, black eyes. Vampires hid for centuries until Edgar had decided to finally emerge and take what was rightfully his. In the early 1700's vampire hunters came to light, to hunt the dead and protect the humans.

Hundreds were lost, hunted and killed for simply being the creature humans had created them to be. For the humans had lost their grasp on controlling the vampires and the easiest option for them was to eradicate the entire existence of them, wipe them from the history books.

Riots began, vampire sympathisers rose and fought alongside the vampires. The minority won and the vampire population thrived. Slowly they began to overtake the continent, infecting each country they could get too. The only problem they faced was the dwindling numbers of humans. For their own gain, the vampires went underground once again and let the human numbers thrive once more.

Finally the vampires came to an agreement with the humans, for peace. To try and co-exist without the blood shed from either side, a council was created and I was on that council, with my dear old friend Kalabhiti.

I stop reading, my heart pounding. This was personal. Did Kal know she had her diary here? Was he really comfortable with letting just anyone read it?

Should I?

I mean, I know she's my ancestor so technically I have a right to, but it feels wrong. Like I am invading her personal space. A larger curious part of me wants to know everything I can about her and Kal. I find the sections about him.

It is the turning day for Kalabhiti and I'm deeply saddened. I sit in my chamber writing this while the sun rises outside my window. A sun I can't stand to be in anymore.
Will Kal realise what he's sacrificing? Only time will be able to tell, although I do not wish this burden upon him. He is too sweet, yet troubled. I fear the darkness will like him far more than it does the others it takes.
He doesn't know I had influence in choosing the sacrifice and he must not know for, I chose the most pure and innocent girl I could find. I will not corrupt him with more evil. Ah, there we are. The bells are chiming, in a matter of hours he will be bitten and in a matter of days he will be changed.
Changed for what purpose?

Cassidar knew the girl, found her. I had so many questions and no one I could retrieve the answers from, I highly doubt Kal would have known what she was up to and how much she was looking out for him.

His golden eyes have now been turned a putrid black. He's sitting at the back of his cage like an animal and I suppose in this moment, he is one.

I sit outside his cage on a wooden stool, passing time. He'd drained thirty females of my choosing now and he still wasn't showing any signs of the humanity that he once held. His parents are not pleased, but I assured them it would take him time. He was, in a sense, only human.

Humans are fragile things, like Kal is. I have a long journey ahead of me but I know he has an even longer one and for that I will stay by his side, it is the least I can do.

I hear the front door open and quickly push the book under the blanket. I beg my heart to slow as Kal opens the sitting room door. His eyes me warily and I cross my arms over my chest as I watch him from the couch.

"What?"

He shakes his head, dragging a hand through his hair, "Nothing, I'm just surprised you're still up at this hour. It's late for even I." I manoeuvre the book between my legs so if he were to come closer he wouldn't see it.

"I couldn't sleep so I thought I'd just sit in here where it's warm. How was the meeting?" he comes around the couch, I scoot up and quickly put the book behind my back.

He takes a seat, sprawling very un-kingly beside me. I rest my feet on his thighs as he gets comfortable.

"Long. Annoying. You know this King thing isn't all it's cut out."

"Yes I can imagine, it must be so hard." I tease, nudging a foot against him. It wins me an easy, warm smile. I like this, whatever is happening between us.

"Should try it some time." he pulls the hair out of his face and puts it in a loose, low bun. His hair is much nicer than mine and definitely well taken care of.

"I'd be a pretty hot King, not gonna lie." I shrug when he looks over at me.

himself to feel the love he craves and deserves.
Life with Tobias is good, he is just and does not judge me or
criticise me and he truly loves me. I long ago gave in to my
human ways, us vampires are far from evil or monsters. We are
as human as the rest of them and we deserve the love we all are
destined to feel.

My dear Kal if you are to ever read this you snoopy bastard, I
have always loved you and will continue to love and protect you.
Though I will not be by your side for this journey and the long
road ahead that awaits you, I hope you find your light to guide
you and show you the way.
You will always be in my heart and I will protect you from afar.
When your light finds you, you will know. She will challenge you
in ways you've never been challenged and will make you
question your very existence as the creature you are.
She will show you things I will not.
Do not fear, for she needs you to be her light as well. Together
you will fall apart and be mended. My dear Kal I leave you with
this.
   Open your human heart my dear boy, open it and reap the
rewards of love, life and the joy it brings. I know you're scared, I
am too. I promise I will be here every step of the way, from
heaven to earth and from dust to dust. Goodbye, Kal.

Tears stream down my face as I reread over her last entry, the
last words she'd written. She had loved Kal, and I wish I could
hug her. I wish I had known her. I wipe the tears away and put
her diary back where I found it. I drop my hand and close the
door to the sitting room, was I meant to be the light she
mentioned? I wasn't sure if I *could* be Kals light or if he was
mine, but at this point I knew I wanted to at least try. There's no
harm in trying, although the thought of being so vulnerable to
him makes me want to run to the dark.

I'm not sure, and I can't dwell on it. I can only try, and if I fail then I fail.

For I am human, after all.

13

Allison

M y dreams are plagued by nightmares, my past actions
continuing to haunt me. I wasn't sure when the nightmares
would end but I sure as hell hoped it would be soon. I pull my
black tights on and suppress a yawn; I'd barely slept a wink last
night. I am hoping the training session won't be as gruelling as
yesterday; my entire body still aches from it.

I pull myself up from my bed, slip on my shoes and leave my
room; the castle is silent around me. I reach the garden, Kal
nowhere in sight. I pause. Has he forgotten? Last night crashes
back into me, causing me to blush as I think about dinner. I had
no idea what had overcome me, how was I meant to act around
him now? I groan as I head through the garden. My heart also
aches for him in my chest, what I'd read about him. I couldn't
shake the feeling Cassidar knew who I was and that I would
come. I did not want to make things weird.

I reach the opening and look into the forest, letting my eyes adjust. No sign of movement or life seemed to be waiting for me in the darkness. I cautiously make my way towards the training room, keeping my senses on high alert.

The training room comes into sight, I sigh and hurry towards the door. I open and close it behind me, leaning my forehead against the smooth wood. I always felt safer in the light.

"Lesson one; always take in your surroundings before you let your guard down." Kal's breath hits my neck, his words a whisper. I open my eyes, my body rigid. I feel him step back, I turn slowly and look at him. He is dressed in his black leathers again.

"Do you ever wash those?" I ask, blurting out the question. He grins; his hair is pulled up in a high pony tail. His eyes hold mischief. My heart beat picks up.

"Only once a year." I roll my eyes at him and walk towards the middle of the room. I spin in a circle.

"So, are you ready for today's session?" I stop spinning and look at him. His arms are hanging loosely at his side as he watches me.

"Yes. Do I get a prize if I win?" I ask, he strides over to me; confidence in each step. I swallow hard as I marvel at the muscle that moves beneath his outfit.

"A kiss," he says simply, stopping in front of me.

"And if I lose?"

"You tend to Dominic until the night of the gathering." I'd almost forgotten we were having the higher ranking vampires over. I'd lost track of time, but I knew the day was sometime soon.

"Okay, deal." I hold out my hand, he raises an eyebrow as he looks at it.

"You have to shake on it." He places his hand in mine and shakes once. Before he lets go I pull him closer, my face millimetres away from his as I slowly reach my foot around behind his legs.

"Lesson two; never let your guard down." I whisper before wrenching his feet out from under him, I slip my hand out of his at the last second. He falls back in surprise, landing on his ass. I grin down at him and as he looks up at me, he bursts into rich laughter. He pulls himself up and gets into position.

I attack with all my force, back and forth we dance around each other as he deflects my advances. My breathing becomes heavy as my muscles begin to ache. I didn't want to lose. Not because I wanted a kiss.

Totally not for that reason.

His hand shoots out; aiming for my stomach. Without thinking I flip backwards through the air, skidding as I land in a crouch. I look at him in surprise.

"You're getting better." He cocks his head to the side as I stand on shaky legs. I brush my palms against my tights.

"Yeah, well isn't that the point?" I scratch my head and straighten. Sweat has gathered on my forehead and my upper lip, I am out of shape badly. I wipe my forehead as he approaches me.

"You win this round. But I want to practice with your power today." He takes my face in his hand and angles it towards his. His eyes look at me in question. I stand on my tip toes and close the distance between us. I press my lips on his gently and shut my eyes, he kisses me back as his hands rest against my lower back. Our kiss mingles with saliva and sweat as it deepens.

I pull back for a breath, he pouts his lips and frowns.

"Such a sook. Do you think we could just spend the rest of our session doing this?" I ask, not wanting to touch my power. He is a good distraction. I trail kisses against his jaw, nibbling on his ear gently. He growls low in his throat, his hands tightening. It still feels surreal to me that I am touching him like this, yesterday I hated him and today I can't keep my hands off of him. How had I caved in to him so easily?

"Allison…" His voice is rough in his throat as I pull my face back and puff out my bottom lip. Giving him my best *"please just kiss me"* expression that I can muster.

"Your magic won't work on me, darling." He kisses my forehead gently before letting me go and stepping away. I groan as I watch him put distance between us.

"Now I want you to summon your power, have it in your hands. My shadows will be here to protect you." At the mention of their name his shadows pool around his feet. I take a shaky breath and shut my eyes. I dig deep, finding the vault I'd mentally locked it in.

Come to me.

The vault opens and my power comes rushing to my call. I open my eyes and gasp as it hits me full force. Blue veins run underneath my skin, I look to Kal with wild eyes.

"It's okay, you're okay. You're in control." His voice is calming; I look back down and open my hands. I focus on my palms, slowly the blue veins begin to gather and my hands turn a rich blue.

"Now what?" I ask, my voice shaking.

"Now you need to beckon it out of you." I shut my eyes again. I can feel it wrapping itself around my mind, something else settles against my mind as well. Something I can't touch, and have no control over. I frown slightly but ignore it.

Out.

I open my eyes to see the blue veins spill out of my hands; flowing over and hitting the floor but still connected by a thin stream.

They swim in dormant circles, waiting for an order.

"See? You're in control. You shouldn't be scared of what you can do, the more resistant you are the more you're out of control." I look up at Kal, around us his shadows had formed a barrier. I nod once, afraid to speak.

"Now call them back in." I shut my eyes and visualise them going back into my hands. Slowly I begin to feel them fill me up again, the warmth spreads through me as they gather back inside of me. I take a shaky breath and open my eyes.

"Now we're going to continue doing this, in and out. Get you accustomed to the feeling of them, have you in control of them. Understood?"

"Yes, understood." I say. He nods once and I shut my eyes. We repeat this process until Kal's shadows are forced to guide them back into me. I use the last of my strength to lock them back in the vault. I sit down in a heap and then lay down, Kal lies down beside me. My breathing is heavy as I adjust to being normal again.

My mind is exhausted, this was the first time I'd ever tried to deal with my power without having to attack anyone or defend myself.

"What is your power?" I ask, still half breathless.

"My shadows?"

"Duh," I grin, what else could I have meant? He sighs.

"They came when I found my humanity, as does every vampire's little ability. Mine is stronger than anyone I've ever met, I'm not sure why. I assume it's because of my royal and pure blood, but don't hold me to it." I tilt my head and look over to him, his shadows dance above us, shaped as horses and small people, running side by side like a cloud.

"They're mesmerising." I reach out and brush against them, they swim gently around my hand, but even so I feel the power they hold.

"Yes they are, very demanding as well. Sometimes I feel they control me more than I control them. I haven't used them in their full ability for a very long time now, but the shadows can transport me instantly to places when I focus. Like that day by the stream. That's winnowing and I'm the only one capable of doing it, which is probably for the best. They tell me secrets they hear in the dark, they're my eyes more often than not."

"So you're a spy?" I ask, lowering my hand back to my stomach. He chuckles.

"When I want to be. I don't think it would be in the best interest for the King to be a spy."

I'm more than aware of how close my body is to Kals. Although his skin is cold to touch, it always helps me cool down. I felt too much like fire without him around.

"Thank you." I roll my head to the side and watch him. He faces me as well, a smile tugging at the side of his mouth.

"You're welcome. I can say today's lesson went fairly well." I roll my eyes at him, although he is right.

"Whatever, are we training again tomorrow?" He contemplates my question.

"You can rest tomorrow. You have five days until our guests come, I can't have you too sore for it. They wouldn't know why, and I can only imagine their assumptions." I gasp and a blush stains my cheeks as I look away from him.

His naked body presses against mine, kisses litter my neck. I run my hands along his defined back, my nails digging into the soft skin.

I push the fantasy out of my mind before I get flustered. I'd never been with a man before. I'd pecked Xavier and I'd only gone as far as the other night with Kal. He wouldn't know that though and I wasn't about to tell him. I stand up and start to walk to the door.

"Does that conclude our lesson?" I call over my shoulder, not trusting myself to look back. Every part of my body is heightened and I would have no self-control if he was to touch me. As if he knows this, he's suddenly in front of me. I skid to a stop, bumping into him.

I scowl as he wraps his arms around my waist but I allow the touch, welcoming the coolness of him. I rest my hands on his chest.

"Yes, our lesson is over. I have duties to attend in the city until later; will you be okay by yourself?" He asks, his eyes searching my face. I force a smile.

"I'll be fine, thank you. I'm sure I'll find something to occupy myself. I could even go for a nap." Doubt flickers across his face, but before he can reply I press a kiss to his lips, silencing him. He melts into me after a moment, a hand comes to my face and he cups my cheek gently.

Minutes tick by as we stand there, I pull back for air. He grins down at me.

"Come on, let's get you cleaned up. You stink." He crinkles his nose at me; I swat his arm and laugh. As we walk back to the castle he intertwines our fingers.

I don't let go.

14

Kalabhiti

A llison.

    My thoughts are still fixated on her as I enter the conference room in the largest tower of the city. Zuriel, Zeke and Cassidy sit at the long dark oak table. Still no sign of the twins and with Nardia on leave; I'd have to relay all the information to them at a later date. They were currently on a mission to find more of Dominic's kind, so if we were to face a wipe out, we would have a chance.

I take a seat at the head of the table; Cassidy had left abruptly last night after giving me vital information about the human camp. Their numbers had increased, with abnormalities as well.

"So Cassidy, relay exactly what you saw," I say. Zuriel cocks an eyebrow as he looks at her. Zeke turns to her and she straightens in her chair and clears her throat.

"Well when I walked in, you were on top of our innocent

Allison, sucking her lips off—" she starts, Zuriel coughs as he fights his laughter. Zeke scowls as I clear my throat.

"Not that. You know what." I say, fixing my eyes on her. She sighs and flips her hair over her shoulder.

"I was doing the usual rounds; anyway I scaled a tree and got a look into their camp and it's overflowing with humans. That boy that escaped at the river is there, in charge it seems. I can't remember his name. Their eyes were all green, it's hard to explain and their skin has a green tinge to it as well. And they are fast, almost as fast as we are." She looks to me, her black eyes creased with worry.

"I think whatever they're doing, it's going to match us. If we don't interfere and eradicate them while we still can, I don't think our kind are going to fare well in the next run in."

"But we have our powers. Surely they can't one up us on that." Zuriel jumps in, drumming his fingers on the table. I had that same thought, although it was worrying.

"With the rate they're progressing, it wouldn't surprise me. How long until they discover how to enter our city? We would have nowhere to run or hide," she exclaims, looking fiercely at Zuriel, he rolls his eyes at her.

"You were always one for dramatics. First we can always alter the requirements if that were a threat. Secondly, no other human camps or towns around us are experiencing the same problems. Zeke and I returned to Penrith, there's a slight rise in grobblers but other than that everything is how it was when we were last there." He sits back and arches an eyebrow at her.

"Yes but—"

"He's right Cassidy; I haven't been able to find anything." Zeke says, crossing his arms over his chest. His eyes flicker to me.

"Well that's even more of a reason to get rid of them while it's contained. What will we do if we can't drink their blood? We can't survive off animal blood for the rest of our days." They all look at me.

I'd tasted Ali's blood; it tasted like normal human blood. But would it still after a mouthful or two?

"Capture one, take some blood. Return here with it, and someone can volunteer to drink it over the course of a few days. We'll see how it affects us and if it makes us sick." I know Ali would not approve if she knew what I was allowing but I had to look out for my own race.

"And if we can't?" Zuriel asks. I sigh heavily.

"Then we will wipe them out." Cassidy looks visibly relieved as she sits back in her chair. Zeke nods once.

"Ah well, what can you do?" Zuriel shrugs. He raises an eyebrow. "But, have you told Ali any of this?" Zeke watches me steadily. Fear flickers across his face, he still cares for her.

"No, as far as I'm concerned it doesn't have anything to do with her. I need her to focus on herself right now; she doesn't need to be bothering with official business just yet." I say calmly, picking my words wisely. I would tell her, once I deemed her well enough to handle the information.

"I think you're over stepping your boundaries with her. You're a king and leader of this city. What I walked in on the other night didn't seem very professional." Cassidy raises an eyebrow at me. Zeke clenches his jaw.

"Wait, you're telling me… you and Ali are…?" Zuriel asks, leaning against the table; his eyes wide with amazement. I rub my temples as I look down at the table. I had no idea what we were.

"It's complicated," I say. I wasn't about to rush anything. I may be overstepping my boundaries with her but God when she looks at me the way she has been lately it's hard to keep my hands off of her. Cassidy snorts.

"I knew it!" Zuriel exclaims, hitting a fist against the table.

"Zuriel, please," I say. He grins ear to ear at me.

"If you hurt her, my King or not I will have the pleasure of kicking your ass."

"I wouldn't expect anything less from you. Anyway, what does Allison and I have anything to do with this?" I ask, pointing the question at Cassidy.

"I just don't think it's professional to be fucking her when we brought her here for business. You may be forgetting our main goal, but I'm not." Cassidy storms out of the room, Zeke watches her go.

"To clarify, I'm not fucking her," I say to both of them. Zuriel laughs but Zeke is silent. He avoids looking at me. He stands and goes after Cassidy, leaving me alone with Zuriel.

"As long as she's happy and is getting better, I could not care what you do with her. She's like a little sister to me; I'd do anything to protect her. Even if it meant kicking some King ass."

"I don't doubt you. I am needing a favour though, and I trust her with you more than anyone else. Would you be able to take her into the human world tomorrow?" I ask.

"Yeah, of course. What for?" Zuriel asks as he stands up.

"She's missing the sun, and I'm sure she'd be more than grateful to get some fresh air with a friend for a day. Get her in the morning and return her that night, in one piece please."

"Of course, I'll be there early. You can trust me; she's safe in my hands." I nod once before he leaves me alone.

I tap the table in thought, could I trust her though?

15

Allison

I lay in bed thinking. Kal hadn't returned until what I assume was late last night. He'd looked even more tired so I didn't bother him. I let him know I'd made his bed and there was a bottle of blood waiting for him beside it then he'd kissed me on the forehead and disappeared. If it was a normal day I'd be getting ready to train, but I could well and truly just stay in bed all day if I wanted.

I roll over and get comfortable, preparing to go back to sleep. A knock comes from my door. I frown and roll back over.

"What?" I call, sitting up. The door opens to a smiling Zuriel.

"Come on missy, why are you still in bed? We have a day full of adventure awaiting us!" He exclaims, grinning. He was wearing black jeans and a long sleeved black shirt. I raise an eyebrow at him.

"What do you mean?"

"We're going into the sun today, orders by the King." He fakes a salute as he says this, causing me to grin. Kal was letting me go to see the sun. I squeal and leap from my bed, it's been far too long. Maybe I could even go to a trade and get some more human clothes.

Zuriel steps into the hall while I get dressed. I pull on a pair of black shorts and a white blouse. It isn't ideal but I could not care how I look right now, I pull on my slip-ons and find Zuriel in the hall.

"Okay, I'm ready. Let's go." I run towards the front entrance, Zuriel laughs as he begins to run after me. He has no idea how much I need this. I skid to a stop as Kal comes into view, arms crossed over his chest with a smile playing on his lips.

"Thank you, thank you, thank you!" I squeal as I launch myself at him, engulfing him in a hug. He hugs me back, his chest rumbling from his chuckles.

"I literally owe you one." I pull back and look up at him. Do I kiss him goodbye? Is that the kind of thing we did now? Before I can see if it is, Zuriel strolls in. Kal sighs and looks away from me.

"Boss man, it's good to see you. I'll be taking your damsel in distress." I turn to see Zuriel bow low, a smirk on his lips. I roll my eyes at him, stepping out of Kal's arms.

"Please just return her in one piece," Kal sighs, stepping away from the door. I link my arm with Zuriel's and drag him to the door, looking over my shoulder at Kal and smiling. I'd be safe. I always am.

We leave the castle and run through the forest. I stay close to Zuriel, not wanting whatever that thing was from last time to find me. Before I know it we're on the busy streets of Dafria. Zuriel doesn't slow down, so I keep pace beside him.

Slowly the platform comes into view. Its grand white stairs

welcome us onto the circular platform, a blackness that's too dark to see sits in front of us.

"Are you ready?" Zuriel asks. I nod once and take his hand in mine. I was holding onto Kal last time I went through. As we get closer, the blackness begins to swirl and come to life. We step through.

Blinding sunlight hits us full force. I buckle to my knees and cover my eyes. What in God's name?

"Yeah, that gets easier once you're accustomed to it." Zuriel says, helping me get to my feet. My eyes water as I adjust to the light, my bare skin already warming up. Birds chirp in the distance, a soft breeze ruffles my hair. I take a deep breath, inhaling the forest around me.

"So are you ready to begin our adventure?" Zuriel asks. I look to him and survey the forest.

"What are we doing for it?" I ask as Zuriel begins to walk. I follow behind.

"There's a small human town close by, I was thinking we could do something there."

"Penrith, how far away is Penrith?" I ask, my heart aching at the mention of my home town.

"A few days give or take, why? Did you leave something behind?" He moves a branch out of our way.

"No, I just miss it I guess. Especially having my own house." I say, side stepping a rock. The low shrubs around us scratch at my bare legs.

"It was a cute little house wasn't it?" His voice sounds far away even though he's a few steps in front of me. I hadn't seen a grobbler since I was in Penrith, and I planned to keep it that way.

We continue to trek through the forest in silence. I wasn't sure what direction we were heading, but the path around us had been used enough to leave a trail.

"How is Nardia?" I was dying to see her. I had to know she was still okay and no one was really giving me any answers.

"She's managing, she's always been strong. One eye makes it hard though, especially considering she's had both for the last three hundred years." He looks back over his shoulder at me. "I think Luke was the one that removed it, I can only assume after the way she ended his life." I don't let my memoires surface of that day by the river. I block it out of my memories, not wanting to know.

"When can I see her though?"

"She's different from the rest of us; she likes to be alone while she heals. She deals with everything herself before asking any of us for support. Don't take it personal, I'm sure she'll come around eventually." He looks forward again, the trees around us begin to thin out and in the distance a make shift wall has been built, intending to replicate the cement one Penrith has.

We stop at the tree line and survey for any guards or threats. The wall in front of us isn't very high and is made up from a vast amount of different metal and wood. Undergrowth has begun to fill in the gaps, allowing small white flowers to bloom.

"Are you sure anyone lives here?" I whisper, trying to find or hear any movement of life.

"Yes, I'm sure. They're very well hidden. Their town doesn't operate like yours." Zuriel begins to walk straight for the wall. I catch up with him, not wanting to be alone.

At the wall he reaches down and unhooks a large wooden board, exposing a small enough space for us to crawl through. He winks at me and gestures. "Ladies first."

I sigh as I get down on my hands and knees; I crawl through the small space to find myself tangled in overgrown grass. Zuriel crawls in behind me, replacing the wooden board.

"What the hell," I whisper, pulling grass from my hair.

"I told you it was different," he whispers back. He stands up and helps me to my feet. The grass is taller than us, giving us the advantage of not being seen.

I follow him as he moves forward, it's eerily quiet here. I stay close to Zuriel as we move through the grass, suddenly we enter a deserted street. Grass has grown through the broken pavements and the gravel road. The small buildings are covered in dust and cobwebs, their broken windows long forgotten about. Zuriel breaks away and peers into a rundown diner; the sign words are faded and unreadable.

"Zuriel, where is everyone?" I ask, looking towards the other buildings. It's like they all up and left and abandoned the town.

"They're here; they just don't like new guests," he calls back. I frown over at him, he's tugging on the dining room door.

"What do you mean? Do you come here often?" I ask, coming closer. The door opens inwards, no trace of dust can be seen inside the diner as sunlight streams through the windows.

In the back corner is a group of six people huddled around a table, a small person is lying unmoving on top. Their heads cock towards us.

"What's happened?" Zuriel asks, rushing over. I follow him slowly, not wanting to scare them. Their clothes are filthy and the stench coming from them makes my eyes water. They eye me cautiously, their bones stick out from under their clothes. My heart aches, I was once in their position.

A woman with a thick Scottish accent says to Zuriel's right, "They came to us, offering salvation at a price. Wee' lad here wanted to test it for us, foolish child making such a large sacrifice." She's gripping the boy's hand. Her orange hair is a matted mess atop of her head, her thin features sharpen her bright green eyes.

"Who are they exactly?" I ask, coming closer. They move away from me, Zuriel shuffles over so I can see the boy on the table. I gasp as I come closer. His skin is tinged a dark green, his black hair is stuck to his forehead from his excessive sweating. He doesn't look to be older than ten.

"The Order, as they like to call themselves," the woman says. The others growl at the mention of them. My heart beats wildly in my chest; could this be Xavier's work? Would he really continue to carry on Luke's legacy?

"How bad is it?" Zuriel asks as he presses his fingers to the boys pulse and lets out a sigh. "He's still alive."

"They came a few days ago and when they return, if he's still alive, they will be taking us with 'em"

"Yolanda you can't be serious?" Zuriel turns to her, clearly baffled. She places a delicate hand over his, her green eyes focusing on him. Something passes between them; I turn away from the intimate moment.

"Zuriel, we don't have a choice. I wish we could stay 'ere more than anything, but we're starvin' and dyin'. I need to think of the children." I look back to the boy, his breathing is so shallow his chest barely moves with each breath.

"What did they give him?" I ask and she turns her eyes to me.

"Some sort a green liquid, a large amount at that." She frowns and looks back to the boy.

"He'll be okay. When he wakes he'll be... different." I say quietly. When I was in the camp they were giving the green doses to everyone; including the children.

"How do you know that? Are you a part of it?" She stands and steps towards me, Zuriel grabs her gently by the shoulders.

"No but I was once a member of the camp. The dose will give him similar advantages to a vampire, make him stronger and faster. They gave it to me each day, and they gave it to the children as well. They didn't handle it very well, but after a few days they woke up and were fine. The first dose is the worst." I cringe at my own words, what sort of monster could do this to children?

"So he'll be okay?"

"Yes, but if that's the case you'll all be injected with the same thing." I whisper. They mumble back and forth with each other.

"Yolanda you can't, it's too dangerous." Zuriel says, resting a hand on her cheek. She looks up at him, her emotions smeared on her face.

"I have to. I'm sorry. They have food and shelter and can look after us and if that's the asking price, it's a small price to pay." Zuriel's jaw tightens and a muscle ticks.

"I won't be able to visit," he says softly, stroking her cheek. Tears well up in her eyes. I'm taken aback by the affection he shares with her, a human girl. There is so much I don't know about Zuriel.

"I know, but I have to put them first. Maybe we will meet again." Her voice is barely a whisper. I clear my throat and take a few steps back.

"We must be off, I'll return before you depart." He drops his hand and glances at the boy before turning and heading out of the diner. I quickly follow after him.

I stumble, trying to keep up with him.

"Zuriel slow down!" I shout, breaking into a run to catch up with him. He stays silent as he storms through the grass towards the exit.

"Not here," he says. We leave quickly and head into the forest. I grab onto his arm, pulling him to a stop.

"You're in love with her, aren't you?" I ask and he frowns and looks away.

"It's nothing to be ashamed of," I whisper, releasing his arm.

"I'm not ashamed. But it's hard, I've offered to turn her, with Kal's approval, but she refuses. Now she's going to live with those *animals*." His eyes flash with anger as he looks at me. "I know the horrors they put you through, I can't be there to protect her or any of them. I won't know if she breaks, I won't know what happens to her after they leave." He turns and continues to walk, slow enough for me to keep in stride.

"Have you told them what they do?" I ask.

"Yes, but they have no choice. They're too weak to hunt and have nothing left to trade. I've been binging them food for the last year, begging them to stay where I can protect them.

Yolanda doesn't understand the consequences if they join, not fully."

"So she's willing to give up whatever you have for the children?" I glance over at him and he looks ahead; his eyes far way.

"Yes, but I don't know that I am."

Before I can ask any more questions, we reach the entrance to Dafria. We enter in silence, a million questions swirling in my mind. Zuriel is in love with a human girl. The Order is growing and evolving; if they were reaching for others outside their camp this far, they must be working on building their army. Why now? What were the vampires doing to go against this?

What side would I be on when it came down to it?

16

Allison

The days pass by me in a blur, my thoughts are consumed by Yolanda and the Order. I'd improved in training. I now had control of my powers and was nearly equal to Kal in combat. The more time we spent together the more I was growing attached to him, letting my guard down.

He'd been chipping away at the wall I had built around myself and was worming his way into my heart like a parasite.

We'd been spending far too much time together; we were currently sitting in the living room. My legs are draped across his lap, his hand idly caressing the bare skin while he reads a book.

"They'll be here soon, won't they?" I ask, watching him. His eyes never leave his book.

"Correct. Are you ready?" I look away and around the room.

"No, not really. I don't have a choice though. What am I even going to wear?" I lean back and look up at the ceiling.

"I'll have one of the maids bring you a dress and they'll do your hair as well. It's important to look the part of a queen as well as act the part of one."

"Okay, thank you. Who is going to be there?" I ask.

"Everyone of importance. Nardia is also coming to help you prepare." I sit up, Kal looks up at me from his book; raising his eyebrow inquisitively.

"Nardia is coming?!" I ask. Finally I could talk to her and have my friend back. He gives me an easy smile, his hand still stroking my leg.

"Yes, she will be here later. She's happy she gets to see you again, I'm sure you both have plenty of catching up to do." I swing my legs off the couch and stand up, stretching my arms above my head.

"Awesome, I need to prepare myself then." I turn to him, placing my hands on my hips.

"From now until the guests arrive I don't want you to see me, I want it to be a surprise. Also just send Nardia to my room when she arrives." I grin before turning and heading towards my room.

"Yes, your highness." Kal calls behind me; I roll my eyes and hold back a retort. Once the guests arrived I had to be on my best behaviour, and act more like a vampire than I ever had before. I squirm at the thought of being surrounded by high ranking vampires, they may not be as lenient as Kal is with me.

I open my door and pull a bag out from under the bed, I begin to pack a few sweaters and tights and anything else that could aid me in my grand plan.

I couldn't sit back and watch Zuriel's heart break, so I only had one option: I was going to the camp to protect Yolanda until I could get her and the others out. I knew the ins and outs and I was the best one for the task. I was leaving tomorrow, leaving a note for Kal. I knew he'd try to stop me, but I had to make amends for the wrongdoing I caused. I had to save them from whatever the Order would do to them.

A soft knock comes from my closed door and before I can hide the bag Nardia walks in, closing the door behind her. Her green gown flows around her as she turns to me, her hair is a vibrant red and sits in loose curls around her shoulders; her eye surveys me and then the bag.

"Running away are we?" my heart swells as I engulf her in a hug.

"I've missed you so much," I whisper, breathing in her rose scent. She wraps her arms around me and squeezes gently.

"I've missed you too dear, have you noticed our bond is weakening?" she lets me go and holds me by the shoulders. I briefly search my mind and come back empty, I frown.

"Why?" I ask. Her mouth twists as she thinks.

"I heard you that day when I was with Zeke, in that alley. I think your power broke a part of it to protect me." She touches my face gently. I gulp, I didn't realise I was that powerful.

"I'm so sorry about that, I didn't think you'd hear me," I say, stepping back. I zip the bag up and stuff it back under the bed.

"Don't apologise. Now we're this close it should strengthen. What's the bag for?" She sits down in the now empty space as I lean against the chest of drawers, folding my arms over my chest.

"I'm leaving tomorrow to go back to the Order. They've taken the girl Zuriel is in love with and I need to get her and the others she is with out of there," I say simply, not wanting to complicate it. She frowns.

"The Order?"

"Oh, that's what Xavier now calls the camp. I know he'll let me back." I look towards the window and sigh, another bridge I'd burned.

"Ali, you can't be serious."

Before I can reply a soft knock comes from the door. "Come in," I call. The door opens to one of Kal's many female maids; she sashays into the room holding a black gown and jewellery.

"Miss, the King has sent these for you. I am to dress you." Nardia moves closer to the pillows as the maid sits the dress down. I nod and undress, blushing when I'm down to my underwear. Nardia rolls her eyes.

"I'm over three hundred years old, love and trust me when I say I've seen plenty of boobs." I shoot her a furious look as the maid helps me into the dress; my black gown makes her green gown look simple. It's strapless with a corset waist, diamonds glitter in flower patterns over the breast plate leading down in a trail to the skirts of my gown. It puffs out slightly above my hips;

the multiple layers of black cloth are smooth against my legs. The top layer is sparkled with gems like the night sky, trailing a metre behind me.

"My god, I can't wear this. I'll ruin it." I exclaim, running a hand against the skirts.

"Nonsense. It's ordered by the King. This was once the Queen's dress so it's rather fitting for you. Here, let me help you with your shoes." She bends down and helps me into a pair of simple black heels.

I stay still as she straightens my hair with a hot brush, places a diamond choker at the base of my throat and slips a pair of earrings into my ears. I hiss as she breaks the skin, I'd never had my ears pierced.

"You look beautiful. The guests have begun to arrive so your presence is needed in the ball room whenever you are ready." She bows low before leaving the room.

"Now, why on earth would you think that would be a good idea?" Nardia asks, sitting at the end of my bed. I pace back and forth in front of her, my heels clicking as I go.

"God, I don't know." I groan as I look at her, the shadow of who she was is long gone. She rolls her eye at me.

"Clearly not, how does Kal feel about this little choice of yours?" my stomach twists.

"I haven't told him, I can't until I'm gone. I need to do this without vampire influencers or it won't work, and I need it to work."

"Well I don't think it's a good idea leaving it until last minute. I'm sure he'd understand." She stands and touches my arm lightly, her green gown swirls around her as she moves; the tight waist exaggerating her breasts.

"I can't tell him now, not with all of those other vampires down there," I hiss, frowning. It was finally the night to meet higher ranking vampires from the other cities. She tilts her head to the side and gives this thought.

"Mmm. You need to tell him, if you don't he will drag your stupid human ass from that camp and bring you back."

"Nards, I know you mean well but have you seen Zuriel with her? I need to get her back for him, I can't have any chance of ruining that." while I was there, I was seeking peace between both races. If Xavier had any hint I was there on vampire business I'm sure I'd have a bullet in me before I could blink.

"I know sweetie, but if it goes pear shaped, where does that leave you?" She lets go of me and crosses her arms.

"I can take care of myself."

"Yeah I'm sure you can, but you don't have to anymore. That's the point of all of this, so you're not alone. You have us now, we're your family." She sighs and walks to the door, holding the door knob in her hand.

"We'll talk about this later, but for now we need to go down there and you need to make them believe you're the best damn Queen we could ever have." I nibble my bottom lip but nod and follow her.

Nardia leads us to the ball room, already my sensitive ears pick up the smooth piano and voices. I fiddle with the diamond choker at the base of my throat, I don't know what I was more nervous about; Kal seeing me like this or having to meet new vampires. I tuck a stray strand of my straightened hair behind my ear, taking a deep breath.

Nardia swings the large double doors open and sashays into the room, she's immediately enveloped by the crowd. I walk in hesitantly, breathing in the sweet scent of blood. Every vampire I can see is holding a glass of it and dressed in brilliant dresses and suits. All eyes turn to me. Kal moves out of the crowd, his hungry eyes taking in every inch of me.

I straighten my shoulders as he comes closer, his black suit a nice change from his training leathers. His black hair is pulled back in a tight ponytail, all business and class tonight. I breathe him in as he steps close to me, the vanilla and pine scent of him helps calm my nerves.

"You look beautiful." he says softly, his breath tickles my exposed neck. I look at him and tilt my head slightly.

"Thank you, you look handsome yourself." he smiles as he offers me his arm. I loop mine through and we as begin to move through the crowd, the vampires go back to talking amongst themselves. Kal leads us to a group of three closest to the piano, immediately their power hits me. My own begins to rise, not liking the challenge. Kal tightens his arm.

The three vampires turn towards me, looking me up and down.

"Gentleman, this is our to-be Queen, Allison." the first man extends a hand towards me. They all wore suits, I shake his hand firmly.

"It's a pleasure to finally meet you, we've heard plenty of things about you. I'm Mathius. I'm the ruler of the city of Onyx." Mathius seems to be a simple man, his bald head and pointed nose direct the attention away from his beady eyes that are too small for his round face. He's wearing a crisp dark blue suit, a gold chain hangs around his neck.

"Yes, a pleasure. I'm Kalum. Ruler of the fortress Xaydia, hidden in the moutains." Kalum doesn't offer me his hand and I don't complain. His white hair is thin and long enough to touch his shoulders, his narrow face sharpens as I feel his power swell and prod at me. I clench my jaw and restrain mine. I look him over, he's in a maroon suit with gold trimming. He seems older than the other two here, especially his power.

"Well Allison, when is your official Queen ceremony?" The third one interrupts, I look at him and smile tightly.

"We're still figuring out those details."

"Ah yes of course, well it would be an honour to attend. It has been too long since we've had a Queen in our mists. I'm Sven, pleasure. Ruler of Mortarth, hidden in the hills." Sven's the most casual of them, his golden hair sits in ringlets around his face; his eyes crease in the corner as he smiles at me. He doesn't prod or poke at me with his power, I smile back. He's earnt my respect. And I like his dark green suit, it brings out his eyes. Even though they are pitch black.

"So, are you full vampire?" Sven asks. A waitress walks past and silently offers us a glass of blood. Kalum narrows his eyes at me; I quickly take a glass and nod my thanks. I keep my expression blank as the suffocating stench of fresh blood invades my senses.

Sip it. You know you want too.

"I don't think that's an important question." Kal answers, resting his free arm around my waist. I lean into his touch slightly, we could pull this off.

"It's a very important question. If she is to be our Queen she cannot be a human. We will not have split rulers," Kalum answers calmly. His power still prods at me, aggravating my own.

"Yes, I'm vampire." I say, well aware they can probably sense my human blood and hear my heart beating a million miles an hour.

"Prove it." Mathius says, sipping his blood. I look to Kal for confirmation, what the hell was I meant to do?

"I didn't realise this was show and tell gentlemen," Kal says smoothly, sending out a small wave of power. Sven sighs and rolls his eyes.

"Just show us your fangs, easy. If she doesn't have fangs that answers our question," Sven says. I hadn't had an incident with fangs since those creatures attacked Dominic. I didn't even know if I could just simply summon them.

"That's rather personal for me, I apologise. I also do not appreciate being prodded and poked at like a caged animal. I am not some side show you can throw rocks at trying to get a bite," I growl, narrowing my eyes at Kalum. His power doesn't stop.

"But dear, you are a caged animal currently." He takes a long sip from his glass, never taking his eyes off of me. I let my power rise to the surface. Without taking my eyes from him I can feel the blue tendrils swimming just below the surface of my skin.

"Oh, now isn't that interesting?" Sven asks, stepping closer. Kal's arm tightens around me. Mathius and Kalum look at it as well.

"And what does that do?" Mathius asks, cocking his head to the side. I decide to show them, if they wanted me to prove my worth, I'd do just that.

I will my power to leave me, it floats a centimetre above my skin; the blue tendrils moving and twisting lazily. I focus my attention on Kalum.

In the blink of an eye the blue swirls surround him, caging his power in their tight vortex. As much as I want to squish the vermin, I make my power only cage him and leave him unharmed. His golden, electric power tries to break from my prison, but I strain and make sure it doesn't.

They wanted me to show them if I was a vampire, I'd do one better.

I'd show them I'm so much *more*.

123

"I'm as much of a vampire as the rest of you, regardless if my heart pumps or not. I will protect you with my life, and I will not let your people down. I have one purpose in this world and it's to make a difference and bring peace. You either stand at my side or you go against it, the choice is yours." I pull my power back inside myself, it swims back into me and rests deep inside me. Satisfaction fills me as I watch their shocked expressions.

Kalum scowls as he looks at me, his power doesn't prod at me again.

"You came here to meet me and you've done that. I would not be here if I didn't care, I mean no harm to any of you but I will not tolerate disrespectful questions or interrogations. I'm to be your Queen, so I highly suggest you start to treat me like one." I turn away from them and into Kal. He smirks at me, a shimmer in his eyes.

"I'm going to go and find Nardia, I'll catch up with you later." I say softly. Before I can turn away he brings his lips down to mine gently. I pull him against me with my free hand and savour the velvet feel of them, his tongue flicks teasingly against my lip as he pulls away.

"Yes my love, stay safe." I step out of his arms and nod once more to the three others before leaving them behind and melting into the crowd.

My love.

Was that for show or did he mean it? I put it down for show, he had to show them I was going to be Queen and I'm sure a King that loves his Queen would be a force to be reckoned with.

Each part of my body is alight with nerves as I try to find Nardia. The other vampires keep their eyes on me as I walk past, I keep my head high. A part of me wants to be their Queen, to show them even with human blood I can handle it.

That I can lead them to a better future, and with Kal by my side that distant dream of mine finally feels like it could be in my grasp.

I find Nardia over by a blood drinking fountain; she drains her glass as I approach her. I hand her my full one as I stand beside her and look out into the crowd.

"How did it go?" She asks, sipping from the glass. I sigh and fiddle with my dress.

"I have no idea. I sort of snapped at them, Kal was trying to defuse the tension when I excused myself. God, some vampires can be so rude," I puff, not wanting the bad encounter to ruin my night.

"Eh, old grumpy bastards they are. Kal included, you haven't seen him on days he wakes up on the wrong side of the bed." We both giggle at that, I could imagine a grumpy Kal so easily.

"Speaking of him, how are you going to tell him you're leaving? I know you don't want my input but it honestly seems too dangerous. We just got out, and you've just started to come out of your shell again. I'm worried you'll come back changed." She whispers, leaning her shoulder against mine.

"I don't know Nardia, I really think he's better off not knowing until I'm gone. He'll try and stop me and I can't allow him too. If I don't go I feel the worst will happen to Yolanda and the others. Trust me, I don't want to step a foot even close to that camp but I can't shake the feeling that I need to go." I try to explain, she nods slowly a few times.

"Plus, you know. I'll update you down the bond if it isn't too far away and you can keep Kal in the loop. But he can't find out, I wish I could tell him but I already know how he'll react." I cross my arms over my chest and look out at the crowd, I vaguely see Kal through the group of vampires; laughing and drinking. He's having a good night and I'm not going to ruin it. I haven't seen him this much at ease since I'd arrived and it made me happy to watch him laugh and joke with the others.

"I still think this is the worst idea yet, but I'll support you. Come tomorrow morning though I'm telling him everything, I don't need him thinking I coaxed you into this." She refills her cup of blood.

"Why would he think that?" I ask. She sighs.

"Because it's been really hard for me to bounce back, after what they did to me, what I went through; I'd love for nothing more than to see that place and everyone in it burn to the ground." Her voice fills with emotion, her hands shake as she goes somewhere deep inside herself. I put my hand on her arm and squeeze gently. She brings her glassy eye to mine, tears threaten to spill.

She doesn't hide the jagged scar of where her other eye once

125

was, she wears it like a badge to let everyone know she was a survivor. I admire her for that, she is so strong and I am so proud to call her my friend.

"I am so sorry for everything that happened to you, I'm sorry I couldn't be there to stop it. What they're doing is wrong, if I don't try to stop it nothing will change. I'm doing this for both of us and both races. No one deserves to go through what you did. You know I'm always here for you, Nardia." I search her face as she nods her head, she takes a few deep breaths to calm herself. I let go of her arm and search for Kal, only to find his eyes already on me. He begins to move between the crowd toward us.

"Please don't say anything." I whisper, keeping my eyes on him.

"I promised I wouldn't," she whispers back. My heart swells for her; I don't know what I did to deserve her friendship. Kal approaches us, full glass in hand.

"Ladies, how are you this evening Nardia?" he asks, stopping in front of us. My heart involuntarily speeds up. A small part of me is afraid she'll spill everything to him.

"Just superb, good to see you've finally come to spend time with your queen," she says playfully with a smirk, I sigh in relief and grin at him.

"I couldn't have her changing teams now could I?" He teases, winking at me. I blush deeply; I'd forgotten to fill her in on *that*.

"Oh love, it's funny you think you even have a chance." She rolls her eyes and bows deep. "I must be off; a tall blonde is calling my name." She winks as she disappears back into the crowd. Kal finishes his glass of blood and sits the empty glass down on the table. I've grown accustomed to the smell. He holds out his hand to me, I raise an eyebrow in question.

"What? Have you never danced before?" He asks, smiling. I take his hand hesitantly.

"No, I haven't. I don't think I'd be any good. Really. You should go dance with someone else; you have a large variety to choose from." I scan the crowd; multiple female vampires have their eyes latched onto Kal not caring about me beside him. A growing part of me is jealous.

"If I wanted someone else I'd be with them, but I'm here with you. So come and dance with me, Allison." I reluctantly follow him into the crowd, once we reach the middle of the dance floor he pulls me to his chest, resting both of his hands on my lower back. I wrap my arms around his neck and rest my head on his chest. We sway back and forth to the piano.

"Thank you for tonight." He whispers into my hair.

"That's okay; it's the least I could do. I'm sorry about being so resistant when I first arrived here. You've helped me a lot, more than I could ask for and I never thanked you." he holds me tighter to him. I look up into his eyes.

"You have nothing to apologise for. Nothing. I would help you in any way I could if you asked. It's been nice getting to know you, the real you." a small seed of guilt plants itself in my chest; tomorrow he wouldn't be thinking this. He'd be thinking how much of a human I am and how I haven't changed a bit. What if he thinks this is all for show?

"I agree. I sort of felt almost connected when I first met you at the camp, it's hard to describe." I bite my bottom lip as I think about it; it's as if his blood was calling to mine.

"That's why I guess I was so hard on you. I didn't know how to handle someone being nice to me, after everything I did. I didn't feel like I deserved it. I'm still not sure I do." I cast my eyes down and focus on the top of his suit shirt.

"Oh Ali, you deserve everything and more. I know it will take time to forgive yourself. I still have things that haunt me to this day from my past. Each day gets easier, you learn from your past so you don't repeat the same mistakes. It's what makes us human." I look back up at him.

"Do you ever miss it? Being human?" I ask. He breaks eye contact and looks out to the crowd.

"I didn't, until I realised I had someone worth losing over it." His voice is barely a whisper, but I hear every word crystal clear. I'm not sure when we became so close, I can't pin point the moment I started letting him in. I can't remember when I let him get under my skin and make a home in my chest. Losing him would hurt like hell.

"I think you'd get sick of me annoying you forever," I say lightly, trying to lighten the mood. He looks back down at me with sad eyes. I didn't want our last night to be sad.

"You're probably right." He smirks, kissing me gently on the forehead. His eyes are clear as he pulls back. My feet begin to ache, as does my body.

"I think I'm going to call it a night, my whole body is aching. I didn't realise the physical strain of being a queen," I laugh as I pull out of his grip. He chuckles with me, rolling his eyes.

"You're something else aren't you?" he brings his arm around my waist as he escorts me to the main doors. Everyone was still alive and the night was still young, perks of being a vampire I suppose.

"I thought you would have figured that out by now." I smirk, playfully pinching his nose. It's good to see him more carefree, not on high alert. He snorts at me, which causes me to laugh again.

"Trust me dear, I've figured plenty of things out about you." He raises his eyebrows and focuses on my lips; I blush and bat my hand against his chest.

"No cheeky business in public," I whisper, failing to contain my smile. The thought of Kal wanting me sends my hormones wild. We reach the door and I turn to him. I've never felt more confident within myself and my body from the way Kal looks at me, and the wholeness of him.

"I'll save it for the bedroom," he whispers, tucking a piece of loose hair behind my ear. I feel my cheeks turn scarlet.

"Goodnight mister." He leans down and presses his lips against mine, letting them linger longer than necessary. They're soft and wet as I move my mouth slowly against his, I open my mouth slightly; his tongue slides over my bottom lip. I feel my body heighten and warm, my common sense flies out the window. He pulls back, much to my disappointment.

"Goodnight beautiful. I'll be in bed shortly, you know where to find me if you need me." I nod and gather my thoughts; I smile and turn and quickly leave, heading straight for the shower.

17

Allison

I toss and turn for what seems like hours. The party ended a short while ago and I can't find it in me to go to sleep. The conversation I had with Nardia still consumes my thoughts. Was every loss worth every gain? I groan and get out of bed, I wasn't sleeping anytime soon. I head to the training room, wanting to clear my thoughts. I needed a clear head space for tomorrow.

I'm sitting alone in the training room, looking up at the hundreds of glowing balls of light. I've been left alone with my thoughts, which isn't the best idea. The swell of emotions in my chest is making it hard for me to breathe normally, and I'm not sure how to deal with them. I thought coming here would help get rid of them, not exaggerate them.

As of late my life hasn't been horrible, I've been laughing and smiling and enjoying myself. So why now do I suddenly feel so alone? Why do I feel like my chest is so full that it could burst

129

any moment? I stare down at my trembling hands; I am in one of Kal's overly large white shirts. It swallowed most of my body.

My hair falls around me like a curtain, my bottom lip quivers. "You're okay. You're okay. Don't cry," I whisper, struggling against the tears that are pooling in my eyes. My vision blurs over as the tears win my battle. I stay still as they roll down my cheeks, landing in droplets on my hand.

I sob once and come undone; I bring my hands to my face and let it all out. The pain and guilt of everything I'd done was more than I could deal with. I let those people and vampires die. I'd lost everyone I cared about in the process. I'd lied and cheated and deceived to get where I am now. I didn't deserve any of it, maybe all the horrible things Cassidy said about me are right.

My breathing comes in hiccups as I cry harder into my hands, I rock back and forth as I sit there; needing to move.

Stupid girl.

You're a liar.

You'll only get them killed as well.

You're never good enough for anyone and you never will be.

Do you really think Cassius wanted to die?

Did you really think all those vampires you left behind were going to be saved? You doomed them. You doomed them all.

"Oh God," I cry out as I scramble to my feet, it was too much. Everything is too much. Tears stream down my face as I run to the castle; I let my feet carry me. I don't know where I am going but I needed to run as fast and far away from myself that I could manage. I swipe at my cheeks in half an attempt to stop the tears but it's no point. God, how did I become so useless?

Without realising it I come to a stop outside of Kal's bedroom. A sob wracks my body as I stand there; I reach for the door handle but hesitate.

He has enough troubles; I can't just dump this on him. No, I needed to go, be alone-

The door opens inwards, Kal's standing there shirtless in white slacks; his hair a messy bun on top of his head. He blinks in shock as he takes my appearance in.

"Ali, are you—" I cut him off as I throw my arms around him, I cry into his neck as his arms wrap around me. I heave and sob and my entire body shakes with the sadness that won't seem to budge. He holds me tight against him, rubbing a hand up and down my back.

"Hey, shh. It's going to be okay." He whispers into my ear, I squeeze my arms tighter around his neck. I wanted so bad to believe he was telling the truth.

"Come on, come to bed." He wraps his arms tighter around my waist and picks me off the ground. I automatically wrap my legs around his waist as he carries me to his bed. He pulls the sheet back before gently placing me down, I reluctantly let go of him. He pulls the sheet up around me and turns and shuts the door, leaving us alone in darkness. My eyes are swollen and I'm still trembling and Gods be damned I did not want to be a mess the first time I'm in his bed.

Somehow my eyes adjust to the darkness and I can vaguely make out his figure, he climbs into bed beside me; pulling the blankets up on both of us, before he pulls me towards him. I roll over and curl into his body, resting my head and arm on his chest. One arm rests on top of my own while the other is stroking a hand through my hair. Although his skin is cold to touch I hadn't felt warmer in a long time.

The tears had finally subdued, leaving me with a blossoming migraine behind my eyes. I sigh as I shut them and I nestle closer to Kal.

"Are you okay?" He asks, his voice barely a whisper. I think over his question, I most certainly was not okay. But how could I explain that to him?

"I don't think so, everything is just...so much. I can't escape it. Some days are so good and at the end of them I feel like I don't deserve them." I whisper back, the tears threaten to fill my eyes again so I squeeze them shut tight. He takes my hand in his and rubs his thumb over my own, the gesture calming me.

"I know, I'm sorry I've had to put you through this." His voice is raw in his throat, a hint of emotion I hadn't heard from him before.

"It's not your fault, I make my own choices." And how poor my choices have been.

"Choices at the hand of my manipulation."

"You couldn't stop it, I was quite literally born for this. I think it was going to happen either way." If I could have gone back and changed my choices, would I have?

"I know how hard it can be, having a large burden with no one to share it with. I was lucky to have Cass but when she was taken from me I had no one. I know that guilt, regret and shame come hand in hand." His voice is quiet; we'd never really spoken about his past in detail or depth. I stay silent, hoping he continues. I remember her diary entries, she was there for him and loved him so strongly.

"I still remember the first human I killed, turning me. I was twenty four at the time, our whole royal family had just been turned and I was the last in line. I was nervous, but above everything else I was terrified. I'd known what vampires had done to our city and the surrounding villages. I knew of the plague they carry with them.

"She was only seventeen, and had offered herself to me. Had said it would be an honour." He almost spits the last words out, as if it's anything but an honour.

"I couldn't deny her, and my family wasn't going to pass on the opportunity. I remember her fear, I was already half turned once she was brought to me. I was crazed and starved; they'd locked me away for more days than I could count. I had to drain her of every single drop of blood that she carried.

"A lot of my human rationalisation was already lost, so once she stepped into my cell and the door locked behind her there wasn't much time. All I could hear was the pounding of her pulse and I could taste the fear coming off her in waves." He pauses, lost in the memory. My heart aches; he is trusting me enough to tell me this. He'd stopped stroking my hair and rubbing his thumb.

"I was upon her like lightning, I latched onto her throat and I didn't let go. In her final moments before she fell unconscious I think she regretted her decision. I wish it could have been different. It should have been different, I still could have ruled as a human, not some leech.

"They found me the next morning still latched onto her throat, my hunger had barely been quenched and now a full vampire I needed blood more than anything." His voice shakes as he swallows hard, I rub his hand gently trying to offer whatever comfort I could.

"It's a blur after that, it took me three months of constant feeding until I could think rationally again and control my thoughts. I was stronger than anyone else in my family line, they weren't sure why but they were more than delighted. Cass was at my side every step of the way, she used to sit outside my cell and tell me stories to help guide me back to myself." He takes a deep shuddering breath. I rub my thumb over his.

"I still think about her and all the other deaths I've caused, I didn't even know their names. I only remember their faces, and I think that's the worst part."

"I'm so sorry Kal, I didn't know," I whisper, he'd been alone for it all. What a heavy burden to give to someone so young, it wasn't fair.

"You're the only one that does. I only ever told Cass about that time in my life and the struggle I had to go through... those first three months were so dark. She'd been through it as well, which brought us closer. She was the sister I'd never had."

"I wish I could have met her, she sounds lovely."

"She would have really liked you." I hear the smile in his

words; I think I would have liked her as well.

"So know, Ali, that I'm always here whenever you need me. I don't care what time it is or what's happening. I will always be a word away from being at your side; you don't have to share the burden alone anymore." I savour his words, feeling a small weight lift from my shoulders. Only to be replaced by the guilt of what tomorrow would bring.

"Thank you. I'm here as well, you're not alone either. I'm meant to be Queen, remember?" I tease, trying to lighten the mood. He begins to stroke my hair again.

"I guess I could arrange something, there's a line-up of girls that would love to be queen but if you want it..." I snort at him.

"Sorry love but I don't think you have a choice in this one. I don't think you ever did." I have the sudden urge to look at him, needing to see what those depthless eyes are holding. I go rigid as I fight the urge.

"I've never been more delighted to finally not make the big decisions around here." His voice is warm and god damn me to hell I need to see him. I sit up on my elbow and look down at him, my hair fans around both of our faces.

The darkness of his eyes is endless, even with my vampire sight. I wish I could have seen them before he was turned, I bet they could hold the entire galaxy in them. He raises both eyebrows slightly as his eyes search my face, I feel my cheeks heat slightly.

"Thank you Kal, for everything." I whisper down to him.

"Always." His hand reaches up to my face, he strokes my cheek gently; I lean in to it, savouring his touch.

"May I?" He asks, his voice breathless. His eyes flicker to my lips. Involuntarily my heart beat picks up pace as I lick my lips. I nod once and lower my face, his breath tickles my nose as I go closer.

He draws my face down, pausing a hairs-breath away from my lips. Please, please just kiss me for the love of God. My insides are strung tight in anticipation. He shuts his eyes so I do the same, and then our lips connect.

His lips are cool and wet against my own, smooth to the touch. I move my lips against his softly, hoping I am doing the right thing. It still feels clumsy to me. His tongue traces my bottom lip as he pulls back; I open my eyes to find us both breathless. I blink once and gather myself. I wish I didn't wish for more.

"Let's get some sleep now. If you have any nightmares I'm right here." He reaches up and plants a firm kiss on my forehead, I lay back down and face away from him. He rolls to his side and folds himself around me, his arm reaching around me while his hand fits snuggly between my breasts. I sigh and move back against him, this was my safe place.

"Goodnight, my King." I whisper, sleep already beginning to invade my thoughts. I close my eyes and relax.

"Goodnight my Queen."

I liked the ring it had to it.

My Queen.

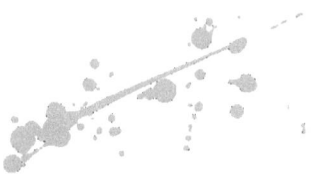

I wake to Kal's still body entrapping mine, a twist of limbs. I am not completely sure which part belonged to who. I hold my breath as I wiggle away from him and pry myself from his grip. I had to go. If I didn't go now I wouldn't be going at all, not if he could do anything about it. I slip off the bed and look down at him, his face peaceful and still, his hair a knotty mess around him. My chest aches as I force myself to leave the room, this is what I wanted to wake up to every morning, but I wouldn't allow myself the luxury of that dream. Not yet.

I still didn't believe I deserved that dream. I don't know if I ever will.

I slip into my room and change quickly into a pair of tights and a singlet; I pull my hair into a bun and pull my bag over my shoulders. I take a deep breath; it was time to save Yolanda.

Nardia, are you there?

I wait patiently for her reply.

Yes I am, what on earth are you doing awake this early?

I smile; her voice barely a whisper through my mind. I begin to make my way swiftly to the front of the castle.

It's time for me to leave. I never told Kal, can you please tell him once he's awake? I couldn't bring myself to do it. I'm sorry I've left it to you.

I reach the door and pry it open, my eyes adjust to the darkness as I begin to run towards the forest. My ears pick up the slightest movement deep within the forest and nothing more.

He's not going to be happy, you know that right? He'll tear the damn world apart looking for you if you don't come back.

I leap over a fallen tree.

Yes I know, I will return. Once I have Yolanda out safely. I don't know how long it will take but I'm hoping a few weeks at the latest. I'll keep in contact if I can.

I break the forest and keep my pace as I head down the busy street; the other vampires barely spare me a glance. Good, I didn't need word getting back to Kal yet.

I'll give you two weeks, if you're in any trouble send word and I'll find you. Okay?

I slow down as I take the steps two at a time, nearly free. I feel a small thrill at the thought of the wind brushing my face.

I promise. Thank you Nardia, for everything.

I don't hear her reply as I step through the swarming darkness of the portal. Sunlight immediately burns my eyes. I squeeze them shut as I regain my thoughts. I take a deep breath of the fresh forest air and then open my eyes.

The sun is sitting low in the sky, the forest trees casting long shadows around me. I begin to walk straight, once I reached the river I'd have to rely on my senses alone to find Xavier's camp again. I can do this, I have to do this. There is no turning back now.

Kalabhiti

"I don't think I'm hearing you correctly," I say calmly. Allison wasn't in my bed when I'd woken, but what Nardia is telling me has to be impossible.

"I'm sorry, Kal. I wanted to tell you as soon as she told me. I couldn't stop her, she's a stubborn thing when she sets her mind to something. You should know that better than anyone," Nardia explains, crossing her arms over her chest. She'd arrived as soon as I'd woken, barely giving me enough time to fully wake up.

"So what, she's gone?" I ask, masking my fear and worry. Why would she leave and not tell me? After everything we've shared, after how close we've become. She still doesn't trust me.

I turn away from Nardia and pace back and forth in the sitting room, she takes a seat on the couch and sighs.

"She's coming back, in two weeks. I said if it was any later I'd be coming and dragging her back. She wanted to tell you, she just knew you'd stop her," she says softly, trying to soften the blow. It still stings.

"Of course I'd try and stop her! Has she gone mad?" I throw my hands in the air, trying to wrap my head around this. What was I meant to do now? Sit around and wait?

"No she isn't mad, she's trying to be a good human. I didn't realise how much the whole thing fucked her up. I didn't know it left such a dark mark on her. She thinks she has to redeem herself." I look at her, how could Allison think that? She did her damn best and saved those vampires. How could she still feel guilty?

"Who is she trying to redeem herself to?" I say the question out loud, I don't stop pacing. If I stop I'm afraid my tether to rationality will snap and I'll hunt her down. Two weeks. I could handle two weeks.

"Herself. She has this stupid idea that she's some sort of monster. Kal, what if she always thinks that?" Nardia looks up at me, I sigh and sit beside her; bringing my arm around her shoulder.

"It isn't your fault. This was always meant to happen. She's strong, she'll live with it. It won't be what breaks her," I say softly, trying to comfort her. I knew Nardia had enough to handle, without worrying about Ali.

"I really hope not. I really like her, she's so good and she doesn't even see it. When would one of us ever try and help a complete stranger out? Just because we knew it would make one of us happy? Not one of us would. You, maybe. We used her to find out if she was really the descendant and it still hasn't broken her." She leans into me and rests her head against mine.

"I hope she's okay," I whisper, allowing myself the small vulnerability.

"You really do feel something for her, don't you?" she asks. I struggle with the truth inside of me. Allison is my vulnerability; a King shouldn't make his weakness known. But I trust Nardia.

"Yes. I do," I whisper, looking into the fire pit at the raging orange flames. It looked similar to the burning I felt inside of myself.

"Don't let this one get away." I shake my head and sigh. So much complication for such a simple feeling. Before I have a chance to reply, the sitting room door opens and Cassidy's cherry scent fills my senses.

"She isn't even gone for a few hours and you're already shacking up with her best mate. Classic," Cassidy drawls as she enters. I stand up and roll my eyes.

"Cassidy it's like you think I'm his type for some weird unknown reason. Do I look like Allison to you?" Nardia fires back, Cassidy snarls as she sits on the couch. Nardia grins smugly between us.

"Now that the little blood bank is gone we can finally discuss real business. We have a human that's been injected with the grobbler blood. Zuriel has volunteered to be the test monkey for the four days." Nardia nods along.

"Why only four days?" I ask, running a hand through my hair. Cassidy's eyes roam over my chest as I do this.

"Because if it's poisonous to us, four days is short enough for it to not do any real damage. Plus we have no idea how to reverse it if it is poisonous and I don't want us taking our chances."

"Good, this is good news. Has there been any word of those creatures?" I ask, my mind immediately goes to the fight against them with Allison. I don't think she realises just how powerful she really is.

"I've sent Zeke and Zuriel out to scout the deeper parts of the forest, hopefully they come up with something. But I just thought I'd stop by and catch you both up." Cassidy looks over at her nails, Nardia sighs as she stands up.

"Well I'm off; I'll let you know if I hear anything Kal." she nods goodbye and leaves. I sit down beside Cassidy and rest my head in my hands.

"How long is she gone for?" she asks smoothly. I feel her eyes fixated on me.

"Two weeks, doing a human mission vampires couldn't interfere in." I sit back and look over at her.

"Finally, it'll be back to how it was before she arrived." She grins, thinking we would go back to how it was. I look over her face; she is beautiful I can't deny that. But I find myself missing ruby eyes, silver and red hair and a heartbeat.

"She's not gone forever Cassidy, and if things go well she'll be staying here with us for good. You have to accept that." I don't understand Cassidy's dislike for her.

"But why?" she whines, pouting her bright red lips. I shiver at the thought of the things those lips have done to me. I push those memories away before they can surface.

"Because it's just how it is. I don't understand your dislike for her, I really don't. She's so sweet and innocent. How can you not like her?" I ask as I stand, I had to search the forest with the others today; we had to find something regarding the monsters.

"It's easy not to like her. She's hiding something, I just know she is. She's human and they're all the same." She raises an eyebrow at me, I roll my eyes.

"Yes and if she believed all vampires were the same she'd think we're all monsters. Is it because she's human?" She looks away, her blonde ponytail swinging with the movement.

"Look Kal, I still care about you and I always will. I'll always be here to protect you, while I'm around your safe. I'm not taking my chances with her just because the idea of her infatuates you. So no, I don't like her and I don't have to. I was by your side from the start, I always have been." She stands swiftly and straightens her shirt, exposing her cleavage.

"Just be nice to her." I sigh, jealous girl drama wasn't something I'd considered I'd have to worry about and deal with.

"Thanks but no thanks. I'll see you out there, you'll track us easy enough though I'm sure." She smiles sweetly before she leaves. I rub my eyes and head towards my room, needing to change into my training leathers. I enter my room and take a deep breath, the whole room smells of Ali, a mellow coconut and honey scent. I want more than anything to go after, tell her I'll help; anything to have her close enough to protect again. I can't deny that she is a good fighter and nearly matches me, but the thought of her with those animals alone sends me into a fury.

Why couldn't she just trust me? I would have tried to understand, if it was her in that camp I'd do anything to get her out again. Anything. I pull my training leathers on and square my shoulders, now wasn't the time to be a love sick man, it was time to be King.

19

Allison

I find the camp easily enough, it takes me two days and one wrong turn but I finally reach it. Only to come face to face with a large chained grobbler. I hide in the shrubs as I watch it pace back and forth in front of the entrance, chains are latched around its ankle and belly; only having a small worn down dirt area to wander.

When did they decide to use grobblers?

I keep my mental guard up so the grobbler can't invade my thoughts or detect me. The camp had expanded since I'd last been here, but they still use the wooden fence with large spikes on the top. I also had to be careful for the silver bombs hidden in the ground.

I extend my senses, inside the camp life flourishes but no one is close to the entrance. How was I meant to get in? Did I just shout out to them? I take a deep breath and step out of the shrubs, this could only go two ways.

As soon as I'm in the open I have the grobbler's full attention, it immediately begins to scream out; alerting the humans. In seconds the wooden entrance gate slides open, revealing Xavier and two other male members I'd never seen.

His eyes widen as he takes me in, I can't imagine what he'd be thinking looking at me. Red eyes, different hair, lean body. I adjust the straps on my bag nervously.

"Uh, hi," I say, attempting a smile. The other two raise their guns at me; I frown as I look at Xavier. He hadn't changed much, his hair seemed longer but I couldn't tell from the bun it was in. His stubble had taken over a majority of the bottom of his jaw.

"What are you doing here?" he asks, his voice deeper than I remember. The grobbler stills as he holds his hand up to it. I can see his skin is tinged green. I cringe inwardly, this couldn't be good.

"I've come back," I say, unsure if I could trust myself to speak the truth. He wouldn't let me waltz in and run the show. I wasn't sure how I was going to be able to worm my way back in.

"Why? To spy again? Destroy us and kill the innocent humans here?" he spits, I don't look away from him. I know what I've done wrong. I was here trying to change that.

"No, it has nothing to do with that. I'm not working for the vampires and I am so sorry for how that entire thing went down. I didn't want anyone to die, vampire or human. How could you sit back and let Luke torture them? Rip their fangs out and starve them?" I ask, my temper beginning to rise. I leave my hands at my side, I couldn't come off as a threat.

"Sorry means nothing. It still happened. We lost children, Allison! Children!" he yells, the veins in his neck strain. The two other men look at each other and back to me, adjusting their guns.

"And I'm sorry! I wasn't here! I didn't kill them! If I was here I would have made sure there were no casualties on either side!" My voice begins to rise, and I have to take a deep breath to calm myself. Shouting at each other isn't going to get me anywhere.

"Well it still happened. You still hold responsibility for their lives and you always will. Tell me truthfully why you're here or I will set the grobbler onto you." he says, calming himself. I can vaguely feel the grobbler trying to break down my mental ward.

"I came to protect a certain member." I say, not wanting to mention her name.

"You really think I'm just going to let you come back in like nothing happened? I'm not as naïve as Luke, I'm the leader of the Order now. I have to think of the safety of others. You are a danger."

"Please, I just need a week," I plead. A week and I'd get her and the others out if they'd come with me. The second week would be spent getting to Penrith and setting them up in my old home.

"A week? That's all you want?" he asks, eyeing me. I sigh.

"Yes a week. I just need to make sure they're safe."

"How do I know you're not here to get Intel? We're not after peace Allison, we're out for blood." My blood chills in my veins, how was I meat to talk sense into him? He isn't the same Xavier I left behind.

"Because as much as you may think I'm running back to the vampires, I'm not. Have you forgotten I let you go that day by the river? I protected you. I could have let them have you, but I didn't. That has to count for something," I say. He thinks about this for a few minutes.

"And still you left with them." he says coldly. I can't blame him for being resentful.

"You don't know what I had to go through Xavier, you have no idea. There was so much I didn't know and questions I needed answered. You'll never understand the sacrifice I had to make." My hands begin to shake at my side, talking about the sensitive part of that ordeal.

"Why are your eyes red?"

"You won't like that answer if I tell you, Xavier," I say wearily. I hold my hands up in innocence. This would make or break him accepting me back for a week. He crosses his arms over his chest.

"I want the truth."

"I'm the descendent of the vampire Queen. I didn't know. When I helped Nardia she had to bite me and it sped up the process of my eyes changing. I'm mostly human, but I do have vampire and grobbler blood mixed with mine," I say quietly. His eyes widen as he looks me over with a new perspective.

"You're the next in line to be the vampire queen?" he asks. The two gun men begin to look back and forth; I knew they wanted to shoot me.

"Yes. I don't want it. That's why I went with them, so I could get answers. I don't have to do it, they've been without a queen this long and I doubt I would make much difference." I lower my hands and look towards the ground.

"I don't trust you but I will allow you a week. You will be watched; even when you think no one is watching. The moment you pose a threat you will be executed without hesitation." I look back up at him, shocked more than anything.

"I know you're not a bad person Allison, and if you're here to protect a friend I will believe you. Don't mistake my kindness for weakness; the beast in me is sleeping. Not dead." I nod silently; the two men lower their guns as I walk forward.

"Thank you Xavier, this means a lot to me," I say weakly, I walk in step with him as we head through the camp.

Above us in the trees are more makeshift homes as well as on the ground; the small tents are still how I remember them. We receive a few odd glances from others that walk past us, everyone seems to be busy with something.

We approach an empty fire pit, a fresh set of logs were waiting to be lit. He comes to a stop.

"You'll be in the same room, no roommate. The only thing that's changed is the number of members and homes. You still bathe in the stream, I'm sure you remember everything else." He avoids looking at me as he says this. A few people whisper as they pass us, I don't catch what they say but I see the fear in their eyes. I frown. I'm not what they should be afraid of.

"Thank you. When's dinner?" I ask, I was already starting to feel hungry again. The apple I'd brought along hadn't lasted me long.

"Sundown, we've just entered winter so I hope you've brought along warm clothes." He looks at me now, really looks at me. His eyes roam over my face, no doubt noticing the lack of my chubby cheeks I last had when he saw me. I hadn't changed, I don't know why he felt the need to examine me.

"Alright thanks. No I didn't really but I'm sure I'll be fine." I nod and turn, heading towards my old room. It isn't hard to find. When I enter, there's only a single mattress on the floor. It's better than nothing. I sit my bag beside the bed and stretch, it was time to find Yolanda.

I head back the way I arrived, surveying the tents in the trees. I smile as kids run past me, squealing as they play together. I wonder if Kal had kids, or if he ever wanted them. I roll my eyes at myself, of course I'd be thinking about him.

It makes me wonder though... is he thinking of me? I have no idea what we are, but it seems like something that could go somewhere. We click, or at least I think we do. He is going to be so pissed at me when I return; at least Zuriel will be grateful.

As if the thought of his name draws her out, Yolanda enters the path in front of me with the same kid I saw that day, holding onto her hand.

"Yolanda. Hey." I say, stopping in front of her, she looks up abruptly and immediately frowns. She looks around wildly before stepping closer to me, I was happy to see they'd been given new clothes.

"What on earth are ye' doin' ere?" She hisses, talking low enough so others can't hear. The little boy looks tired, dark circles are under his eyes.

"I'm here to get you out and take you somewhere that is genuinely safe. I can't let you stay here," I whisper. The little boy's eyes are wide as he watches me, his skin had already started to tinge green.

"Did he set you up to this?" She whispers, pulling the little boy closer to her.

"No of course not, he doesn't even know I'm here. Look, you have to trust me. This place isn't safe." I try to emphasise my words, she doesn't have half a clue what sort of place this is.

"They feed us, they give us shelter and protection. They gave us clothes. All they ask is for our loyalty to the humans." I rub a hand through my hair.

"Yes I know. I've joined this camp before. I only joined because Zuriel and Zeke asked me to come here and spy for them to see if they were kidnapping and torturing vampires," I whisper, not wanting others to overhear.

"And were they?" She asks, her voice a whisper. I hadn't had a good chance to pay much attention to her, but under all the dirt and grime she is gorgeous. Her bright green eyes shine against the orange ringlets that hang against her face.

"Yes they were. They ripped out one of Zuriel's friends eyes. I had to get her out, and they got as many as they could out. Unfortunately, the humans decided to kill half the vampires they'd starved and tortured." The more I explain it to her, the more my temper begins to rise. How could they do that? Take away another being's free will and keep them like an animal. The thought infuriates me.

"My god," she mumbles, thinking about what I'd said. I stand

147

back and wrap my arms around myself, the sun was beginning to set and a cool breeze had begun to pick up.

"Come with me, I'll give you a jumper." she turns with the little boy and I follow her into the trees. At the base of a large one, she pulls against a wooden rope ladder. She helps the little boy climb up before she does. I step forward as she climbs onto a wooden platform.

"Come on, climb up." her head disappears from sight as I begin to climb. Once I reach the top I stand warily, although the platform is sturdy under my feet, I'd never been one for heights.

"It's only about five metres off the ground," she calls from the tent. She pulls back a flap to reveal a bedroom the same size as mine. I enter. The little boy is lying on the mattress under a thick blanket; a small gas light sits on an old upturned basket. She sits down at the end of the bed and pulls a jumper out from under the mattress.

"Here, have it. I figure you didn't realise it was going to be winter." she chuckles as she passes me a dark green jumper, I pull it over my head and immediately begin to warm up. I sit down on the wooden floor.

"Thank you. No, I didn't. It's hard to keep up with anything while I'm living in the vampire city. There's no sun there so I get a bit lost," I admit. I pick at a hole in my black tights.

"Tis' alright. I can imagine how confusing it would be in there. I know I couldn't do it." She moves to lie beside the boy, he was already asleep.

"How has he been? He looks a lot better, so do you."

"He's okay, seems a bit shaken but I'm sure he'll be back to normal in no time. We've already started injections. They make me feel funny but after about an hour I go back to feeling normal. Were you injected?" she asks, studying me.

"Yes, I was. The liquid has grobbler blood in it, which explains the vampiric like powers you gain from it after you take it long enough." I think back to the fight with Cassius, how it had turned him.

"Oh. I didn't know that." she frowns as she looks down at the boy, running a pale hand through his black hair.

"I don't imagine any of you do. Do any of them know about you and Zuriel?" I whisper, in case anyone had the hide to eavesdrop on us. She looks back at me with wide eyes.

"No. They can't. I won't be able to stay if they do." her voice shakes.

"I could take you to Penrith, my old home town. You could live in my old house. It has two bedrooms; and there's a stream that runs right behind it for baths. You'd just have to look into trying to get a small job or learning to trade, but the attic is full of goodies you could trade." I feel a pang of home sickness at the mention of my old home, my room. I'd spent a majority of my life in that house.

"I don't know…we just arrived here and got settled in. It's so easy here," she admits.

"I know, easy isn't always better though. I could help you get settled and stock up on food at the trade and show you the tricks. You'd have your own house to yourself; you can take the others with you. Zuriel would be able to visit you."

"Would he?" She whispers, leaning forward with a glimpse of hope in her eyes.

"Yes he would, there's a sewer system that navigates under the town. A sewer drain is directly outside my house and at the wall." I stretch a leg out and stretch my arms above my head, I supress a yawn.

"I still don't know. I don't think a lot of us are strong enough to make that journey again. But what about the injections? What if they're going to be a benefit?" I twist my mouth as I think about her words.

"I don't know what it turns you into and I'm honestly afraid to find out. I want peace for both humans and vampires; I'm still figuring how to go about it though." I sigh as I stand up, she follows me with her eyes.

"I'd rather find out over being vulnerable. I have to think of the kids, if I can't protect them who will?" I look down to the boy sleeping, feeling a pang of loneliness.

"I'd do whatever it took to protect my kids if I had them, but losing me wouldn't help them. I doubt the formula is even stable. But please, just think about it. I'm only here for the week and then I'm going back home. I'll find you in a few days and we'll talk again." I pull back the flap. The sun is setting, lighting the sky up in an array of blue and pink and orange. I missed this so much.

"Thank you. I'll think about what you've told me. I never caught your name?" I look back over my shoulder.

"Call me Ali." I smile, earning a smile back.

"Have a good night, Ali."

"You too." I climb back down the ladder and head to my tent, wanting more than anything to rest my bones.

20

Allison

A cool breeze jostles me from my thoughts. I blink slowly as I take in my surroundings; yet again forgetting why I'm here. My purpose of being here. Shadows from the fire dance around me, I step out of the safety of my tent and head towards the warmth. The winters were cruel and unrelenting, each one being worse than the last. My thin sweater does nothing to keep the constant chill out. Everyone has gone to bed, except Xavier. I cautiously approach him, his eyes stay trained on the fire. I take a seat beside him, pressing my hands between my thighs. We both watch the fire as minutes turn to hours; I'm unsure how much time passes. It warms me to my core, heating my face up.

"So, how are you settling in?" he asks. I blink slowly at his words.

"It feels... different. But I'm getting there. I'm only here for another few days so I don't want to get familiar with it," I say quietly. I had one goal of being here. Exactly how I had one goal the last time I was here.

"Different how?" There's an edge to his voice. He hasn't forgotten.

"Luke isn't here; things don't seem as bad as they were..." my voice trails off; I push away the conjuring images of the tortured vampires. I couldn't think about them now or I'd think about him.

"It was a lot to handle, you know. Coming back and being leader, I don't know how Luke did it as long as he did." I look towards him, his beard has grown out and his hair was in a wild, messy bun. We'd both changed in the months apart; we weren't the same people we once were.

"I could imagine it wouldn't be easy, especially with the camp expanding as much as it has been lately." and expanding is putting it lightly, the camp now stretched into the forest around us, makeshift homes were built high in the trees. They no longer manipulated vampires or tortured them, which I was relieved to find out but that doesn't stop them from hunting them. He shrugs like it's nothing.

"Why go to such lengths, what's the point of it all?" I ask. I turn away and look back into the fire. The gold and orange glow is a comfort in the darkness that seems to suffocate the place.

"I'm starting to think there might not be one. I once thought humans would come out on top, but now... I'm not so sure." I can feel his eyes on me, roaming over my body.

"Who said coming out on top would be the victory?" I whisper, wanting him to understand my reasoning. Vampire and humans could coexist, I knew they could. I'd seen it with my own eyes, hell I'd been happily living with vampires in the last few months.

"Anything less would be a failure Ali, you know in the end it would never work." I look at him and catch his eyes, the emerald green is bright. The soft tinge of green on his skin reminds me that he's as less of a human as I am.

"You missed dinner as well." he says, looking away from me.

"Give it to the elderly or the children, from what I observed they need it more than I do." He sighs at my words.

"I don't know what to do. The dosages have increased but we're running low on food, casualties are becoming high." I feel sick to my stomach knowing he'd so easily sacrifice innocent lives.

"You know exactly how I feel about that, Xavier. You shouldn't be playing God." we sit in silence.

"You know, we're not so different. You and I," I say finally. I stand up and wrap my arms around myself. I wasn't here for a war, I was here for peace. I step out of the fire pit; I glance at him once more.

"We're completely different," he says, but in his eyes I see the truth. I glimpse the same man that I had once known.

"We both want peace, I don't think that makes us very different at all. Goodnight, Xavier." I turn and head towards my tent, wanting to be alone and to hide in the confines of the darkness. I get into my tent and crawl into bed, pulling the sheets tight around me; my body shivers. I miss the softness of my mattress at the castle, I miss the darkness. I miss seeing Kal every morning for breakfast and training by his side.

I close my eyes and let the heaviness leave my body. I focus on Kal. I hadn't tried to get in contact with him through a dream for a while, so I could only hope it works. Xavier wasn't the only one with a few tricks up his sleeve.

Once the world around me clears I'm standing in the sitting room at the castle, everything looks exactly how I left it. Only a small candle lights the room, casting a dull glow around me. I turn slowly, a small ache forms in my chest. Home. The door clicks open and Kal steps into the room; his shirtless form takes me by surprise. I feel a blush rise to my cheeks. God damn him. His sleek black hair flows around him with such grace it was hard to not see him being supernatural. He closes the door and finally looks up, his eyes widen when he sees me. I smirk.

"Miss me?" I tease, crossing my arms over my chest. I hadn't seen him since the day I'd left, the day I'd agreed to this. This is the first time I'd been able to connect to him in my dreams, and Gods be damned if I hadn't tried.

"Ali?" His voice is a whisper, as if he's seeing a ghost. I roll my eyes.

"At your service, your majesty." I bow low mockingly, suddenly I'm being crushed in his arms, they wrap around my waist and pull me close. He takes a deep breath as his head nestles into the base of my neck.

"It's really you," he says, lips skimming my shoulder. I shiver in anticipation, hands tightening on his back.

"Of course it is, you buffoon." I pull him closer and savour the coolness of him, I breathe him in. Savouring his scent, even in dreams he was powerful.

"How?" he asks, pulling away to look down at me. His eyes are pitch black, as dark as the night sky. They search my face.

"I'm asleep currently; you were the last thought before I fell asleep. If you were thinking of me as well I can connect to you. Clearly I've been the last thought to come into your head." I growl the last part.

"Jealous, are we?" he smirks, I narrow my eyes at him.

"I'm gone for a few days and you've already forgotten about me?" I mock, raising an eyebrow.

"When you look this good, it's hard to forget." He leans in and presses his lips to my forehead, I sigh. The kiss lingers as he pulls away, he twirls a strand of hair between his fingers.

"Which should be all the time mister." I say, smiling at him. He doesn't smile back, a shadow falls across his face.

"What's wrong?" I ask, trying to read his face. As fast as it is there it disappears, I hold back my growl of frustration.

"Nothing your pretty little head needs to worry about. Now how is it there? What's been happening? Are you okay?" He asks as he leads me to the couch, he pulls me on to his lap. I rest my head against his shoulder and run my hand absently up and down his muscled chest.

"You know I hate it when you keep secrets from me." I say softly.

"I know, and I am sorry. It's just not something you need to worry about and I promise to tell you all about it once you return."

"Fine, but you better keep your promise or a finger is coming off." I growl the half-hearted threat at him, his chest rumbles slightly with laughter. We both knew I'd never be quick enough to get a finger off of him.

"So, how are you?" he asks; his hand runs up and down my leg, drawing patterns as he goes.

"I miss this, I miss my bed. I miss you." I whisper.

"I miss you too."

"Not much has happened, they've been recruiting more people and injecting them but the dosages are larger than normal. I think they're desperate. The food is starting to get a bit thinner so portions have been cut back. I try and give mine to the people that need them." the kids and the elderly are the ones that usually don't survive the dosages, I try and give them my food and hope it helps them become strong enough.

"Kal this world is ruined, I don't know if it can ever recover," I whisper. This was a thought I could never admit to myself. I didn't even know what recovering would look like. All I'd known was a broken world.

"Shhh, don't think like that. There's still hope, you know this more than anymore. You can't give up on me just yet." I look up at him and bite my lower lip.

"I'm not giving up, I just... I'm lost Kal. How do I get them to understand?" I ask, needing some sort of direction.

"You give them hope, how you've given it to me. It's not easy and it never will be, but you're strong and you've always been a leader. You know in your heart what you must do, believe in yourself like I believe in you Ali." his words wrap a warm blanket around my heart, I'm unsure of how I managed to wedge myself into his and show him the possibilities of a better world. I don't think he knows how either.

"Together?" I whisper, focusing on his eyes. Darkens begins to creep into the corners of my vision, my heart beats in a panic. I wasn't ready to say goodbye, not yet.

"Together. Always." I tilt my head back and reach up to his lips; I savour the velvet feel of them as they move against mine. I close my eyes, welcoming the darkness. His lips are the last thing I feel.

I wake groggily, my brain thundering against my skull. I groan as sunlight streams into my tent, the camp is alive with noise as everyone continues on with their day. I push the sinking feeling of longing to be home deep inside of me; I could not show a single one of them that part of me.

I slink out of bed, wishing I had warmer clothes. Although the sun was up there was no warmth for us here, it was a mockery. I pull on my boots and head out of my tent, people pass me barely noticing me. Their green tinged skin doesn't go unnoticed. I knew the serum had to do with grobbler blood, but surely they weren't just injecting grobbler blood into people.

I wander around the tents, I am a ghost here. The people who remember me steer clear to avoid me, the ones who didn't know me don't bother trying to. I leave the ground tents and walk into the trees. Up high, people walk on makeshift rope and wood paths. Kids run around on the forest floor, running faster than any normal human child should be able to run.

I shiver as I continue; I didn't take the dosage like the others. I refused, I didn't care what Xavier said. I would not go through that, not again. I think he understood.

Xavier didn't trust me. I doubt he would ever again, but we'd both saved each other what feels like a lifetime ago. We owed each other this much.

21

Kalabhiti

"Still nothing?" I ask as I enter the dining room for breakfast. Everyone apart from the twins is present. We'd spent the last few days searching every inch of the forest, still coming up empty handed.

"Nothing, it's like they've just vanished. The marks that led to Dominic's feeding chute seemed to disappear into thin air." Cassidy huffs. Zeke runs a hand through his hair.

"I couldn't find anything either, it's like they're only around when Ali is." Zuriel says, leaning back in his chair. Nardia raises an eyebrow at him in question. I do the same.

"What are you saying?" I ask.

"He's saying that without a human nearby they're going to be dormant. They're drawn to her blood, which would be why they came as close as they did to the castle," Zeke explains for him.

"Why would they attack Dominic then?" Cassidy asks. She

reaches forward and pours herself a glass of animal blood. I take a seat at the head of the table and pour myself one as well.

"Because she'd been in there with him, grooming him and most likely giving him a cuddle. She's a sucker for animals," Zeke says with amusement. She definitely would be the type of girl to cuddle a large bat creature.

"Yeah but she didn't bleed on him." Cassidy rolls her eyes, Nardia frowns at her. Zuriel takes a sip from his green bottle, which is full of tainted human blood. Zeke and Cassidy had managed to capture one of the members from the Order.

"Her scent would have been on him." Nardia clarifies it for her, crossing her arms over her chest.

"God why does everything have to be about her?" Cassidy whines, puffing out her bottom lip.

"You're just jealous it isn't about you anymore." Zuriel grins at her, she flips him the finger.

"Well, what are we going to do today then?" Zeke asks, looking to me. I sigh and run through my options.

"We could use some of her clothing and leave it as bait? If they're after her scent I'm sure her clothes would be good enough. What if they're just drawn to humans in general?" If that is the case, if these creatures multiplied and escaped I feared what that would mean for the humans. I don't know where my care for other humans was coming from but I knew I'd been around Allison for too long.

"Yeah that could work; we should set up two spots for traps. One with her clothes and the other with some blood from the human mutant." Cassidy chimes, finishing off her cup.

"You know Cassidy, that's actually not a bad idea," Zuriel remarks, clearly impressed.

"I'm not just my good looks you know," she growls. Zuriel bursts into laughter, Nardia tries to hide her grin.

"Girl, you aren't even that." He roars with laughter, nearly spilling his bottle. I chuckle along as Nardia joins in with Zuriel.

Zeke fights a smile as he watches her.

"Oh fuck you all, I don't know why I bother with you blood suckers. I'm going to get blood from the human. Zeke, are you coming?" She stands from the table, Zeke nods and gets up as well.

"We'll gather some clothes. Leave the blood at the forest edge near where the tracks disappeared. We'll leave her clothes near the back garden in the first tree line," I say, rising from the chair.

Zeke and Cassidy leave without another word; we'd kept the human contained in a small section in our business building. I couldn't risk having them here, not when Ali could be back without me knowing.

"Nardia, can you please grab a few items from her drawers please? Ones that smell like her." Nardia nods and leaves without a word. Zuriel stands up and skulls the last of his drink. He grimaces as he puts the empty cup back down.

"That bad?" I question, scrunching my nose up. He looks at me and runs a hand through the light blonde of his hair, letting it fall over the right side of his face.

"It's even worse than you can imagine. Drinkable but it definitely has a funny aftertaste." The human had been a pale green, a young man with full health. We still fed him and gave him a place to sleep, we're not total monsters. He's just a donation bank at the moment.

"One more day and it'll be over. Then we'll find out if this new form of human is sustainable for us," I say, heading out towards the front of the castle. Zuriel keeps in step beside me.

"What if it isn't? What if it's poisonous to us?" he says softly. I hadn't debated that, or given it much thought. I'd spent most of my morning thinking about Ali and our late night dream encounter.

"We still have animals. It's not ideal, but it does work."

"I'd rather drink animal blood for the rest of my life over gross mutant human blood." he fake gags at the mention and I roll my eyes playfully at him. Nardia is waiting for us at the front door, a large white shirt over her arm.

"Is that mine?" I ask, raising an eyebrow in question. She grins at me.

"Looks like someone prefers sleeping in your shirt." Zuriel elbows me lightly; I take the shirt from Nardia and put it over my arm. The scent of vanilla and honey and Ali hit me immediately. I faintly pick up my musk; she mustn't have washed this shirt since she'd been here. A swell of emotion forms in my chest, one I'm not familiar with.

We walk around the castle, to the back garden. Owls hoot in the distance, as well as the occasional deer breaking shrubs. There's no hint of noise from any other creature. We stop at the tree line, opposite the opening of the garden. I place the shirt on the lowest branch and step back; I hope she won't be mad at me for using her shirt. Well, my shirt.

"Now we wait," I announce. We head back to the garden and take up positions looking out into the night. Silently waiting, like the predators we are.

22

Allison

I've been here for four days and in that time I've been able to establish two things; one, the camp can't keep up with the demand of the people they have here and two, they're sacrificing the elderly and young kids that aren't surviving their dosages.

I run at a human pace to Yolanda's tree home, hoping to catch her. It was already lunch time, my body was having a hard time adjusting to the sun and having something similar to a clock to go by for sleep.

I climb up the ladder and stop once I reach the top.

"Yolanda?" I call. The flap moves and she pops her head out.

"Oh it's you! Come in, come in." she pulls the flap back for me as I walk in; the little boy is gone today. My heart picks up in my chest. Maybe he was just playing with the other kids.

"Have you thought about what I offered you? I also have new information you'll want to know." I say quickly, needing to get the words out. She sits down on her bed.

"Tell me your information first and then I'll decide."

"Okay so the camp is running out of food, they can't keep up to the demand. Everyone is growing weaker, it may not seem like it but the portion sizes have been cut back. It won't be long until they run out of food all together." I begin to pace the small area, needing to move.

"The second thing is, when they inject the elderly and the kids, a majority of them aren't surviving. I don't know what they're telling everyone when a kid or grandma goes missing but they're killing them."

She looks at me with wide eyes.

"My boy," she whispers. In the blink of an eye she rushes past me and hurls herself down the ladder.

"What?"

"He's getting his shot *now.*"

Allison

I follow quickly, keeping pace up with her as we run into the main camp, she leads us through to a large tent that's hidden behind the others. She bursts in. It was the same one I'd been in when I'd first met Kal, it seemed like a lifetime ago since I'd been caught in his shadows.

"NO!" She screams as I rush in after her. Everyone in the room freezes and looks at us. On a wooden bench her little boy is laying, his breathing is laboured and he's sweating. Xavier is holding his hand as he looks down at him.

She runs forward and throws herself over the boy, whispering in his ear as she cries. Xavier steps back and looks over at me; my blood boils to breaking point

In a flash I'm inches from his face.

"You're a fucking monster. Another innocent child is dying because of you," I growl. I feel my fangs breaking through the skin of my gums. I wouldn't be able to hide them once they'd come down the entire way.

"He was the last one… the others did so well we thought he'd be fine," he says weakly. The man that injected the boy had left; the others that were in here had left with him, leaving us and two guards inside the door. I notice their guns rise silently towards me.

"No no no no no," Yolanda whimpers. I snap my head towards her. The small boy takes one last shaky breath. He doesn't take another one. Before I can do anything, Yolanda lunges at Xavier and shoves him backwards.

"He was all I had and you've taken him from me!" she shoves him again and begins to beat at his chest. He tries to grab onto her hands but she's a machine of anger and hate. The guards point their guns at her. I turn and snarl at them, knowing my fangs are out.

"Don't you dare point that gun at her." I use my fangs to my advantage; they train the guns back on me. I was the real threat.

"I'm so sorry I didn't know; I was just trying to help." Xavier says softly, trying to calm her down. I take a step towards them.

"Yolanda…" I whisper, she turns to me; tears streaming down her face. My hearts break for her, I didn't understand her loss but I could never imagine going through it.

"He's… g-gone." she chokes on her words as she runs to me, wrapping her arms around my waist. I hug her back, running my hand over her curly hair. She sobs into my chest, squeezing me tight. This was wrong. So, so wrong. I look back to Xavier, his eyes train on my fangs.

"This has got to stop Xavier. You can't keep doing this," I say. He shakes his head and looks to his guards, motioning for them to put their guns down.

"It can't Allison. We have no hope if we stop."

"Give me a viral of the serum, I'll take it back with me and I'll find a proper scientist who can make a correct concoction that isn't going to kill everyone." I say.

"No, we can't trust it in vampire hands." He pulls off his jacket and places it over the boy's green face. I look away.

"Xavier they're your only chance at a correct serum. You can't keep taking a shot in the dark with it. You know I'm right. They're not going to make it to weaken you; I'll make sure they make it stable enough to give humans equal physical abilities with vampires," I say calmly. If humans could become equal in strength with vampires, I'd have more chance at equality and reasoning with them.

"How can I trust you, though? You're more vampire than human in my eyes right now," he asks, eyeing me. I try and call my fangs back in, failing. The vampire in me was a protector and she would protect Yolanda at any cost. I needed to at least look human for him.

"I was angry; sometimes they come out when I can't contain my emotions. I have vampire blood in me, doesn't make me a full vampire." I sigh, I think of Kal; needing his thought to calm me. His voice rings through my head sweetly, *come back to me.*

Slowly my fangs recede, leaving me human once more.

"Problem solved," I smile weakly; Yolanda has stilled in my arms, her body still shaking. I keep my arms tight around her.

"I want a vial of the serum by the end of today. Then I am gone. If Yolanda chooses to stay that's her choice but I'm giving her the option to leave with me," I say calmly. She pulls back and wipes her swollen red eyes.

"I'm coming with you," she says; her voice raw. She avoids looking at Xavier as she rushes from the tent. He sighs and runs a hand over his face.

"Just give me a chance to show you that I'm being honest about wanting equality. I don't know how long it'll take for them to create a stable serum but I promise I'll bring the first batch straight back to you. You're out of options Xavier and I'm not leaving without that vial." I straighten and hold my head high, holding his eye contact.

"Fine. I'll give you one vial, that's it. If you don't bring me something by the end of winter nothing will change. I'll continue injecting what we have. Winter is three months. I'm sure by then you can have something." His words run through me and give me hope; trusting me to do this. I wouldn't let him down. Before I know what I'm doing I wrap my arms around him; hugging him to me. I hear the guns click, no doubt aiming at me.

He relents and gently wraps his arms around my shoulders.

"Thank you. I won't let you down," I say as I step out of the hug, embarrassed by my outburst of emotion. I head towards the door, narrowing my eyes at the guards. I open it.

"You would make a great queen if you went through with it, Allison. If you do, I hope you keep your word about finding peace between the races," he says softly. I look over my shoulder at him. I give him a small nod and leave the tent.

I wander back to my own and gather my things, I'd have to find Yolanda soon and get her ready to leave. I couldn't take her to Penrith now; I'd have to take her back to Dafria. I'm sure Zuriel wouldn't mind that.

I'd received what I'd come for, now I just had to hope I could keep my word.

24

Kalabhiti

Hours tick by as we wait; Zuriel had taken it upon himself to build a small stick house while Nardia had begun counting the flowers. I'd stayed focused, listening to the animals move around in the night.

"What if it was a one off thing, a fluke?" Zuriel finally whispers, I look over to him from my spot near the opening. I have to say, his stick house is rather impressive.

"I don't think so. Two encounters seem too close to be a fluke. We just have to be patient," I whisper back, not wanting to scare any away if they're close.

"Why don't we just get Ali in on the plan when she comes back? You know she'd offer to help."

"Which is exactly why I don't want to ask her. It's too dangerous." I frown at him, why would he want to risk her getting hurt?

"You need to stop wrapping her in cotton wool; she's stronger than she looks," he fires back. I turn towards him fully now.

"I am not wrapping her in cotton wool. I'm protecting her from unnecessary harm," I say, almost in disbelief at his words. He stands up, knocking his stick house over.

"You are so—" he's cut off by Nardia approaching us, her hand raised in the air. I raise an eyebrow at her.

"Can you hear that?" She breathes out slowly, I look back towards Ali's shirt on the tree; a small breeze moves it gently. I listen for any sign. Nothing. Zuriel frowns.

"I can't hear shit," he says.

"That's my point," she whispers and we all turn to the shirt and focus. Slowly we hear them, twigs snap in the under bush as they come closer to her shirt. I begin to hear their low snarls and snaps as they communicate.

"What's the plan?" Zuriel whispers as they come to stand beside me.

"We follow them back to their lair or wherever they're hiding. There's no doubt they'll take the shirt back with them. Alright? Stay low, keep your guard up and we stick together." Slowly three of the creatures emerge from the thicker trees and head towards the shirt, walking on all fours as they break into a gallop. Their white bodies seem to glow in the moonlight.

They stop at the shirt, sniffing and pulling at it. One snatches it off the branch with its mouth, its nostrils flaring. The other two fight the first one for it; nipping each other trying to get a good grip.

The one holding the shirt rips it from them and gallops off into the night, the other two follow its lead. That's our cue. We run after them, keeping our steps light as we them through the thick forest. It's not hard to follow as they gallop along, destroying everything in their path.

The wind blows their scent towards us, keeping us hidden. It's worked perfectly in our favour. As we get deeper into the forest, I come to realise we've never explored this section. I'm sure how we missed it, considering it's directly behind the castle.

Who could have stopped us looking here?

We come to a halt as the trees begin to thin out, revealing a large rocky wall. Above it are more trees, continuing on. We stop at the tree line; the creatures climb half way up the wall and then vanish into thin air.

"What the hell…" Nardia whispers.

"They're gone?" Zuriel whispers back, confused. I frown, from here it looks like it's just rock.

Behind us a twig snaps. I twirl around; ready to attack, only to see Zeke and Cassidy walking this way. Both covered in blood.

"What happened to you guys?" Nardia questions as they stop in front of us. Zeke frowns as Nardia tries to wipe the blood from her face.

"They went into a frenzy over the human blood, a fucking frenzy. Once it ran out they freaked out, we stopped them in their tracks. If we keep the bodies I'm sure we can dissect them and learn more about them." Cassidy says, scowling.

"We followed three here, they climbed half way up the rock wall and then they vanished. Almost like they dropped from thin air," I say as I look towards the rocks. Where could they have gone?

"Well we know where their lair is now; we should regroup tomorrow and figure out where they've gone. If there's more wherever they're gone we wouldn't have a chance against them," Zeke says, focusing on the wall. Nardia and Zuriel nod in agreeance. One more day wouldn't hurt to wait.

"Alright, tomorrow morning we'll meet in the dining room again. Zuriel, make sure you keep up on the blood as today is your last day, I'll want a full report by tomorrow; Nardia let me know if you hear anything from Ali. Zeke and Cassidy go get cleaned up. We're officially done for the day." I give them their orders before we run back to the house. Cassidy bickers with Zuriel on the run; Nardia and Zeke talk quietly together at the back. My thoughts end up on Ali again, frustrating me. I wanted this problem gone before she came back, it wasn't her concern.

She'd be more than happy to bait them if it meant helping us, and I know she could hold her own. I'd seen her fight, she was damned good at it. I don't know why all of a sudden I'm so worried about her, she was out doing god knows what currently and I was waiting for her to come back like a lost puppy.

I wasn't entirely sure what we were doing. She hadn't mentioned if she was going to take the offer to become Queen or even transform fully into a vampire. I know she doesn't like the idea of it, but what happens to me if she decides to stay human? Would she regret her choice once she's old and frail and has to leave me behind?

I know I will support whatever choice she makes a hundred percent, even if it means having to say goodbye to her one day. My chest aches at the thought of her disappearing forever, it's a funny feeling. I hadn't felt anything close to this since Cass had been killed.

We reach the castle and go our separate ways, I head into the empty castle; greeting the silence. I head to my bed chambers, exhausted from the day. I pull my shirt over my head and let my hair flow loosely around me; Cass always said I look better with longer hair.

I lie down and pull the blankets over me, letting my thoughts drift back to Allison again.

25

Allison

I find Yolanda with her bag over her back, ready for the night's trek. She didn't want to spend a minute longer in this place, I couldn't blame her. We'd spent the afternoon burying her little boy by the stream; she'd vanished again once he was buried. I'd offered to carry him back with us but she'd refused.

"Are you ready?" I ask, double checking with her.

"Yes, I just want to leave this place far behind me." She looks towards the entrance of the camp. The wooden gates are open; the giant grobbler paces back and forth. We make our way to the entrance, stopping once we're at the gate.

Xavier walks up behind us, the glow from the fire just reaches were we stand. He passes me a black pouch, I take it; feeling a long heavy tube in it.

"Three months Allison. That's all I'm giving you." He steps back and looks at Yolanda.

"I'm so sorry for your loss. If I had known he wouldn't make it I wouldn't have allowed Mark to inject him," he says softly. She stays silent as she watches the grobbler; her eyes narrow slightly at his words.

"Thank you Xavier. I wasn't sure what would happen when I arrived, I'll look into the serum as soon as I get back." he nods and clasps his hands together.

"Have a safe journey." he whistles to the grobbler; it moves back and allows us a clear path to cross. We waste no time as we begin to jog into the forest; the sun is beginning to set.

As soon as we got back I'd be finding someone to look into the serum, if I could get something stable in less than three months I'd be cheering.

"It's about a two day journey, so we'll have to set up camp at some stage soon and rest. I'm assuming it gets fairly dark here," I say between breaths. I keep my pace even with hers; the training with Kal has done wonders for my stamina.

"Tis' okay. I just want to go as far as we can for now," she murmurs, focusing on the path in front of her. We stay silent as we move through the forest; I revel in the fresh air and the chill of the soft breeze.

This is what I missed, the freedom of the world and what the elements have to offer. I don't know how Kal could live in that shell of his, the imitation weather can't even begin to compare to what this feels like. Even the thunder storm seemed fake.

As the sun disappears and the moon begins to rise, I slow down. We needed to set up a camp and rest, mainly for Yolanda's sake. I'd like nothing more than to power on and get home.

"Yolanda, we need to stop now. We've covered a heap of ground. If we keep this pace as soon as the sun breaks in the morning we'll be there by sundown," I say wiping the sweat from my brow with my jumper sleeve. My eyes adjust to the darkness as it thickens; she stops and turns to me.

"Yes okay, would you be able to set up a fire? I can't really see." she fumbles around as she takes a seat on a piece of large wood. I drop my bag beside her and search for some things to start a fire; I grab twigs and some large logs. The longer the fire burned the better, all we had was a blanket each, the clothes off our backs and the few we'd arrived with at the camp.

I come back to the clearing and pile all the twigs and logs in a small circle. I pull out the matchbox I'd taken from the supply room, no reason why they'd miss it.

I attempt to light the twigs, and fail. I sit back and sigh.

"Do ye' need some help?" Yolanda asks. I turn towards her; it was weird to me that she couldn't see right now, that it was all black for her.

"Yes please, I can't get it to light." I reach out for her and guide her to the fire; she takes a seat beside me as I pass her the matches. She reaches out and feels for the wood.

"Would you be able to get some dead leaves or dried grass?" she asks. I nod and stand, I find what she needs easily enough. Once I return she sits them on top of the wood, as soon as the flame touches the dried grass the fire begins.

I watch in fascination as she keeps it going, blowing on it here and there to grow the flame. After a few more matches we have a stable fire.

She sits back from the fire and sits her bag beside her; I move over and lie on my side and use my bag as a pillow as I watch the golden flames. In the night the wildlife is alive with noise, it occurs to me that we have no protection if something were to attack us.

"So, how did you and Zuriel meet?" I ask, flicking my eyes to her from the fire. She runs a hand through her red curls.

"At the camp, he and a few others had come to suss the area out I suppose. I was hiding in my room under the bed when he'd come in, by himself. I had a pan in my hand, when he turned to open the cupboard that my little boy was in I crawled out and swung the pan at him." she pauses as she smiles faintly at the memory, I smile as well. It seems the past held better days for both of us.

"It bounced off his back, not doing any real damage. He'd just turned around with this huge stupid grin on his face, and I swung again. He'd stopped the pan and talked to me, telling me he wasn't there to hurt me or the little human he could smell in the cupboard.

"I'd relaxed but still held the pan. He explained that our town was worse off and that he and his companion wanted to help, they'd bring us food and whatever else they could once a month.

It kept us all alive for this long. How did you meet him?" she asks, focusing on me while her hands pull at the grass in front of her.

"In Penrith vampires were just a myth, no one had ever seen one before. One day I was in town for the local trade and was handed a flier saying three were to be executed in the old shed out of town. Of course I went, I don't believe in killing them. When I arrived there, all three were strung up on stage.

"Zuriel was stabbed with a silver stake, Zeke's sister was ashed and disintegrated but Zeke was able to escape which caused everyone to freak out. I took the only chance I had and tried to help Zuriel, Zeke appeared and got him out of the chains he was in and I took them back to my house." I pause at the memory, thinking back to how long ago it felt. Everything was so simple then, so easy for me.

"Zeke left him with me for a few days to get some medicine for his wound, and we just formed a strong friendship. I was glad I was there to help them." I finish the story and look away from her, I'd rather not relive the moment I walked in on Zuriel draining the corpse of that homeless man.

"Well, I'm glad you were as well. If you didn't help him everyone in my town would have eventually died of starvation. So thank you, for not only saving him but giving us more time," she says softly, the fire crackles in the silence around us. The animals had all gone quiet; the breeze brushes a stray piece of hair against my nose. I push it away and look back to Yolanda, and that's when I see it.

My blood runs cold.

Crouched behind her is a large black cat, its yellow eyes the only sign that it's there.

"Yolanda, whatever you do don't make any sudden movements. There's a large cat behind you, larger than I've ever seen before," I whisper. I rise slowly as her eyes widen. The cat doesn't pay attention to me as it falls back to its hind legs; ready to pounce.

Time slows as I leap towards Yolanda at the same time the large black cat does. It yowls as it flies towards us.

Yolanda's broken scream fills the night as I shoot my power out towards the animal.

175

As its large claws connect to her shoulder and neck my power rushes it, snuffing its life out before it can do any more damage. I crash to the ground and am up and at her side in a heartbeat, the large cat lays unmoving behind us.

Blood pours from her shoulder and neck as she gasps for air. I cradle her head in my lap as the overwhelming smell of blood invades my senses.

There's so much blood. I reach my power out to feel her life force; it's weakening drastically.

Oh god, she is dying.

"Shh, shh. It's going to be okay, I promise I won't let you die Yolanda." my whole body shakes as I watch her skin begin to pale; I rip my jumper off and press it against her neck trying to stop the blood. God there is so much blood.

Think Allison, THINK.

The blood slows but I know she's running out of time. Blood coats my hands and upper arms and I do the only thing I can think of.

I bite her.

26

Kalabhiti

Nardia bursts into the dining room as I'm having breakfast; I sit the glass back down and look at her. Her breathing is coming in gasps as she tries to catch her breath.

"Did you run all the way here?" I ask, amused. She nods and comes to the table.

"Kal, Allison fed on a human last night. I can *feel* it. Last night I could sense something down the bond but I didn't know what it was, but I know that feeling of sating hunger. It was the same feeling." she rushes out; I sit back with wide eyes.

"You're sure? Allison would never feed from a human, we both know that. Not voluntarily." I say, trying to figure it out. Why would she now? Was she attacked and left with no option? Was she forced?

"Yes, I'm sure," Nardia snaps.

"I was just clarifying. Can you find out how far away she is for me please? We still have a few things to deal with while she's gone." I finish my glass off and set it down; there was always something on top of the other. I never got a damn break.

"What do you need to deal with?" she asks, following me out of the dining room.

"The creatures on that rock wall, where they've gone and how we can get rid of them. They endanger both humans and vampires," I say calmly.

"What about Ali?" she asks.

"I can't do anything for her until she's here, can I? So until then I need to focus on one problem at a time. I'm not invincible Nardia, I'm just one man," I growl. I'd need to get a hold of Zeke, Zuriel and Cassidy and get them to meet me at the same spot we left yesterday.

"I understand that, I'm sorry. I'm just really worried about her," she says softly. We reach the front of the castle.

"Just focus on getting in contact and seeing how much time we have. Can you get a hold of the others and get them to meet me at the same spot we left yesterday? Come once you receive word from Allison." she nods once and disappears in the forest, heading towards the city.

I follow the path around the castle and head into the forest opposite the garden where Ali had first discovered the beauty of those plants. Life wasn't all bad in the darkness.

I run along, being cautious of my surroundings and listen for any of the creatures. The last thing I'd need today is to be ambushed by those monsters, although a fight could help with the turmoil I was currently feeling inside.

Does Ali know the consequences of drinking human blood with vampire blood in her veins? Does she know how hard it will be for her to come back to her human side if being a vampire isn't what she wants?

I let out a frustrated growl, I had to have trust in her and trust in the fact that she knew what she was doing. I had to hope she hadn't snapped and caved in to the craving. I know she'd be considering how human blood would taste; I know the vampire in her would now want it more than ever.

I reach the clearing near the rock cliff and wait for the others. In no time they arrive; no Nardia. No luck so far then.

"Alright, what's the plan?" Cassidy asks, flipping her blonde ponytail over her shoulder. Zeke and Zuriel look towards the wall.

"First, Zuriel report. We can wait a few more moments." I turn to Zuriel.

"I went to my check up this morning and the blood isn't stable, it had begun to break down my organs and nervous system. Whatever is in it isn't good for us, the doc said I was lucky I didn't exceed the time frame I was given as it would have killed me. So yeah, no the blood is bad. BAD." He wipes sweat from his forehead.

"When do you get back to full health?" Cassidy asks, watching him carefully.

"A few days since I've stopped and I'm only to drink human blood until my vitals are stable again. I have to go see the doc again in the next few days." I nod as I listen, this was bad.

"Alright, thank you. I'm glad you're okay. Let's focus on the task at hand." we all turn back to the rock wall.

"All we can do is scale it and hope we don't get bombarded with them, look for any sort of hole or gap they could have squeezed through. We end this today," I say. I nod once and they follow me to the wall. I jump to the spot the creatures disappeared into the wall, breaking the lose rocks and making a groove to hold onto. The others follow. Zuriel moves to the exact spot and begins to poke and prod at the rocks. So far I see nothing but rock wall above us.

"This is no use." Cassidy grumbles from beside me.

"That's not the right attitude to have," Zeke calls, slightly above us as he tests the resistance of the rocks. Cassidy huffs out a breath as she continues to try and find a clue.

"Uh guys, I found something," Zuriel calls to our right. We slowly make our way over beside him, slightly caved into the wall is a small black hole; the smell of decay wafts out. I hear someone gagging behind me.

"Good job, I'll go first and call once it's safe to enter." Zuriel moves over for me as I align myself with the hole. I'd just squeeze through.

"You can't be serious right? I don't want to go in there, it smells bad." Cassidy's whining voice echoes around the small space as I begin to crawl. Slowly the hole begins to open more, the stale air is stagnant as my eyes adjust to the darkness; the light no longer reaches in this far.

The entryway opens up to reveal a large cave; I stand and brush my hands against my pants. No creatures are in sight. I crouch back down and look towards the entry.

"Come in, coast is clear," I call out. I move back as I hear them begin to climb in. I suss out the cave, seeing that it continues to go deeper into the mountain. How on earth had I missed this? Ripped pieces of clothing and dead animals, what I could hope is animals, litter the floor of the cave.

"Oh god it smells even worse in here." Cassidy gags as she stands up, Zeke ad Zuriel climb in behind her; covering their nose as they go. I pull my shirt up over my nose as well.

"It goes deeper, be ready to fight." my voice is muffled from my shirt but we begin to delve deeper into the cave.

"I hope this is the last time we have to come in here," Cassidy groans beside me, kicking a few stray bones out of her path. Zuriel snorts behind us.

"That's what every guy must think when they're inside of you," Zuriel calls. I hear him and Zeke snicker as she turns and glares daggers at them. I shiver inwardly, although the sex was good with her I'd never once finished inside of her. I push the thoughts of us from my mind as I focus ahead; there was no need to reminisce.

"Go fuck yourself," she growls, flipping the middle finger at him. I grin under my shirt, I was glad Zuriel kept her on her toes. Ahead of us the cave ends and in the centre of the cave a cluster of the creatures are sleeping. I spot my shirt in the middle of the pile in the hands of one of the creatures.

"What the hell?" Cassidy hisses, as they all come to a stop beside me. Bones litter the floor, which are stained a dark red from the animals they had been bringing back to feed on. From this angle, the creatures almost looked human.

"Alright, let's make this quick and easy. I'll suffocate them with my shadows and then we can examine the bodies," I say softly. They agree, as Zuriel puts his shield around us. I send out my shadows, they fill the small area in front of us. I take a deep breath and blow it out of my mouth. The darkness in front of us changes as it's sucked into the creature's air ways.

It moves and puffs out as the creatures die one by one; this was the most humane way to kill them that I could think of while keeping us safe. I pull my shadows back to me while Zuriel brings the shield down.

"Let's have a look." we step towards the creatures; now lying unmoving. I bend down to the closest one and roll it on its back, its black tongue falls out of its mouth and exposes its dark yellow stained teeth.

"You know, they almost look human," Zeke says quietly as he looks over one. I grab one of their arms and feel how the joints connect at each spot, definitely close to our skeleton.

"Kal, look at their necks," Zuriel says, getting closer to the neck of one of the creatures. I lean down and do the same; I stretch the skin on the right side of its neck and see two small scarred holes. It couldn't be.

"Is that…?" Cassidy trails off, the others stay quiet.

"Someone is trying to turn humans and is failing, clearly. Which is creating these…things. Zeke can you carry one back into our lab? Take Cassidy with you. We need every scientist we can to help see if our assumption is correct. Don't let anyone see it, stop by the castle and wrap it in a blanket as well as the others you killed. The more we have the better. We don't want whoever is doing this to know we're onto them." I stand up and scan the room, no other sign of a vampire. I take the lead as we head out of the cave. I crawl through becoming desperate for fresh air.

Without thinking, I free fall to the ground, twisting to land on my feet at the last minute. I hear a small feminine gasp in front of me. I rise to my feet, surprised to see Nardia and Allison standing there.

Only Allison is covered in blood and her fangs are shining in the moonlight.

27

Allison

"I didn't have a choice, I freaked out. How could I not? She was dying in my arms!" I throw my hands up in the air as I pace back and forth in Kal's bedroom; the two candles on the bedside table illuminate the blood still caked on my arms. No doubt whatever I missed around my mouth as well.

"It's okay Allison, you did your best." Kal says calmly, he's sitting at the end of the bed wearing a loose white shirt and loose black pants.

"Did I though? I should have made her wait until sunrise, god I was so stupid." I grab my hair and pull at it, if she doesn't live I don't know if I'd be able to forgive myself.

"You weren't stupid, she lost her child. No mother would want to be anywhere near the killer," he says softly. I glance over at him; his eyes seem far away. I clear my throat, he snaps back to reality.

"She'll be fine, a week at most and she'll be back on her feet."

I stop pacing and sigh. A week, except she wouldn't be the same Yolanda.

When I bit her and fed from her it unlocked something dark inside of me. I wasn't sure what I was doing, but I came to know I could inject something with my fangs. I don't know if it's poisonous or would help her but I had no option. When we reached the city I'd met with Nardia and we'd taken her to their medical ward.

I also hadn't realised that the building belonged to Kal and his business side of things. Another secret he might have not wanted me to know about. Once Yolanda was settled we left to find Kal. I'd hid the vial of liquid in my room before we'd gone there.

"She won't be the same though, will she?" I ask, finally coming to a stop. Immediately my nerves begin to creep higher again. He sighs as he stands up, running a hand through his hair.

"No, she won't. Not exactly. It will still be her though. It's the only thing that could save her, and I'm sure Zuriel wouldn't have just let her die. Even if it isn't what she wants."

"Will she be angry at me?" I ask softly, I hadn't even considered that she might have rather die than to be a vampire. He comes to me and wraps his arms around me. I rest my head on his chest and sigh; I leave my arms at his side; not wanting to stain his shirt.

"No I don't think so, we'll find out once she rises. You won't be able to go near her until she has her hunger under control." The breath from his words tickle my neck. I take a deep breath; frowning when I detect a hint of decay under his usual vanilla and pine scent.

"What was in the cave?" I pull back, looking up to his face. His eyes search mine as he struggles to find the right words.

"I didn't want to worry you with it." his voice is soft as he tucks my hair behind my ear. He licks his thumb and scrubs gently at a small spot on my cheek.

"You don't get to make that decision, I want to know. What happened while I was gone?" I demand, stepping out of his arms. He rolls his eyes at me.

"You're so stubborn, do you know that?" he moves around the bed, grabbing a black jumper from the floor. Since when did he leave his clothes on the floor?

"Yes, I do and you still haven't answered my question," I chime, raising an eyebrow. He pulls the jumper on and grabs my hand, pulling me towards the door.

"Where are we going?" I ask, reluctantly following him but not letting go of his hand.

"To the sitting room, I'll start the fire. It's starting to get colder." He walks at a human pace which I'm thankful for, my legs still burn from the run back. I hadn't stopped, no matter how many times I wanted to or felt like my legs were going to break. I just hoped it was worth it.

"Mmm." I hum; his mention of fire momentarily takes me back to the fire in the woods, the large black cat hunting Yolanda like she was a small rodent in the forest. I shiver; it could have easily been me in her place. Instead I would most likely be dead by now.

"Are you thirsty or hungry?" as we reach the sitting room, he drops my hand and flashes over to the fire. I walk over and sit on the couch, I groan as I look down at my arms. I still hadn't had a shower.

"What?" he turns from the fire, which was slowly growing and already beginning to heat the small room.

"I still haven't washed myself, I must stink." I pout, having no energy to even move. He comes and squats in front of me, putting his hands on my knees.

"You stink no more than usual." he smiles, I swat at his shoulder and fail to hide my smile.

"Ha ha. You're funny aren't you?" I say, sitting back into the couch and crossing my arms over my chest.

"When I want to be. Why don't you go and have a shower? I'll make you a hot chocolate and we can get comfortable on the couch and we can talk." he rubs his hands up and down my thighs, relaxing me.

"I have no energy to walk there, better yet scrub all this blood off of me." I sigh, leaning my head back and looking towards the ceiling. It would be good to have the hot water beating down on my broke body though, more than anything right now.

"Alright, come on." he says softly, I look back at him in time to see him stand; wrapping his arms under my legs and back. He lifts me into the air effortlessly, I wrap my arms around his neck without thinking.

"What are you doing?" I squeak, watching his face. His eyes flicker to me before focusing in front of him. The dark shadows don't go unnoticed; I wasn't naïve to think it was because I hadn't been here.

"I'm carrying you to the bathroom, I'll run it for you and get it ready and once you're finished I'll come and carry you back to the sitting room." we turn down the hall for the bathroom and my heart picks up in my chest. The last time I'd had someone this close to me and water was Xavier.

He unlocks the door and glides in, shutting it behind him. He stands in front of the mirror that covers the wall from floor to roof and catches my eyes. I let my eyes roam freely over us; he looks like a protector with me in his arms. His hair sticks out wildly from his low bun, his black jumper and black pants are bright against the grey cobblestone wall.

He slowly sets me down, his hands lingering on my waist before he turns around. He walks over to the basin and pulls a small cream block out.

"What's that?" I ask, wrapping my arms around myself. I'm not sure what to do, do I start to undress? Do I wait until he leaves? He walks towards the shower.

"Honey and coconut soap, your favourite," he says as he sits it in a crevice on the back wall before turning back to me.

"How'd you know?" I ask, raising an eyebrow at him. He gives me a mischievous smile.

"Well when my soap starts to diminish faster than it usually does it's a dead giveaway." my cheeks go red at his words; I roll my eyes and smile weakly. Even that was taking effort. He comes over to me and places his hands on my cheeks, raising my face to his.

"Get undressed; I'll get the water running for you. Only if you're comfortable, if not I'll leave the room." he plants a small kiss on my forehead and turns around to press the button. I ignore my race car heart and begin to undress, pulling my tights off first and then my shirt.

I unclasp my bra with shaky hands then pull my underwear off. I gather the dirty blood stained clothes and toss them towards the small bench. I cover my breasts with my hands, tuning to look in the mirror.

I let my eyes roam over my naked body; they linger on the bare skin of my slim stomach where I know Nardia first bit me. I follow the curve of my hip down my legs, currently covered in small cuts from the run back. I suck my bottom lip as my eyes go back upwards; in the mirror I catch Kal's eyes. He watches me silently, as still as that black cat was. A predator.

I gulp.

He'd never seen me this exposed before.

He walks towards me slowly, stopping behind me. A large hand comes to my hip while the other pulls my hair to one side; exposing the soft skin of my neck. I involuntarily turn my head for him. His eyes flicker to the skin before returning to me.

"You're so beautiful Allison." he whispers, sending a chill down my spine.

"Thank you." I say softly, my lips damp. He kisses the skin against the pulse in my throat. I know my heart is beating a million miles a minute. A new rush of adrenaline now finding me.

His kiss lingers as he feels the pulse.

"Do you want to know a secret?" I whisper, his eyes search my face. He waits silently.

"It does that whenever I'm around you. I can't seem to get a hold of my heart," I say softly, finally admitting it out loud for the first time. His lips graze the skin as he peppers kisses across the top of my shoulder. Here I was fully naked, with the vampire King kissing me. I never would have thought I'd ever be this lucky.

I watch him intently in the mirror as his kisses fill me with electricity, he is so beautiful and unearthly and my blood sings to his. This is what I wanted forever; this is the one thing I would always fight for.

He straightens himself and I let out a small whimper, missing the contact. He breathes heavy behind me, his chest pressing against my back. He rests his chin on top of my head.

"If you keep looking at me like that I'm afraid I might lose control." he says; his free hand skims my arms. I'm extremely aware of how close he is to my breast. I squeeze my legs together.

"Will you help me shower?" I ask. His eyes widen at my offer. A few moments of silence pass and I begin to regret asking. Oh god I was a fool-

"Yes." his voice is deep as he lets go of me, I watch through the mirror as he pulls the jumper and shirt over his head; the muscles along his shoulder and chest ripple, his defined abs moving as he lowers his arms back down. I'd see him shirtless before, but this time it felt more intimate.

He pulls his pants off next, but keeps the thin material of his boxers on, leaving little to the imagination as the length of him is hard and tight against the fabric. I tear my eyes away and try and focus on my uneven breathing.

I focus on myself again, not knowing where the burst of confidence came from. He clears his throat from behind me.

"Are you ready?" he asks, his voice is thicker than usual. I nod once, not trusting myself to form a coherent sentence. He reaches a hand out for me, I move my right arm around to cover both breasts and place my left hand in his.

He leads us to the shower, opening the glass door. We step in; I drop his hand as I move to the back wall towards the soap. The water is hot and begins to steam the glass up. I'm nervous to turn around.

He comes up behind me and turns me towards him, the water droplets run down his face and neck; leaving the trails of loose hair behind. His hands rest on my hips. His mouth is slightly parted as he looks down at me and I almost have to pinch myself to remind me this isn't a dream.

"Tell me about the camp," he says. I frown at him. That's not what I was expecting. He reaches behind me and grabs the soap before taking my hands in his, he begins to scrub at the blood on my arms.

"It was different, they have grobblers as their guards now and I'm guessing they'd use them in other areas. I had a chat with Xavier one night by the fire." A low growl comes from him at the mention of Xavier's name. I smirk a little.

"Someone jealous?" I tease; the muscle in his jaw twitches.

"No, I was clearing my throat," he grumbles. He finishes washing my arms and puts the soap back before his hands move and rest on the back wall on either side of my face; encasing me in. I want badly to touch his chest and to feel the muscles there but then I'm fully exposed to him.

"I get jealous too," I whisper, looking down. His boxers stick to his skin, although the spray from the water mainly hits his back. I still feel like my skin is on fire.

"You have nothing to be jealous of Allison, nothing." I draw my eyes back up to his, I nibble my lip. Of course I did, I knew what Cassidy looked like and God knows whoever else he'd been with. I was just some impure half breed human.

"I do. I see the way the other females look at you." I wish I could take the words back after they leave my mouth, God I was a downer tonight. I have this sexy man in front of me and I'm feeling sorry for myself.

"And do you know who I'm looking at?" his right hand comes to my face as he strokes my cheek. I shake my head slowly. He rests his forehead on mine.

"You. Always you." His answer makes my heart swell in my chest, I had no words.

"Oh." I whisper dumbly, embarrassed with myself.

"Come on, I'll wash you and get the rest of the blood off you." He straightens and reaches for the soap behind me again. I look down at my arms; most of the blood had washed away already from his earlier attempt, only leaving a few stubborn patches.

He stands back with the soap in hand.

"Do you trust me?"

"Yes." My voice is barely a whisper. It terrifies me how much I do trust him, how easily I had fallen for him and was still falling for him. I don't know if he feels the same, but for right now I am going to pretend.

I let my arms fall to my side, fully exposing myself to him. I watch as his eyes roam over my bare chest, taking in each curve and imperfection.

He reaches out for my left arm and begins to run the soap along it. Bubbles form and turn red as he removes the grime and dirt. He raises my other arm and repeats the same gesture, cleaning them thoroughly.

"Could you... wash the rest of me?" I ask softly, his eyes widen as he nods once. I let my arms fall to the side as I turn around. He runs the soap up and down my back, over my shoulders. My breathing gets shallow as his hands reach around to my stomach, with the soap in his hand he begins to go higher. He stops just shy of my breasts.

"Are you sure?" he breathes into my ear, with each rise of his chest it touches my back; I hadn't realised how close he'd moved.

"Yes." I look over my shoulder at him; I don't take my eyes from him as one hand cups my breast while the other roams over them with the soap. He sits the soap back in its crevice and takes my other breast in his hand; he begins to knead them softly.

The pulsing between my legs picks up, I squeeze them together to try and find some release from the pressure that is beginning to build up deep inside of my stomach.

Each slow knead is more torturous than the last, his fingers are gentle as he skims my hard nipples; nearly sending me over the edge. To where, I wasn't sure but the rise was nearly greater than the fall. My breathing comes in uneven gasps.

"God... that feels amazing," I moan, letting my head fall back against his chest. I expose the right side of my neck to him, also letting the water beat down against my chest, each droplet helps feed the fire he's started inside of me.

"I would do anything to hear you moan again." He slides his lips up my neck, his hands never relenting. I lean back, arching my ass into him.

"Fuck." he swears under his breath. I'd never felt this wound up before, I had no idea what to do but my body seemed to.

"Kiss my neck." my breathing comes in gasps as he kisses my neck, gentle at first. Obeying my command. I wonder what it would feel like if he were to... bite me.

"Oh god, Kal." I groan, shutting my eyes. He rubs himself against me and I don't hesitate as I roll my hips in sync to his, the length of him nestling between my ass.

He goes to kiss me again, but instead of his tongue I feel his fangs graze across my pulse. All rational thought flies out the window as one hand begins to travel down my stomach; he gropes the inside of my thigh gently. If only he'd reach higher.

"I'm not going to have sex with you tonight, my queen," he whispers in my ear, before taking it between his teeth and tugging gently. His hand drops from my breast as he turns me to face him, he pushes me against the back wall; holding me up with his thigh. I whimper at the pressure and pleasure that comes from him nestled between my legs.

"Bite me then," I gasp, tilting my head back to look into his eye; water catches on his long eyelashes. His fangs gleam in the light. He stands there panting, his eyes snap back to mine. I wasn't sure were the primal urge came from, but I needed it.

"Allison..." I can tell he's pulling away, back to his sensible self. I didn't want sensible right now, I needed dangerous. I needed him.

"Please bite me, Kal." I beg. My hands reach out and pull him closer to me, I begin to grind myself against his thigh. He moans low in his throat as he watches my breasts bounce with the movement. I rack my nails down his back, I can tell he is about to snap.

In response my own fangs emerge, pressing against my bottom lip; I lean forward and pepper small kisses along his collar bone, grazing my fangs along as I go.

Bite him, sink your fangs into the soft flesh and make him yours.

He is yours. Forever and more.

Claim him.

I try and fight against the urge but it's pointless, I let the more vampiric part of me take over. I plant a kiss at the base of his throat and shoulder and press my fangs down softly; silently asking permission.

"Ali, there's something you should know before you do that... before we do this." he groans, he doesn't move away though.

"Tell me after." I say against his skin, my voice a purr. I knew he wanted this as much as I did. I'm not sure where my fascination came from to be bitten and bite back, after I bit Yolanda it's like something deep inside has woken.

"Allison..." my name is a blessing and a curse on his lips, breaking me away from any rational thought. I sink my fangs down, immediately my mouth fills with blood and the feeling is pure euphoria. I groan as I drink from him, the taste of his blood drives my senses wild. It tastes better than heaven.

He grinds against me as I grip his back, racking my nails down. A growl rips out of his throat as he pulls away, I gasp as blood leaks from my mouth and no doubt is smeared across my teeth.

He takes in the sight, his eyes wild and unlike the Kal I'd grown to know. He swallows, hard.

"Please, Kal," I pant, needing this. My fangs retract on their own, knowing they're not needed anymore.

"I don't want you to regret it." his voice is rough, still fighting the primal urge. I expose the right side of my neck to him, knowing he could hear how erratic he's making me.

"I won't, I promise." my voice begins to whine now, I needed some form of release or I was sure to go mad. Everything inside of me is wound up and ready to explode, drunk on him.

"If at any moment you want me to stop, tell me and I will. Okay? I need you to promise that." he leans his forehead against mine, his hands grip my hips as he pulls me up higher; I wrap my legs around his waist. The length of him rests between our bodies, right against the warmest part of me.

"I promise." I lick my lips as one hand comes to my shoulder; he lowers his mouth over my throat. He grazes his fangs along the sensitive skin, I moan.

He comes undone.

He slowly sinks his fangs into me; I feel the blood begin to run down the front of me. I gasp and moan, moving my hips fast against him. My body begins to ignite deep inside of me. He groans against me. Deep in our state of pleasure I feel a connection form between us, it snaps into place.

"Oh god yes, Kal…" I moan his name like a pray, over and over again as the pleasure explodes until it ebbs away. I feel him drinking my blood, once I still against him he unlatches. I hiss as his fangs leave, the two small holes continue to bleed slowly; mixing with the water. He pants as he looks down at me, blood runs down his chin.

"You taste divine." he slows his breathing as he takes control of himself, slowly his fangs retract. He leans his forehead against mine while we both stay there panting. That was incredible.

"I'm ready for that hot chocolate now your highness." I say weakly, smiling lazily up at him. He dips his face down and pecks me on the nose.

"So am I." he lowers me to the ground and takes my hand in

his as we leave the shower; he passes me a black towel as he pushes the button off. I look at myself in the mirror, my pale skins seems to glow; the two small bit marks still leak. My wild eyes and damp hair look nothing like me.

He wraps a towel around his waist, leads me out of the bathroom and towards his bedroom.

"Picking up where we left off?" I tease, squeezing his hand. He shakes his head. I know there's a smile on his lips. He opens the door and leads me in, I stand there while he moves around the bed. He picks up one of his usual white shirts and passes it to me; I drop my towel as I pull it over my head. I breathe in his scent.

"Are my boxers okay to wear?" he asks, turning towards me as he pulls a black pair from his draws. I nod once as he throws them to me, he dresses in his usual long white pants and pulls a dark green long sleeved shirt on.

He scoops me up in his arms before we head back to the sitting room, I snuggle into him. I gently run my fingers over the two fang marks on the side of his neck; identical to my own. What had he said again? What did I have to know? My eyes grow heavy as I relax, exhaustion finally catching up to me.

I finally found my home.

28

Allison

I wake to a hand running through my hair, I enjoy the moment before everything from last night comes crashing back into me. Kal carrying me to the shower. Kal washing me. Kal biting me. *Me biting Kal.* Oh God. My eyes fly open, only to see Kal leaning on one arm looking down at me. I relax slightly.

"Good morning sleepy head, how are you feeling today?" he asks, stroking my cheek. I groan.

"I wish I could have slept in a little more." although my body is feeling refreshed my mind still feels exhausted. I had a busy day ahead of me today, first thing I had to do is take that serum to someone I could trust.

"There's plenty of time to sleep, I could wake you up again in a few hours?" he suggests; his hand travels down my neck and rests on my shoulder. His eyes flicker to the spot he'd bitten last night.

"I have a busy day today, I might need your help actually." I sigh and roll on my back; he must have carried me up to his room last night.

"You need my help with something? That's a first." I roll my eyes at him, he'd have to get over the fact I'd left to do my own mission without him. I sit up and stretch my arms, yawning.

"Yes, your help. I need you to take me to one of your most trusted scientists. I have a ... favour to ask of them." he sits up beside me, the sheet exposing his bare chest.

"A favour you say?" I lean my head against his shoulder. Time to open up.

"When I was at the camp the serum they're injecting everyone with isn't stable. They're killing children and the elderly with it. I made a compromise with Xavier. I said I'd bring back a stable serum for them that essentially makes them equal to vampires. He gave me three months otherwise he will continue using the same serum." I raise my head to find his eyes searching my face, deep in thought.

"I know it isn't ideal for you, giving the humans an advantage. But I can't think of any other way to make them equal and eventually have us all coexist." I sigh, needing him to understand.

"Allison, it's not just about having us all coexist. Vampires can't solely survive on animal blood; we still do need human blood. If the serum isn't stable for us to feed, we may as well just wipe out my entire race." I frown at his words.

"Make it so you can still drink it then? In the world I imagine I have us all coexisting; humans own the day and vampires own the night. We could have everyone do monthly donations so the vampires wouldn't have to kill anyone." I sigh, wishing it was that easy. That simple.

"Not all vampires and not all humans would like that idea." he says softly.

"I know they won't but we need to start somewhere. I'd even thought about creating like an underground town for vampires, so through the day they could still do their own thing and not just be locked away in a house." I can see my vision so clearly, vampires could still roam throughout the day and humans could still roam at night if they pleased. If I could live with them why couldn't other humans?

My mind wanders to the vampires that had cornered me, wanting to taste my blood. I shiver involuntarily. If I was a mere human I'm afraid of how that encounter could have ended.

"It still surprises me that you think of my race and try to make sure they're just as comfortable as well. I can see your vision; it's just getting there that is going to be the hard part." he wraps an arm around my shoulder and pulls me closer to him. I manoeuvre onto his lap and lean back against him.

"I just wish everyone could see it how I do, it's so clear in my mind. But can we still please try with the serum? I can't have any more blood on my hands, Kal. If their serum was stable, Yolanda's little boy would still be alive. She wouldn't have been turned. Kal, if I can stop unnecessary deaths you know I'm going to." I lean back so I can look up at him, my eyes stray down to his neck; two puncture wounds stare back at me.

I sit up and turn in his lap; he raises an eyebrow as I sit on my knees. I take his head in my hands and lean it to the right, the puncture wounds still there.

"Kal? Why is the bite mark still there?" I ask, touching them gently. He stills under me, his face turns serious.

"You know how I said you had to know something before we went through with it?" his voice is cautious; I frown and let him straighten his head.

"Yes…" I trail off. When Nardia had bit me the bite marks had disappeared. Why hadn't Kal's? Why had the humans on the street had scars from them?

"When we both do it willingly and feed from one another… it forms a bond, a connection. Like two souls connecting. I should have just told you instead of giving in, if you don't want it the bond can be broken… it's painful though," he says softly. My hands fall to my lap as I try to process this information.

In the moment I had felt something form between us, I just thought it was an intimate moment not our souls connecting as one. I wasn't sure how I felt about it.

"So we're what? Connected? Soul mates or something?" I ask, avoiding his eyes. I reach up and sure enough I feel the two puncture marks from his fangs. I know I liked him, but did I love him?

"This just seems like something people in love would do. But you don't love me, I don't even know if you like me, because I do like you and I don't know how you managed to worm your way under my skin, but you have." I begin to ramble nervously; he rests his hands on my thighs. I stop and look up at him, his face wounded.

"We're connected, yes. The marks won't go away unless the connection is broken. Allison you have nothing to worry about, nothing has changed between us. I do like you, if you want to do more... couple things I would be more than happy. Please don't overthink this. We can take it as slow as you want." he cups my face and strokes my cheeks. Everything had changed though, we had both changed.

"Kal, how could I not overthink this? If whatever this is between us goes any further you'll want me to become a full vampire and right now that's honestly not what I want. I don't know if it ever will be." I bite my bottom lip, would he be angry if I chose to stay human and leave him behind?

"Ali, it's okay. I'm not asking anything of you and I'm not asking you to become anything for me. I like you for you, your smart attitude and mostly your human heart. It makes you, you. If you chose to stay human I would support you the entire way. If this isn't what you want then I will do the right thing and step away. I want to see where we can go, forget about being my queen or us being bound together. If you want to see where we can go then we will; if you don't, tell me and it can stop." I take a minute to process his words. He doesn't care if I stay human or choose to become a full vampire. The thought of him stepping away hurts my heart; the pain is a surprise to me. I didn't want to be without him.

I do trust him, more than I trusted Zeke and Xavier. He is the first person I could be open and be myself with.

"I want to try," I whisper. I reach up and wrap my hands around his neck.

"I want to see where this goes, but please be careful with me. I am broken and still trying to heal," I say softly, rubbing my thumbs against the back of his neck. He brings his forehead to mine and takes a deep breath. I think back to Cass's diary entry. *Do not fear, for she needs you to be her light as well. Together you will fall apart and be mended.*

"You make me so happy Allison, never in my hundreds of years have I felt the way you make me feel. I would wait a hundred or more years for you again. I hope I don't disappoint you." he leans forward and brushes his lips against mine.

"You make me happy too, Kal. I didn't know what it felt like until you came into my life," I say softly, my breath hitting his lips.

"Now let us go and find someone to make a stable serum," he says, before bringing his lips softly to mine. I kiss him back, running my tongue along his bottom lip. My blood ignites as he slides his tongue into my mouth; I pull myself closer to him.

His hands leave my face and trail down my sides, resting on my hips. Reluctantly he breaks the kiss, breathing heavy.

"Sweetheart there's plenty of time we can continue this, but we need to focus on getting that serum into work." I sigh and roll my eyes.

"Why do you always have to be so sensible?" I groan, even though I know he is right. I climb off of him; his shirt hangs part way down my thighs. I'd be able to walk back to my room like this.

"I'll go and get changed and meet you at the front of the castle then, yes?" I ask as I walk to the door, I look back over my shoulder as I grab the door handle. He leans back against his arms, the sheet just covering his waist. I trail my eyes up his toned stomach; his messy bun is nearly undone, sending long strands down the front of him.

In this moment he looks like a god. A god who only has eyes for me. What he saw in me I wasn't sure. Currently, I was thankful for that bond we'd created. I'd never get used to waking up to his handsome face every day.

"Yes, that sounds like a plan." he raises an eyebrow suggestively; I roll my eyes at him in return, wanting nothing more than to climb back to his side.

"You can't walk around town half naked," I groan, opening the door.

"You mean fully naked," he calls as I shut the door behind him. A huge smile settles on my face; seeming permanent.

I walk back to my room grinning like an idiot, as I go to pass the sitting room hallway, I hear voices coming from the room. I pause and look down the hallway, the door opens as Cassidy and Nardia step out. I freeze, realising what it must look like. Nardia catches my eyes and her mouth falls open, Cassidy's eyes travel to the bite mark.

"You've got to be fucking kidding me," she growls.

29

Kalabhiti

I enter the sitting room, adjusting the sleeve of my usual black training leathers. I'd pulled my hair back into a high ponytail, showcasing the mate mark. I look up to see Allison sitting on the couch, dressed in black tights and long sleeved red shirt. Her hair is down, the waves fan around her face. Nardia and Cassidy stand in front of her.

"Ladies. What do I owe the pleasure?" I ask, eyeing Cassidy and Nardia as I stand behind the couch. My hands itch to reach out and touch Ali; I grip the top of the couch instead.

"When were you going to tell us you'd decided to mark her?" Cassidy asks, furious. I stay calm as I look at her. Nardia shrugs. She would have known this was coming.

"It wasn't planned," I say coolly, not that this was any of her business. She scoffs.

"Yeah right, well now that you two are just the best of lovers

I'm sure you've told her about the human you've been keeping here against his will." Cassidy growls, crossing her arms over her chest. I go rigid, looking down at Ali. She looks up at me, her eyes wide. This is not how I was planning on telling her.

"Tell me she's lying," she pleads. Her ruby eyes search my face; her bottom lip quivers.

"Why would I lie? I get nothing from it. I don't know why you think he is a good man, because he isn't. At the end of the day he will always be a vampire, you stupid mortal." I growl at the insult. Cassidy knows nothing of the man I am.

"You will not speak about your King that way and you sure as hell will not talk to Allison like that either." I stand straight, immediately my shadows begin to fan out around me. I'd been slack with them ever since Ali arrived, I'd been trying to change my old ways.

"I can talk to her however I want and you're not one to stop me. She means nothing to me and she never will. You've become soft since she's arrived. You're a piss poor excuse of a King," Cassidy spits. Before I have time to retaliate Allison has her pinned against the fire place. She snarls at her, her fangs extending.

"You can speak to me however you like but I will not sit by and watch you disrespect him. I may be a mortal but I am far from stupid." Allison growls, her hand tightening on Cassidy's throat. I step forward; Nardia sends me a warning glare. I move around the couch and stand beside Nardia, maybe this was a long time coming.

"Get your filthy humans hands off of me!" Nardia shouts, her fangs coming down as well. Ali gives her a wicked smile. She turns still holding Cassidy and sends her flying through the door into the hallway. She sends me a glare full of hate before she prowls around the couch, she hadn't forgotten about the human.

"Finally you've grown some back bone," Cassidy says, pulling herself up from the floor.

"That's what happens when you go through hell and back." Ali stands in the door way, deathly still. Her voice had dropped an octave, turning into something more primal; more vampire.

"You know Cassidy, I never did like you. From the moment Zeke dragged you along to one of our meetings I knew we weren't going to get along. I've done nothing but respect you this entire time and you still seem to find ways to hate me." She stalks forward, blue tendrils spill from her hands; working their way towards Cassidy. In this moment a small part of me is afraid of Ali. I'd never seen this side of her before.

"Nardia, shouldn't we stop this?" I whisper, watching as the blue tendrils wrap around Cassidy's legs.

"She's not going to kill her, but this is a long time coming. She's assured me she's no murderer," Nardia whispers back before looking back towards them. Cassidy growls, Ali hadn't seen the power Cassidy possessed. Not many people had, she was very private about what she could do.

"How could I like you? You let my people die, they were defenceless and you left them behind. My little brother was a part of those who died; I will never forgive you for that." Slowly Cassidy's skin begins to glow a bright red, the air grows hot around us. Nardia raises an eyebrow; I have my shadows ready to diffuse the situation. I hadn't known she had a little brother. Allison stills at that information, I can't imagine the thoughts that would be running through her head.

"I tried to save them, half of them were saved. I'm sorry about your brother," she says softly, her blue tendrils seem to falter. I knew Ali wasn't a fighter and was more of a lover. She already held enough guilt about those vampires we lost.

"I don't want your pity." Cassidy spits, her skin glows a dark red now and the heat in the room is almost sweltering. I feel sweat beads form along my forehead.

"I will never like you," she says, taking a step back.

"Why not?" Ali asks; her voice low. Cassidy catches my eyes.

"Because you have him and ever since you've been here everything has changed, I was here before you. I always have been." She tears her eyes away from mine and turns around, fleeing from the castle. Nardia sighs and runs after her, calling out her name.

As soon as she's gone the temperature returns to normal. Allison calls her powers back into her before turning towards me. I stay still.

"Why do you have a human here?" She asks, her voice blunt.

"Because we needed to see if their blood was still compatible for us to drink. They're staying in a private room in the city, donating it in small amounts. Zuriel had been testing it to see if it will poison us or not," I say calmly, clasping my hands behind my back. I had good reason to do this, but looking at the hurt on Ali's face it just makes me feel...bad. Wrong.

"Have you not learnt a thing from me? Or from our conversations? I am a human, I am trying to find a balance in this world and you do this. You're just as bad as they are!" She cries out, her hands shake at her sides.

"Can you please calm down, the person isn't hurt. We feed them and they have a proper room to stay in. We were only keeping them long enough to see if their blood was compatible and then we were letting them go, but they don't want to leave." I try to show her the reason; I had no other way to go about it. I had to look out for my people just as much as she did. It was my duty as a King; I'd done worse things in my years as ruler.

"Calm down? Regardless if you keep them in good conditions or not you've taken away their free will, a basic human right. Were you ever going to tell me?" I feel the trust we'd formed ebb away and I can't believe I've fucked this up. After everything she's gone through, I throw this in her face.

"I was going to tell you and take you to meet them, since you're human and would have more in common with them. I didn't mean to hurt you; I was just trying to look out for my people." I take a step towards her, she takes a step back. She begins to shake her head.

"Don't. Don't come near me. I can't believe you, you should have waited for me and we could have come up with something together."

"Like how you enlightened me with your little plan where you ran away for a week? How you oh so nicely left without a damn word?" I ask, my voice beginning to rise. She could not point fingers at me.

"I couldn't have vampire influence on my plan, you know this!"

"Yeah and I couldn't have human influence on mine." I growl, my emotions are chaotic in my chest. She has unravelled me and rattled me. She shakes her head in disbelief, I wanted nothing more than to hold her and tell her how sorry I am.

"I shouldn't have given you the time of day to make me believe you could be better than what you are. You're a vampire and I'm a human. I knew this wouldn't work. I should have known you'd never change. Forget about the serum, I'll do it on my own." My face crumbles at her words, she turns around; ready to leave me behind. I begin to panic, all of this for nothing.

"Ali, please don't go. Give me a chance to show you I can be the man you need," I plead, taking a step forward. She doesn't look back; we both know if she did she'd cave. I wanted her to cave. I'd do anything to have her look at me.

"I already did and look where it got me? Another broken heart and broken trust again." her voice is barely a whisper; she takes a deep breath before walking down the hallway and disappearing.

I fall to my knees; tears begin to well in my eyes. It couldn't be over, she couldn't give up on me so easily after how close we'd come. I'd opened myself up to her and she'd done the same, I knew what I was doing would hurt her. I just didn't think I'd lose her in the process.

Maybe she is right.
Maybe all I am is just a vampire.

30

Allison

I grab my things and shove them into my backpack, not caring that they're thrown in a ball. Hot tears stream down my face and make it difficult for me to see but I push through the pain.

I had trusted Kal, and he had gone and taken a human against his will and used them as an experiment. It hits close to home, far too close.

That camp had taken those vampires and done the exact same thing. How could he think I would be alright? Did he know of the suffering they had to go through? That I had to go through?

I grab the serum and shove it on top of my clothes before zipping the bag shut. I couldn't be in this castle right now; I couldn't be near him at the moment. My heart aches in my chest, just as I'd let it heal I go and shatter it again with my own foolishness.

I don't know exactly where I'm going or what I'm really doing, but I'd formulate a plan as I went along. I strap the bag over my shoulders and run to the door, not wanting to see Kal or give him a reason to stop me. I burst through the front door and sprint towards the forest, running as fast and far away as I can get.

I ignore the sounds and animals in the forest, not caring if the creature comes after me. I hit the city streets and slow down; I wipe the tears from my face and head towards the large white platform that will get me out of here.

Maybe I was over reacting, but if he's kept something like this from me who knows what else he's been hiding. As I walk along I begin to look for science buildings or something similar. If I could somehow get the serum to someone who could stabilise it, it wouldn't have been all for nothing.

"Excuse me; do you have a science building in the city anywhere?" I ask a female vampire that stares too long at me; she shakes her head and looks away.

I repeat this question over and over to the strangers on the street, finally an elderly vampire stops.

"Yes we do. It's towards the platform, has a gold lion on the sidewalk. Easy to spot, shouldn't give you too much hassle to find." his greying hair shines in the light around us, his eyes flicker to the marks on my neck. I shift uncomfortably. God damn I was stuck with his mark.

"Thank you so much," I say in a rush. I head towards the platform keeping an eye out for the golden lion he mentioned. Sure enough, it stands on the footpath; a scowl on its face. I look up the tall building, no windows were evident. I cautiously open the glass door, the female vampire behind the counter looks up at me. She adjusts her white lab coat and glasses.

"How can I help?" She asks, beginning to type away at her computer. I come to the counter.

"I need to talk to one of your most trusted scientists; I'm here on special orders from the King," I say. I don't feel guilty lying to her. Kal had brought this on himself.

"Ah yes. Doctor Robert is our most trusted by the King. Were you needing to book an appointment with him?" Under her red fringe her eyes flicker towards my stomach.

"Oh no I'm not pregnant. I just have to give him something," I squeak, my cheeks burn under her gaze.

"Alright, he has an opening now if you'd like to go on through to his office. Go up the elevator to level two and you'll see his name on the second door to your right." She looks back towards her computer, dismissing me.

"Thanks." I mumble before heading towards the elevator. This had to work; I had to make sure I didn't screw this up. The elevator ride is short and sweet, classic piano keeps me entertained for the few moments of the trip. It pings open and I step out into a brightly lit hallway, each inch of it is pure white and nearly blinding. I walk slowly, finding his door.

I knock against the white glass once. It sides open. At a bronze desk a young vampire sits; flicking through folders in front of him. A small black seat is vacant across from him.

"You may enter." his voice is deep, he gestures with a hand for me to come in. I hesitate. I didn't even know if he was for or against helping humans.

"Ah thank you. I'm sorry to take up your time like this," I say as I step into the room, the door slides shut behind me. The room is small, bare of any decoration. As I take a seat I feel like a lab rat. He sits his paper down and looks up at me.

His blonde hair sits wavy against his head; his black eyes are no surprise. He's clean shaved, not one speckle of hair is to be seen. He's good looking in an odd kind of way I couldn't place.

"Now, how can I help?" he asks, surveying me.

"I need your help, I don't know if you're going to like it or not and if you don't I can find someone else but I've been told you're the Kings most trusted scientist?" I ask, gripping the straps against my sides tightly.

"Yes I am. And who might you be?" he asks, sitting back in his chair.

"Allison," I say, not liking his constant need for eye contact. He smiles bleakly at me.

"Alright Allison, how would you like me to help?" He crosses his arms over his chest. I pull my bag out in front of me and grab the vial.

"I need you to make this a stable serum. It's so humans can take the dosage and become equal to vampires in areas they lack." I hold the green liquid up for him to see, this catches his attention.

"Now why would I do that?" he asks, leaning forward as he looks at the serum.

"Because they're being injected and dying from it. If all humans take it and all die that leaves vampires with nothing. I'd rather them have a stable serum than die out completely," I say calmly. He didn't have to know the whole truth about the serum, or that only the elderly and children were dying.

"Has the King asked for this?"

"Yes he has. We want you to also make it stable enough and compatible so when vampires drink it they don't get poisoned. It has to be vampire friendly." he reaches out for the vial; I pull it out of reach.

"I'll only give you half the dosage, so if you fail I can still find a solution on my own." I sit it back down on the bag, eyeing him cautiously.

"Smart girl. Very well, I'll run it by the King himself and if it's what he wishes I will begin. You'll need to pour half the contents into another vial." he opens a draw under his desk and pulls out an empty vial; I take it off him and begin to pour the liquid in. A small amount slips from the opening, he holds out his hand as an invisible power shoots out; grabbing the liquid and pushing it back towards the vial.

I finish pouring half and pass it to him.

"Thank you, it means a lot for you to do this. That's a cool power by the way." I remark as I put my vial back in my bag. He puts a lid on his and slides it back under his desk.

"Yes it's rather handy in this field of work, amazing how much you spill things. Is that all you needed? I have another job I need to be working on." He stands as he says this, straightening his jacket.

"Yes it is; thank you. I'll be back in a month or two too see how you've come along. I have a dead line of three months, so I can't be messing around," I say seriously, pulling the bag back over my back.

"Yes I assure you I will get started immediately, once the king gives me the green light. Thank you for stopping by Allison, have a good evening." He smiles and nods once; I nod back and leave the room.

I leave the building fast, not wanting to hang around any longer. Once Kal knew I'd been here he would come looking for me. I didn't want to be found right now. I just needed some time to clear my head and figure out if he is what I really wanted, even after everything he's done.

I sigh and head towards the platform again; a night or two camping in the woods should do wonders for me. I could even stay in Yolanda's old town if I wanted more security. As I near the platform a backstreet catch's my eyes, a deep red mist swallows the end of the alley; deep thumping music echoes and drifts towards me. I stop in my tracks, vampires and their blood humans mill in and out of the street, making sure to step around me.

A black door hangs open, the source of where the music comes from. Instead of hiding in the forest I could just hide down there, I know this would piss Kal off even more than being in the forest alone.

I walk down the overcrowded street, keeping my head down

and try to ignore the ever growing fear that's sitting deep inside my stomach. I hold my bags straps tightly as I squeeze through the door, if I wasn't part vampire I wouldn't have been able to see the stairs that spiral down only a few steps in front of me.

I cough slightly at the mist; the thumping music grows louder the deeper I descend. The vampires bop their head along to the music as they leave and enter. It's a constant flow of vampires coming and leaving.

Not one of them looks sideways at me or points out the markings Kal had given me. I was a ghost here, almost fitting in with them. I reach the bottom of the stairs and move out of the way for the vampires behind me as I look around.

Red lights sit in every corner, the mist a thin layer at my feet. The open space before me is full of vampires dancing with one another, the ones on the outskirts socialise with one another.

I look over to the bar; I walk through the crowd and take a seat on the red stool. A female vampire stands up from under the counter, her pale skin is covered in tattoos; her red dreadlocks sit in a high pony tail, exposing the shaved sides of her head.

"What can I get ya?" she yells, raising a pierced eyebrow at me. I look around for a menu and come up empty.

"Something to take the edge off," I yell back, placing my hands on the sticky counter. She pulls a large glass out and begins to pour dark red liquid into it. She places a small umbrella in the slush and passes it to me.

"How much is it?" I ask, taking it hesitantly.

"Nothing, it's free Friday night specials. Enjoy." She flashes me a fanged smile before heading down further to serve others. I take the drink and stand back up; I make my way to one of the more secluded back corners and take a sip.

Immediately my senses are flooded with blood, but not human. I take another gulp, my body begins to hum. I finish the drink off with another few gulps, I'd never drunk before and right now it's all I wanted to do.

I move back to the bar and place the empty glass down. I take a seat as the bartender comes back to me.

"Can I get another two?" I ask as she begins to make one.

"Sure. Your first time?" She asks as she shakes a bottle.

"Yes it is. What's in it? It doesn't taste like human blood." I look around the bar; more vampires had come forward to get drinks. A man takes a seat beside me.

"It's deer blood and alcohol, it'll make you buzz but be careful not to drink too much. You'll have a killer hangover tomorrow if you do." She passes me my two drinks and continues on. I take both and leave, I find an empty table and take a seat. I polish off my second drink, loving the humming it was giving my body.

The room around me begins to blur at the edges, either the room is moving or I'm swaying something fierce. I giggle out loud at the thought as I begin to sip on my third drink; forcing myself to go slow.

I feel my fangs emerge, the blood driving my senses wild. I put my bag on the table and finish my third glass. I need to dance. I shimmy onto the dance floor, my body sways to the music. I close my eyes and throw my hands in the air, the smell of blood and sweat drowns out anything else.

Bodies move against mine and I open my eyes as hands wind around my waist; pulling me against a hard body. I lean back into them and lower my arms, putting my hands over theirs.

"You're a pretty little thing," he purrs. His breath hits my neck and sends chills through me. Kal had held me in a way similar to this, except this didn't feel nearly as good. The rational part of me knew I should get out of here before I did something I'd regret but the alcohol in my system threw that out the window.

"Mmm human and vampire." his tongue licks the bare skin under my ear. If he was on the other side of my neck he'd see the marks.

"Do you want another drink?" he asks, I nod as I sway with him.

"I'll be back." his hands leave my waist as he disappears. As soon as he's gone I've forgotten about him. A few other vampires come and dance with me, not caring or knowing who I am.

I'm being led away from the dance floor by a female vampire. I'd forgotten where she said we were going and the room is spinning around me. She pulls back a black curtain, revealing a red love seat. The male from earlier sits on it, two glasses sit on the small glass table.

"Remember me?" he asks, reaching a hand out to me. I reach out and take it; he pulls me onto his lap so I'm facing the female vampire that led me here. Her features are a blur as I try to focus on her. They begin to talk to one another.

Where the hell are you!
I jump in his lap, not expecting to hear Nardia's voice.

"Where are we?" I try to say, not knowing if the words came out in a coherent sentence.

"The Beat," the male says, his hands skim up and down my waist.

The Beat.

You are in so much trouble.
I snort at her comment. I could do what I want.

The female vampire sits beside us and opens her purse; she pulls out a small bag. She makes three white lines on the table, I'm not sure what it is but it looks tempting.

She snorts the first line, scrunching her nose up once she's finished.

"It's your turn love," she says, leaning back. I go to lean forward; I had nothing to lose so I may as well. I lean onto the table, trying to steady myself, the lines blur in front of me.

I lean down to a line, in a swift move I do my best to snort the powder.

I cover my mouth as I begin to cough, she giggles beside me. I haven't finished the whole line. I move from the guy's lap and squeeze in beside them; my head feels a million miles away from me.

He leans forward and finishes it off. He sits back and throws his head back, I notice his fangs out. I reach up and feel my own out.

I frown, unsure of how I got here. What had I just taken?

"What was that?" I ask, rolling my head to look to the female vampire.

"Just a mild drug, nothing harmful," she murmurs. I look back towards the black curtain; the music is slightly muffled by the curtain.

"It makes you feel really good and everything you experience is a thousand times more intense," the guy says. He sits up and grabs onto his drink.

"I can't believe you wanted to try it, hard core lil fox." the girl begins to giggle and I find myself joining in. I can't believe I'd wanted to try it. I have no idea who these people are.

"Are you two a couple?" I ask. I look down at my hands and begin to move my fingers. My body doesn't feel real.

"Eh, something like that," she says. I look back to her. The drug has taken away the harsher effects of the alcohol, so I can see her more clearly. Her blonde hair is cut in a bob, her dark eyeshadow exaggerates her large, plump pink lips.

"Do you care I'm human?" I ask.

"Nope," they say in unison. We all join in laughing, my sides begin to hurt and my face aches from the smile I can't wipe off my face.

The curtain is pulled back and a large male steps in. I turn my head to the side and I'm hit with his scent.

Kal.

I stand and stumble over to him; I throw my arms around his tense form. I nestle my head into the crevice of his neck, his arms wrap around my waist.

"What are you doing?" he growls.

"Having a good night. It's free Friday, have a drink with me," I whisper. I begin to pepper kisses along his neck, tasting his sweat. He must have run here.

"We're leaving. Now." he lowers his hands to my ass and pulls me up into the air; I wrap my legs around his waist but lean back so I can see his face.

His expression is masked but I can see the anger under the thin façade.

"Bye guys, thank you so much!" I lean back and look at them upside down, they're making out with each other. The female pulls away and smiles at me before going back to the male. I pull myself up and watch Kal's face as he leaves the small room.

"You know you need to lighten up. I'm fiiiiine." I drag the word out, whining. I want to dance. I begin to wiggle in his arms.

"You are not. What did you take?" He asks, his jaw twitching. I shrug, I had no idea.

"Can we dance? Please? Then I'll come." I raise my eyebrows a few times.

"Your pupils are dilated," he growls. I bite my lip as I smile.

"Does it look cute?" his eyes flicker to my fangs.

"No." he manoeuvres through the crowd, right through the dance floor.

"Please Kal, one dance," I beg, shaking his shoulders with my hands. No vampire paid attention to us, or the fact their King was down here with a mortal girl.

"One," he grinds out. He places me to the ground and helps steady me, my hips begin to sway to the bass that's thumping through the speakers. I turn in his arms and lean back against him; I raise my hands above me and wrap them around his neck. I grind back against him with my hips, his hands go to my waist as we sway together.

"You've been a very naughty girl, Allison." he whispers into my hair, his voice lights my body on fire.

"Do you have to punish me?" I purr, rubbing back against him harder. Feeling his skin against mine is mind blowing, I didn't know it could feel this good.

"I'm afraid so." he nips at my ear and I moan low in my throat, a few vampires look our way. He growls at them.

"We're leaving now. I don't like people seeing you like this." In a quick movement I'm cradled in his arms. I lean my head against his shoulder and sigh.

"Don't forget my bag," I murmur, my head feeling suddenly heavy.

"Nardia has already retrieved it." he begins to climb the stairs. The cool air chills me to the bone and I begin to shiver. My teeth chatter as we leave the club. Nardia stands there with a coat over her arm. She throws it over me and tucks it in.

"You're so silly." she shakes her head but I catch the small smile she gives me.

"We're going back to my apartment. She'll freeze before we reach the castle. I'll see you in a few hours when she's asleep." he nods once and begins to walk. I look up at the black sky.

"You need stars." I say.

"Yes we do." he mumbles.

"Why are you so grumpy? I'm okay," I say, looking up to his face. His eyes flicker down to me.

"I was worried about you. I had no idea where you went; I thought I was going to be too late when I arrived," he says softly.

"I needed to forget for a bit, it worked. I had fun." I giggle, bitting my lip again. I love to dance.

"We'll get you showered and into bed, we'll talk tomorrow." I close my eyes and nestle into him.

"Alright Kal, just wake me when we arrive." I yawn, my body feels heavy but my mind is alright and alive. I give into the needs of my body.

31

Kalabhiti

I manage to open the door without waking Ali, her small form reeks of blood and alcohol and I can't believe she'd let herself get this bad over one argument and whatever dark thoughts plagued her.

I close the door behind me and walk down the small hallway of the penthouse apartment, it opens up to a large spacious area where the king size bed sits flush against the back wall to. In front of me it's glass windows that reach from roof to floor and the glass door that leads out to the small balcony. I didn't bother with curtains, not with the constant night and being on top of the apartment building.

I turn left and pass the small kitchen, the lights turn on with my movement; causing the white kitchen bench to shine.

I go down another small hall and open the door up into a large bathroom, Ali stays still in my arms; breathing heavily. I was going to have to wake her up soon, hoping she'd be able to stay conscious enough for a bath.

The large spa takes up the back wall, large enough for eight or more people. The small sink and mirror to my right are spotless; a black towel sits on the sink bench.

I gently place Ali down on the wooden bench that sits opposite the sink; I plug the spa and turn the water on; pouring a small concoction of coconut soap into the water. I go back to Ali and sit her up, her eyes flutter as I hold her up.

"Ali darling, I need you to wake up for me," I say softly, I reach up and run a hand down her face; brushing the hair out of the way. She's so warm to touch. So painfully human. Her hands spread and she helps support herself on the bench. She opens her eyes, only a sliver of the red that I'd come to adore is left from her blown pupils.

In this moment she is vampire. Her fangs prod her bottom lip; she blinks slowly as she looks over me.

"Kal?" she mumbles. She reaches up and rubs a hand against her eyes. I lean back, keeping my hands on her knees. I rub them back and forth to help warm her up.

"Yes, it's me. You're safe now," I say and she slumps back against the wall and groans. I stare at the mating mark I'd left her with; I know mine would be showing as well.

"We're going to get you in the bathtub and then I'll put you to bed, you'll hopefully feel better in the morning." I cringe as I say it, after taking the drug you didn't feel better the next day; you felt worse. I'd learnt the hard way.

"But I feel my best now," she whispers, her words almost a slur.

"Yes well enjoy it while it lasts. Come on, bath time." I stand up and hold out my hands for her, she grips them shakily as she stands. She sways back and forth.

"I can't bath myself." She raises an eyebrow at me, pointing towards the bath. "I'll drown," she clarifies; the unformed question in my head evaporates.

"Are you sure?" I ask, hesitant. I didn't want to make her feel uncomfortable with me being here. I know we'd both seen each other without clothes but I feel wrong staying in here when she's in such a vulnerable state.

"Yes I'm sure. It's either your company or death. I chose you."

she huffs, letting go of my hands. She reaches out a steady hand and undresses herself; I force myself to look away.

I hear water splash and look back over, she's sitting against the front of the tub; her small face resting on the edge.

I take a seat on the bench and watch her. She blinks slowly as she looks around.

"I was taken from my family when I was little," she says, I raise an eyebrow at her statement. She diverts her eyes to the floor.

"All because I wasn't registered. If I had just been able to get that stupid chip I'd have been able to stay with them." She sighs as she sits back, lowering herself into the water. The water and bubbles finish just below her shoulders.

"I'm sorry." she waves her hand at me, sloshing water.

"Dad said that one day I'd understand why, why he never let me get chipped. I don't know what could be of such importance that he'd lose me rather than have me know." she looks up at me with sad eyes, her bottom lip quivers.

I sit back and think, I'd been hibernating when she was born. Only recently being resurrected again.

"Do you think it's because they would have picked up on your vampire blood?" I ask, that was most likely the reason. If her dad gave in and got her chipped, she might not be here today. Humans are cruel things; something as small as her having mild vampire blood in her veins would be enough for them to execute her.

"Yes, maybe. I'll never see them again; I can't even remember what town I was born in. All I know is Penrith and its cruel ways. I want to change that, more than anything." I stay silent as she talks, no words I could say would bring her any comfort at this time.

"Like why does it have to be vampire versus human? Why can't we just co-exist with one another? There's no equality. I know there would be deaths but it's in both our natures to kill. I've seen what the humans in my town have done, I know what vampires do. I don't know how to go about shoving them together and making it happy ever after." She swishes her hands back and forth in the water, deep in thought. An idea comes to mind.

"Are you really serious about wanting to change this world?" I ask, leaning forward to look at her. She meets my eyes and although I know she's most likely in another world her eyes are clear as she answers.

"Yes. More than anything."

"Be my Queen." my voice is clear as it rings around the room. She just watches me with those calculating eyes. I'd have to relay this conversation to her in the morning if she doesn't remember.

"Why?" she asks, as still as night.

"Together I believe we'd be a force to be reckoned with. You have influence over the humans whereas I have influence over the vampires, if we unite as one I believe we'd have a sure chance of winning both of the races over and showing them there's a brighter future for us all." I lean forward, seeing it clearly in my mind.

"We can go to the smaller towns and begin to build them to suit both humans and vampires. We can take down those ridiculous cement walls and begin to piece this world back together."

"What if there were towns that wouldn't want to take the risk?" she asks, leaning forward. I knew she could see it as clear as I could, both of us uniting and becoming one in this world.

"Then we show them the way of the new world, the new order. Equality for both, no more registered and non-registered humans. Each human deserves the same treatment, like the vampires have in this city." I'm so engrossed in this idea that I've moved from the seat and am now sitting in front of the spa on my knees.

She moves towards me, sitting her small chin on the ledge again. She meets my eyes and nibbles her bottom lip.

"Is that the only reason you wish for me to be Queen?" Her voice is as soft as a feather, her breath hits my face. I'm surprised by her question.

"I need to know if what we share can go somewhere Kal. I'm not one for games, so if you solemnly swear that me being queen is only to unite the races I will let the fascination I have for you go and keep it professional." I sit back on my heels, eyebrows raised. I hadn't realised that how I felt for her wasn't obvious.

"Allison…" She raises a hand and cuts me off.

"I'm serious, Kal. I can't have my heart broken again, the pain isn't worth it. I don't know if this works the same way for vampires or not but—" I cut her off as I move closer to her, our noses touch as I look into her eyes, peering into her soul.

"Allison, I have been in love with you from the moment I laid my eyes on you. When I saw you at that camp I knew I had to have you, but only if you'd have me. I didn't want to rush you or pressure you into anything you didn't want. I had to make sure what you felt for me was only because of you and not because of my influence." I'm breathless and the world around me seems brighter than ever. I'd just confessed what I'd been feeling; a weight releases itself from my chest as I focus on her and only her.

"You're in love with me?" she squeaks, her cheeks begin to turn red. I grin at her.

"I thought I'd made it obvious." I say lightly, shaking my head. She begins to giggle.

"What's so funny, hmm?" I ask, leaning back. Two dimples appear on her cheeks from her smile. I do everything I can to not poke them.

"I think I'm in love with you too." the force of her words knocks me back, I didn't think I'd ever be worthy of love again. I sure as hell didn't deserve it, not after all the wrong doing I'd caused.

"Be my Queen and I'll spend every day forward being the best damn King I could ever be. Together." The hope in my chest is overwhelming and the happiness comes hand in hand. Cassidar would be looking down on me and smiling, this was exactly what she would have wanted for me. To find that person that makes me a better version of myself.

"Ask me in the morning, for now I'm still processing the fact that you love me. And that I love you. That we love each other." she shakes her head in disbelief, the smile never leaving her face. I rise from the floor and get the towel.

"Let's get you to bed then." I wrap the towel around her as she steps out of the bath; she leans into me as I lead her to the bed. I pull the covers back while she stands there patiently.

"I don't have anything to wear," she says, yawning. I pull the shirt over my head and pass it to her, she drops the towel and pulls it on, the material skimming her thighs. I help her into bed, tucking the sheets around her.

"Will you be here when I wake up?" She asks, holding onto my hand. I sit down on the side of the bed.

"Of course I will, always." I lean down and press a kiss to her damp forehead.

"Kal if I stay human, what will you do?" she asks. I hide my worry as I look down at her.

"I would love you until your day came to leave this earth, and I would carry on your legacy until it was time for us to be united in another world. Now get some sleep." I let go of her hand, the room darkens as the kitchen light goes out. I walk out onto the balcony and shut the door softly behind me.

I lean out and look over my city, the city I'd built from the ground up.

I wasn't alone anymore. I had Ali, maybe not forever but each day with her would last me an eternity.

32

Allison

I awake to pounding, unsure if it's in my head or the world around me as I sit up; I clasp my head in my hands as the room spins. I hear footsteps and the door opens, words are exchanged.

I have no idea where I am or how I got here. I can't remember anything from last night. My final memory is when I'm dancing with that girl, I groan as I drop my hands.

My whole body aches and I feel mentally off. What happened to me last night? I look up as the kitchen light turns on, Kal walks in and slams his hands on the bench. His shoulders heave as he grips the counter.

"Kal?" I croak; my voice scratchy and foreign. He looks up at me, finally realising he's got company. He walks over to me and stops shy of the bed.

"Good morning, sleeping beauty. How do you feel?" He asks,

finally taking a seat near my feet.

"I don't know; it's the weirdest feeling. I can't remember a thing from last night. How did I get here? What happened?" I ask, running a hand through my hair. His face falls, but he recovers before I can ask why.

"I found you at the club, intoxicated and on drugs. I brought you back here, put you in the bath and put you to bed." I drop my face into my hands as he says this, I'd done drugs? Who was I turning in to?

"God I'm so sorry, I honestly don't know what came over me. I was so stupid. Thank you for coming to get me; I can't even remember why I'd gone there in the first place now." for his sake he's lucky I can't recall what drove me to drink, because I have a suspicion it has something to do with him. He sighs and stands up.

"Well we need to get you ready for the day; Nardia has just informed me there's something wrong with the portal so we need to check that out." he walks over to the glass walls and looks out at the city.

"I don't even have clothes." I pull the sheets back and stand on shaky legs, as much as I'd love to stay in bed I needed to help with the portal.

"If you look in the bathroom there's a fresh set, be quick please. I'll wait for you in the hall." he turns swiftly and walks down the hallway, I walk as fast as my legs will allow; finding the pile of folded clothes on the sink. I avoid looking at my reflection as I pull the black tights and red sweater on. I run a hand over my hair as I head into the hallway.

I find Kal leaning against the wall, dressed in his usual leathers; hair pulled back in a tight bun. His eyes flicker over me, he clenches his jaw and begins walking towards the elevator.

A strange silence settles over us, as if something was missing between us. I tap my fingers against my thigh as the elevator goes down, finally opening up to a white tile lobby.

He rushes from the elevator; from me or the silence I'm unsure. I follow after him as we merge into the crowd on the street. We both look up to see the white stairs, the usual black portal was now static; the outside world flickering in and out of existence.

We move through the crowd and make our way to the stairs; Nardia intercepts and begins rushing with us.

"When did this start?" he asks, Nardia shakes her head.

"I don't know, one minute it was working and the next it began to do this. I don't know how long it's been doing it for, I only noticed when I looked out the window and thought it would be best retrieving you." he nods as he listens and I try to push the nausea away, I was walking way too fast. The crowd stands back and make way for us as we walk up the stairs, vaguely on the other side I can make out figures.

"Kal, can you see that?" I ask, pointing towards the closest one, the portal is still too blurry to make out any distinct features. The air around the portal is static and crackling with electricity, a hint of smoke in the air. I walk up to the portal and Kal places his hand on my arm. I look back at him, the muscle in his jaw twitches as he drops his hand.

"Be careful." he steps back and watches me. I nod once and continue through the portal. As I pass, a small spark of electricity courses through me; the hair on my arms stands up. As I blink in my surroundings I'm surprised by the humans standing there, over two dozen all have eyes for me.

"What are you guys doing here?" I ask, trying to find a familiar face. A tall man steps forward, his thin frame obvious in his loose torn clothes. He sweeps his shaggy brown hair out of his face.

"We've come looking for Allison. I'm Sam, and we're former members of the Order." he stands tall as he looks down at me, I raise an eyebrow and look back over the people. It strikes me then, they're terrified. Of what, I didn't know.

"Yes that's me. But why me?" I ask, the static in the air from the portal begins to grow dense; pushing against my back. I didn't have much time.

"Because you're our only hope. You want equality for both races and we're here to help the cause." He bows low, as do the others.

"You do know that's a city full of vampires in there right?" I say, pointing back towards the portal. They all nod.

"We can't go back to the camp, those who have stayed are going to war for this and we want to be on the right side." Sam straightens, puffing his chest out.

"Okay, give me a second." I immediately connect with Nardia down the bond.

The humans want to come into the city, seeking refuge. They can't go back to the camp, I think the rest of the Order are planning a war. The seconds that tick by seem like hours. Finally she responds.

They want to come in here? Full of vampires? She asks in disbelief.

Yes, I know it seems crazy but they're terrified to stay out here and this portal doesn't have much time. Can you talk to Kal please?

"Well?" Sam asks, looking around me.

"Oh sorry, mind communication thing. She's asking the King." A few eyes widen at my words and I'm reminded that no one apart from his inner circle knows who he really is; know how soft he is.

All clear, sending out a vampire that can chip them all so they can pass through.

I let out a sigh and step away from the portal. It shimmers as a small male vampire steps out, his greying hair shines in the sun. He hisses as he moves to a spot in the shade.

"Sorry about that folks, my old age gets to me. There's a few things you need to know, first is that you need a vampire activated chip to enter through the portal." He holds up a small silver diamond device.

"This is placed behind your left ear, it stings for a few moments but then it releases a numbing serum. Secondly, this does not stop the vampires from coming near you." He raises an eyebrow as he looks over his glasses.

Sam steps forward and falls to his knees.

"I'll go first." He turns his head and moves his hair out of the way. The vampire shrugs and uses his sharp nail to make a small cut behind Sam's ear before sliding the device in. Sam stands and instinctively touches behind his ear. Slowly the other humans form a single line, each falling to their knees. I guide Sam through the portal, holding his hand as we pass.

He gasps as he takes in the city and I smile. I remember the first time I entered as well. All the vampires move back, but keep their eyes on the humans that begin to filter through.

I smile down at Kal, he smiles back. My dream was finally being put to the test. Nardia comes forward and greets Sam. Once all the humans and the vampire come through, Nardia introduces herself to each one, shaking their hand as she goes.

My chest fills with happiness, I couldn't be more proud of her.

"Alright, I need-" Nardia's interrupted by a thundering crack. Behind us the portal begins to glow bright, electric flame spits out at us.

"Get back!" I yell, pushing my way to the portal; pulling the humans behind me. Screaming begins to erupt as the air grows sweltering.

"Ali get back!" Zuriel yells from somewhere behind me, but I can't. A small girl is huddled on the ground in front of the portal. I reach her and wrap myself around her small frame; the skin on my back feels like it's melting from the portal.

We both scream as the portal breaks behind us. The blast is blocked by an invisible shield as the portal collapses in on itself and blinks out of existence.

I open my eyes as I sit back, the little girl cries. A woman runs forward and picks her up, tears streaming down her face. She thanks me over and over but the ringing from the portal blocks it out. She helps me stand, I walk towards the end of the platform; Kal runs up and grabs me by the shoulders gently, he asks me something as he searches my face.

I turn and show him my back.

As I turn back his eyes are wide, it must be bad. I lean my head against his chest as I take deep breaths, relaxing the muscles.

He strokes my hair, and hums to me. I'd saved that little girl, and that was all that mattered to me.

33

Kalabhiti

I take in my surroundings and I'm taken aback, I now have over two dozen humans in my city and no portal to the outside world. Ali leans back and I look down at her; her eyes are clear now but God her back is covered in small blisters and a bright red.

"I need to address everyone, can you find Nardia and help get the humans to the closest hotel. Can you do that?" I brush the hair back from her eyes, she nods a few times and steps back. She turns and slips into the crowd of humans; one of them offers her their jumpers. I turn to the city of vampires and clear my throat.

"Attention everyone," I call, my voice raises and echoes around the space. The murmurs and crying quieten as everyone focuses on me.

"It's obvious the portal has broken, and there are humans needing our refuge. We can't turn them away; while they are here they're under my protection. Each one of them that's stepped through the portal is mine and if anything happens to them you have me to answer to.

"Our scientists are going to be working on fixing the portal as soon as possible; figuring out why it's gone and what it's done. Worse-case scenario we have to create a new portal, which might take weeks to become stable." gasps echo around us, some people yell out at me. I raise my hand to silence them.

"There is a new world on the horizon and we will be a part of it. We will be a reason why both races can unite. This is our ultimate test; if we cannot learn to coexist peacefully with the humans, our race is doomed. This world cannot be ruled by a sole species; together is the only way to end this war.

"I know I have changed tremendously over the few hundred years that have passed, but the change is for the better. I need you all to be on our side and to unite. What do you say?" I yell, raising a hand. The crowd erupts in agreeance.

"I can't hear you!" I scream. They raise their hands and scream *yes* back to me. The humans cheer behind me as the vampires clap. I turn back to see the humans following Ali and Nardia to the hotel on the corner but they watch the vampires warily.

I'm about to turn back to the space where the portal once was when I hear a scream, I frown as I turn back towards the crowd. My heart plummets as I see flickers of white filtering through the tree line in the forest.

The creatures break through, hundreds filtering out; their screams pierce the air.

War is coming.

34

Allison

I look towards the screaming and my jaw falls open; hundreds of half vampire creatures bound towards us, their figures almost a blur with their speed.

They can smell the humans.

"Hurry! Follow me!" I scream as I run towards the hotel. I wrench open the doors to a stunned vampire assistant behind her desk. The humans file in, not understanding what's going on.

Nardia comes up behind them, "That's all of them." I nod as she heads back outside.

"You need to get in the elevator and go up a few flights, stick together. Do not come outside unless I or Nardia come and get you." I push them towards the elevator.

"What are those things?" Sam asks, holding open the elevator doors as a load full climb in.

"Floor five." Sam says, nodding at them.

"I'm not sure, they're turned vampires gone wrong. Since you're all human you're all at risk, please don't be brave," I say, tapping my foot as the carriage begins to come back down.

"We won't go anywhere. I'll make sure of it." we both rush more people in. The female vampire comes over and raises an eyebrow.

"What on earth are you doing?" she asks, looking over the humans.

"We're under attack and the portal to escape is broken, the humans cannot leave this building. Okay? Protect them, please." she rolls her eyes and waits for the last few to pile on.

"Can you help me barricade the doors then?" She asks Sam, sucking on her bottom lip. He nods.

"Alright, I'll be back. Be safe. Thank you so much again." I run out of the hotel and into pure chaos. I look back to make sure they lock the doors, they begin to push furniture against the door.

I frantically look around for Kal, not finding him or anyone else familiar. All around me the vampires begin to form a curved wall, the ones at the front flicker their display of powers. I stand there in awe as purple, blue and orange bright flames begin to form a barrier as the front vampire's fuel their powers together.

I breathe in the thick air, full of tension; my headache and aching bones and sore back long forgotten. The white creatures are nearly upon us now, their screams pierce my ears. I rally my power to the surface, wrapping lasso like strands around my hands.

Some vampires shape shift, others grow larger, a female bristles beside me as her skin turns to stone. I don't know what sort of vampires they are but they are not like the story book ones.

I spot Nardia's fiery hair at the front line, talking to a man that had turned green with bright yellow funnelling out of his hands.

This was incredible and if death wasn't so close I would be in awe.

The first wave of creatures hit the shield, they shriek as they're burnt and thrown back. The closest ones shrivel up and turn to stiff charcoal figures as they drop to the ground. The others don't relent and the shield begins to dim.

"Be ready!" Kal's voice thunders out over the crowd, I don't take my eyes off the barrier that is our only protection. My mouth fills with the taste of blood as my heart beat is the only noise I can hear. Sweat beads run down my forehead.

The barrier shutters once.

Twice.

Collapses.

I move through the thick crowd, my eyes wide as I pass three vampires that are joined; their bodies turned into that of animals. The creatures dive towards the first line of vampires, I see Nardia take down the five that are upon her but they're too fast. Slowly, they begin to intercept the crowd, growing ever closer to the hotel. The air rings with screams and fills with the smell of blood as the battle intensifies.

Now was the time to put my power to the test.

I rush forward and push past vampires closest to me, six creatures surround two males; their power was only weak, sending out small lightning bolts to keep them at bay.

I swing my hands towards the creatures and extend my lasso, capturing three in each hand. I squeeze and throw my arms behind me; the creatures squeal as they're thrown back through the air. As I turn two others come at me, I shield my face with my forearm; the creature sinks its long fangs into the skin, grazing the bone.

A scream rips from my throat as I lose hold of my power over the other six. They all come for me, the smell of my blood driving them wild. I throw my head back and scream as my power glows under my skin before exploding from my body, tearing the creatures apart. Body pieces scatter around me; I lower my bloody arm and flex my fingers.

Before I have a chance to recover, three more hurtle towards me, screaming and snapping. A female vampire jumps in front of me; her jaw dislocates and extends down to her stomach. Razor sharp teeth grow outwards. She screams as her jaw wraps itself around one creature; snapping it in half. Blood sprays against me, covering my face.

My power acts on its own accord as it rushes towards the last two, diving straight through their eyes and into their skull; their heads explode in a matter of seconds.

I gasp for breath as I look around, vampires and creatures lay dead around me. Where is Kal and the others? In answer I spot Kal and Cassidy fighting side by side across the clearing, her flames glow against Kal's shadows. Kal's shadows devour the creatures while Cassidy's flame burns them to a crisp. Sensing me, Kal looks towards me, his eyes widen and then I see the shadow fall over me from above.

I dive out of the way as a creature lands where I was standing moments ago. I crawl back as it comes for me; my hands slipping on blood and guts. I bump into a male, he smirks down at me. I watch in fascination as he extends his hand, sending out ice and freezing the creature. He pulls me up before turning back to the mess.

My body is in overdrive with adrenaline and I can barely think straight.

I look back towards the hotel and gasp, over twenty creatures had begun to climb the hotel; no doubt sniffing out the humans. I run back, jumping and sidestepping the others as I go.

I hold up my hands as I come closer and wrap the blue tendrils around the highest creatures, I send them through the ground with a loud crack. The ones on the ground turn to me and lunge. I duck as one jumps and twirl around the next. I pick up a broken metal pole and fight them off as I make my way to the closed door. I stab the closest one through the mouth as it flies at me; I kick its body from the pole and swing it sideways, connecting with the skull of another one.

I was going to need help, I couldn't fight them on my own and still had to get the last few from the hotel down. My power begins to weaken, becoming less and less visible. I look around frantically for help. I blink and suddenly there are six versions of Zeke surrounding me and fighting off the creatures.

"Oh God, thank you." I whisper, half wanting to cry and laugh. The closest Zeke nods and flashes me a quick smile, I look up and use the last pieces of my power to pull down the remaining creatures; sending them flying right in the path for the ice vampire. They freeze mid air before falling and shattering like glass around us. My arm throbs and pain shoots up to my head, I hope their bites weren't poisonous.

A Zeke turns towards me and comes closer, gently looking over my arm. He clicks his tongue as he assesses the damage.

"I don't know how much I have left in me," I say weakly. The adrenaline had worn off and now my body and mind were crashing.

"Come on, I'll take you somewhere safe." He wraps an arm around me. I nearly oblige until I see Kal in the middle of the thickest part of the white creatures.

He stands deathly still as black mist begins to spill from his very form.

Kalabhiti

As soon as the creatures swarmed upon us I lost sight of Ali, only glimpsing her here and there locked in battle with these filthy creatures. The blood in my veins sings with each blow, each death. I haven't been in a battle like this for over three hundred years, and it is painfully exciting to me.

I twirl around Cassidy and slice my blade through the closest two creatures. When I first saw them coming I'd quickly winnowed to grab my sword; it had been too long since it last tasted the rush.

I make my way through to the front where the carnage is the worst, the air thick with death. These things had one purpose and that was to get to those few humans.

I send my shadows out, letting them consume the ones closest to me. Someone had set this up, it's too much of a coincidence for humans to show up, enter the city, have the portal break and then we're attacked by creatures purely driven for human blood.

I wanted more than anything to find and protect Allison, our training sessions would need to be increased after this. I just hope and pray that she is okay.

Now behind a majority of the creatures, I yell out to them, they turn and rush towards me. Under the surface of my skin I can feel that sick, ancient power I possess. We can't keep fighting them head on like this, we'll lose too many. I have to make a sacrifice; I just hope Ali will be able to forgive me for the man I truly am.

I hold out my hands and begin to chant under my breath, the ground starts to shake under my feet as I call forward to the darkest nightmares I could create.

Black mist seeps from my skin, surrounding the white creatures. The vampires scurry backwards; they know exactly what I'm doing. What I am.

Fascinated, the creatures stop their assault and look around blindly. As my chant grows I hold out my hands. I blink slowly and am possessed by the ancient power I'd been cursed to walk this earth with.

My body hums as my eyes glow; the mist thickens and swallows the creatures. I clench my fist and close my eyes, consumed by the hunger.

Large black shadows grow from the mist, their white gleaming teeth the only colour these beings hold. They grow in numbers as they wait for my order. Their anticipation heightens. I hold my sword above my head and plunge it into the ground, breaking the last barrier that is holding my power back.

It explodes from me with a ferociousness so fierce I fear for those white creatures, for my shadows never have mercy. The screaming begins; I stay still as the onslaught continues. My jaw twitches.

I try to desperately grasp onto the person I'd become, but the person I had once been is far too strong. My mind darkens, and I break.

I raise my head and look around; it has been such a long time since I have tasted fresh air. I grin as I take in the battle around me; the screams are like a symphony to my ears. My shadows make quick work, starved from the fight for too long.

The mist begins to dissipate into the ground as I prowl towards the others, only a handful of white creatures remain now and are being handled accordingly.

A girl begins to run towards me, an unfamiliar face but with the eyes of Cassidar. I cock my head to the side as she comes to a stop a few metres in front of me. Her red eyes are stunning as she looks me over, her breathing is ragged and I smell the blood.

Her blood.

Human blood.

36

Allison

I hesitate, not wanting to step any closer to Kal. His eyes seem sharper, he's standing taller and there's this aura about him that I'd never felt before.

"Kal?" I ask, nibbing the inside of my cheek. My hands clench and unclench as I resist the urge to run to him and wrap my arms around him to make sure he's real.

As soon as I lost sight of him the screaming began, I thought I'd lost him. I couldn't take my eyes from the mist, not while he was in there.

"And who might you be?" he asks; his voice deeper than usual. He comes towards me with predator grace. He walks a circle around me, studying me.

"Allison." I keep my head high as he comes to a stop in front

237

of me. Everyone around us is silent, no one daring to interfere with whoever this man is.

"I don't know anyone by that name. You're human," he states, raising an eyebrow as his eyes narrow. I take a step back.

"You don't remember me?" he turns his head away from me and looks over the crowd before looking back to me.

"No." His answer is blunt but doesn't stop the sting I feel. I have to make him remember who I am, what we have. Who he is.

"Let me jog your memory." I take a small step forward; I hear the hints of a growl in the back of his throat. This could damn well get me killed.

"We first met at a human camp; you trapped me in your shadows to see if I was really Cassidar's descendent; which I am. After a lot of bullshit I came here and you took me under your wing, you helped pull me out of the hell I had created for myself and you showed me the light." I take another step forward, raising my hands to let him know I'm not going to do any harm. He doesn't say anything, so I continue.

"We danced together when I met the other important vampires in the ball room, I slept in your bed that night and you held me as I fell asleep."

"Impossible," he says, but his voice is low and his eyes are bright with confusion. He's fighting whatever has hold of him.

"Not impossible in the slightest. I had to go away for a bit and when I returned you helped me shower, where we gave each other mate marks." I push my hair out of the way and expose the flesh where he'd marked. I hold my breath as he closes the distance between us; he touches the mark before feeling his own neck. I look up into his eyes, silently begging for him to come back to me.

"You are Kal and you are my King and my better half in every sense. I need my Kal back, so do your people." I place my hands on his chest, it doesn't move up and down like Kal would make it.

"Why?" His answer is so soft I nearly miss it. But I don't. I take a deep breath and gather my courage.

"Because I love you, Kalabhiti." the words cement in the air around us, I hear a few gasps behind me. This was the first time I'd admitted it out loud and to myself.

"I loved a human girl once." He looks down at me sadly, my cheeks burn and I want to cry. He hadn't said it back.

"I sliced her throat and watched her bleed out on my white fur carpet." his jaw twitches as he looks away and I drop my hands, they shake as I stare at him. His jaw twitches and he frowns. He hadn't told me anything about this before and I doubt he ever will again.

"Why?" I whisper, needing a good answer.

"Because I didn't deserve her and I was putting her through hell, so I killed her because I don't know mercy and I am not a good man." he looks back towards me; the wind brushes a few stray strands from his face.

"That is how I got this scar." He tilts his head and runs a finger along the thin scar I'd always been fascinated with. I feel sick to my stomach.

He takes a step towards me and I flinch but keep my feet planted on the ground. He smiles down at me; nothing kind in his eyes.

"Do you see now Allison? Do you finally see this can never work? I am not good for you." his hand comes to my face and he strokes my cheek, wiping away a single tear.

"You're not the same person you were all those years ago. I know you, Kal. You are a good man in my eyes and those around you." Before I can let my brain stop me from what I'm about to do, I wrap my arms around his neck and force my lips to his.

He tastes of sweat and blood, but I don't stop, not when he parts his lips for my tongue. Not as he wraps his arms around my waist and pulls me closer. I reach up and stroke my thumbs across his cheeks. As I hold his face, tears run down them. He holds me tightly, using me as his hold on reality.

I pull back and wipe my own tears away. "Please come back to me Kal," I whisper. My bottom lip wobbles and it finally dawns on me how much I need him. He shuts his eyes and leans his forehead against mine. Minutes seem to tick into hours as we stand there. No one around us makes a move, watching fascinated to see if his beast can be tamed.

His chest begins to move up and down again and I melt into him with relief. He wraps an arm around me and raises his hand.

Silently they all raise their hands, uniting us all as one. Bodies of vampires and creatures litter the street around us, the damage minimal to what it could have been if Kal hadn't stepped in and taken charge.

The once grey cobblestone street now shines bright red, Nardia rushes forwards; her arms are littered with cuts.

"Oh my god, thank god you're both okay!" she wraps both of us in a hug and I wince, remembering the bite mark. She reluctantly lets go and steps back.

"We'll need to get everyone who's injured to the emergency rooms, get them patched up. Can you get Zuriel and Zeke on the case as to why the portal has disappeared and if the attack has anything to do with it please?" Kal asks, looking down at my arm.

"Yeah of course, I'll keep you updated." Nardia begins to call out orders to everyone. One by one they begin to pick up broken street items, their dead loved ones. The injured follow Nardia.

"Can you patch my arm up?" I ask, holding it against my body. "And my back also?" the jumper irritates the raw skin on my back.

"Of course, come. We'll head back to my apartment and we'll both get cleaned up." he sweeps me into his arms; I rest my head against his shoulder and shut my eyes. My entire body aches and

I'm left wondering if Kal remembers what I'd said to him.

37

Allison

I smile down at my sketch proudly; I'd drawn up a blood donation bank so the vampires had no reason to attack the humans now living amongst them. Unfortunately, my blood is tainted so I can't donate, and the humans only have to donate two litres once a month. I wish I had more humans who would help and try and see if this world can work together.

"Kal! I'm done!" I call from the dining room. He comes in; flour covers his apron and his cheeks. He walks over and looks down at the drawing; smiling.

"That could just work. Good job." he kisses the top of my head. He walks back into the kitchen to continue making his brownies. I relax back into the chair and tap the pencil against the table.

It has only been a few days since the battle took place but so much has happened. I'd found a nice hotel for the humans to stay in that was also mixed with vampires.

A part of me was scared to leave them alone but this could be the only way I'll learn if we can coexist with each other. After Kal had bandaged my arm up we'd gone back to the disaster and helped collect the dead creatures. We started a large bonfire in the middle of the forest to clear the bodies.

We'd only lost a few handfuls of vampires but I'd made it my own personal mission to go to each family and thank them for their sacrifice.

The blood donation bank was going to be along the main city street, and once that was operational it would be time to start looking into getting the humans jobs and setting up a small shop for them to get food and whatever else might be needed.

Kal comes back in, apron gone. He picks up the drawing and looks it over.

"Do you think they'll mind donating blood?" he asks, sitting it back down.

"It's their payment for their apartments. Eventually we'll have to help them get jobs but I've run it past them already and they all agreed. I made the age limit over eighteen, there's only a few children." I'd thought this plan over a million times, now it was just waiting to see if it worked that put me on edge.

"You sound like you're all over it love." he begins to massage my shoulders and I groan, shutting my eyes.

"That feels so nice, my whole body is aching," I murmur, enjoying the contact. He chuckles and continues to massage along my shoulders and up the back of my neck.

"Why don't we celebrate tonight?" his hands stop moving but don't leave me.

"Mmm that sounds good, just us?" I lean my head back and open my eyes, I supress a yawn as I raise an eyebrow at him.

"Tonight it will be just us and tomorrow night I'll get everyone else over, how does that sound?" he raises an eyebrow in turn.

"That sounds good to me, do you even have alcohol here?" I

ask, sitting back up straight again. His hands drop from my shoulders and I follow him into the sitting room. He opens a small cabinet beside the fire and reveals three bottles of liquid.

"It's just the stuff you were drinking the other night, but I'm sure you'll enjoy it more this time around." he pulls out two glasses and the bottle. I make myself comfy on the couch; the fire crackles and warms the space around us.

He passes me a full glass before taking a seat beside me. I manoeuvre on the couch, rest my head on his lap and hold the glass on my stomach.

His free hand strokes my hair as he sips his drink; I lean up slightly and sip mine. The effects don't hit me as hard this time, and I am not drinking as much as I did the other night.

"How's your arm feeling?" he asks. I yawn this time.

"It's sore but I keep it moving to make sure it doesn't go stiff." I hold my left arm up. The middle of my forearm is bandaged, which I change every day to make sure it stays clean.

"Good."

"Kal, I've thought about your offer for me to be Queen." I look up at him; he looks down at me and quirks his lips. My eyes trace the thin scar, he tenses under me and his hand stops moving in my hair.

"And?"

"Yes, I'll be your queen," I say simply. I look back towards the fire. It crackles and spits out small flames. I think I knew all along I was going to say yes to the offer. Especially when I know it's going to help so many people.

"Are you sure it's what you want?" he asks, drawing my attention back to him. I sit up and quickly gulp down my drink, I sit the empty glass on the floor and turn and face him. He stares blankly at me and I know he has his shield up. I reach out and rest my hands on his arm.

"I've never been surer of something in my life. I would like to wait a few more months though, just to see how the human and vampires go together." I bite my bottom lip and look over his face.

"I agree, we'll wait a little longer and hopefully everything runs smoothly." he looks away from me and back to the fire, he finishes the rest of his drink. I lean down and place mine on the ground. I reach out and comb his hair back from his face, savouring how smooth it feels.

"Can I kiss you?" I blurt. He looks over at me and my cheeks heat. He smiles and nods. I climb onto his lap slowly, making myself comfortable. His hands reach up and cup my face, bringing it down to his.

I close my eyes as our lips connect and the sparks fly between us, my whole body has missed his touch. I reach up and wrap my arms loosely around his neck; I pull back and nip at his bottom lip.

His eyes shine as he looks at me, his hands roam over my back and rest on my hips.

"I could get used to that," I say, smiling dumbly at him. He rolls his eyes but smiles; he pouts his lips and makes a kissy noise. I lean forward and kiss him, opening my mouth lightly. I pull myself closer to him so my body is flush against his, his hands now cup my ass; his thumb stroking the thin material of my pants.

I bite down on his bottom lip and he moans low in his throat, my fangs ache to come out again and mark him and taste him, but I refrain. I begin to move my hips against him; I run my hands down his chest and marvel at the muscle he possesses.

I clear my throat as my hand dips lower, sliding into his pants. He arches into my hand as I wrap it around the length of him, I pull back and look at him with wild eyes; panting. He looks equally as wild.

He moves us in a flash, laying me on my back on the couch. I remove my hand and tug at my shirt; wanting it off. He obliges and his fangs come out. He grabs the material with his mouth and rips the shirt in half.

He stares down at my bare chest and takes deep breaths, his hand reaches up and cups my right breast; he rubs his thumb over it gently. I groan as I push my hips against his, feeling the pressure and pleasure building.

His hair falls down around us as he leans down and kisses me with such force it make me breathless, I run my hands under his shirt and down his back.

"I need more," I beg, pulling away from the kiss. He is conflicted as he looks down at me.

"Ali…" he gulps; his apple Adam bobs up and down.

"Kal, please," I groan, puffing my bottom lip out. He always had to be responsible, why can't he just let go and give in to me.

"Not tonight, I want that first experience to be special for you. Not on a couch while you're sore." I open my mouth to complain, he brings a finger up to my lips to silence me.

"Ah ah ah, we won't do that tonight but I can give you more in other ways." my eyes widen as he grins at me wickedly.

He spends the next few hours of the night giving me just that.

38

Allison

"Do you want to make a quick trip to see the humans? They fixed the portal today, so if any are having second thoughts they're welcome to leave." Kal massages my shoulders as I sit on the couch and sigh. I wanted a nap and a back rub but that was far from happening at the moment. Two things are also irking at my mind. I haven't been able to use my power and Kal has kept things platonic for the most part; showing me small bits of affection here and there and sending me absolutely wild last night. I'm afraid he knows what I've said and doesn't feel the same.

"Yeah?" he asks again, pulling me from my thoughts.

"Yeah let's go but I need a nap after this pronto." I stand up and stretch my legs. I wish there was a way to get to the city without having to run. I follow him out of the castle and towards the forest.

"Can we talk while we get there?" I ask, jogging beside him.

"Yeah of course. What's on your mind?" I have no idea how to put my thoughts into a sentence he'd understand.

"Okay well we haven't spoken about what happened to you or the conversation we had while you were whatever you were. I know you're not that person anymore Kal, but that human girl you killed because you loved her... has she been the only one?" I clench my fists as he picks up the pace, not wanting him to see my shaky hands.

"Yes she's the only one. Can we talk about this tonight? We've both had a very big few days and I don't have the energy to bring up the past at the moment." he sighs and rubs his face quickly; the shadows under his eyes don't go unnoticed.

"Yeah okay, sorry. You know I'm here if you ever need to talk about anything," I say softly. The city lights begin to blink in through the forest ahead of us. We stay silent the rest of the way and I only feel worse about bringing it up.

The hotel we'd picked out for the humans is down a side street in a very well-lit area. We come to a stop in front of the large old style hotel; Sam walks out and spots us and waves, coming over.

"Hey guys, what're you up to?" he asks, pulling his jumper tighter around him. The winter breeze doesn't escape us here.

"Just coming to check on everyone. The portal is up and running again and we were just coming to make the offer that any of you can leave if you want," I say, stuffing my hands into my pocket.

"That's kind of you but it's best we don't leave. If they know we've come here and decide to go back we'll all be dead. Plus, you guys aren't bad to live with at all." He shakes his head as he says this, I'm about to launch into questions when something pulls at my mind. I frown and look around.

Kal continues to talk to Sam. I shake my head and go to ask a question when it pulls again; stronger this time. I don't say anything as I follow the pull. It leads me from the street and towards the portal.

I frown as I keep walking, I know I should stop and get Kal because this has never happened before but curiosity gets the best of me; like always.

I walk up the white stairs and towards the blackness of the new portal. I stop in front of it as it begins to shimmer into focus, the pull is stronger here and I stagger forwards.

I couldn't control my own feet.

"Kal!" I cry out, trying to stop my feet from walking forward. I was closer now, I could reach out and touch it if I wanted. I resist the urge as my right foot drags forward.

"Ali? What's going on?" he yells out behind me. I look back over my shoulder and I see the panic on his face.

"Kal please!" I shout. As he begins to run towards me, the force yanks and a scream rips from me as I'm thrown through the portal.

I land on my face and skid across the grass, the sun does nothing to stop the cold wind. I get to my knees and look up; to my horror the assistant from Penrith and Xavier sit on a grobbler each.

"Have you missed me?" The assistant grins, his grobbler screeches as it breaks my last mental barrier; sending me into darkness.

Kalabhiti

The portal blocks me momentarily before I can go through, Sam comes running up behind me. Panic floods every sense in my body.

"What happened?" he asks, looking around for Allison.

"Get Nardia and get the others, hurry." I say over my shoulder before going through the portal. I hiss at the exposure of the sun and shield my eyes. I open them and growl.

Xavier sits on a grobbler, shotgun aimed at my chest. I look towards the other man; I hadn't seen him before. He's dressed in a white suit which isn't practical on a grobbler.

Between them, Ali is on her knees, staring at me with lifeless eyes. Tear tracks stain her cheeks. I feel my shadows begin to emerge, thick and angry. How dare they take my mate.

"Let her go or so help me," I snarl, fangs ripping through my gums. All rational reasoning wants to leave me and let the anger swallow me and tear them apart.

"Now, now you wild beast. Sweet little Allison here is coming with us. If you make any sudden movements Xavier will blow your brains out," the man says cheerfully. He hops down from the grobbler and stands behind Ali. She blinks slowly, her arms are still by her side but I see her fingers twitch.

He reaches into his pocket and pulls out a small knife.

He presses the blade to her throat. I hear a small tear in her skin. I growl and take a step forward, a tree splinters behind me from Xavier's gunshot.

"That was a warning, I don't miss twice," he says, pointing it back to me. Behind me I feel the others. I couldn't let them take her.

No. No. No.

Nardia comes through first, "What on earth is…" She trails off as she sees Ali, I feel her rush forward; I reach out and block her as Xavier trains the gun on her.

"Leave her the fuck alone!" she yells. Zeke, Zuriel and Cassidy file out after her and all freeze behind us.

"Now we can do this the easy way or the hard way. She won't come to you; by all means you can try," the man says, holding the knife steady. The beast in me wants to rip this man's curly blonde hair from his head and make him choke on it.

"What are you doing here?" Zeke asks, coming to stand beside me. He growls as the assistant smiles.

"Oh how ironic this is!" he begins to clap his hands, a small relief comes from the blade not being near Ali's throat. Ali's eyes stare at us, momentarily they flicker to the grobbler beside her.

"You know him?" I ask, looking at Zeke out of the corner of my eye.

"Yes. This is the assistant from Allison's village. He was the

251

one that killed my sister and stabbed Zuriel." Zeke's face darkens at the memory, the assistant looks so happy.

"Yes, indeed. How sad is it though, I had you and she saved you but now that the tables have turned you can't save her. Who knew I'd be a bigger problem."

"Ali babe, you need to come here right now," Nardia pleads. The man grins as he moves back. Nardia shuts her eye and I can only assume that she's trying to speak with Ali. She looks at me helplessly.

"She isn't under your control anymore," Xavier says, aiming it at me. I don't take my eyes off of her.

The front of her shirt is covered in dirt and pieces of grass.

"She never was. She chose to do everything she's done of her own accord," I say calmly. If I can be rational they might leave and not take her with them.

"And now she's been crafted into a weapon, she comes here and you train her and teach her how to use that power. You make her strong, near immortal. You forgot one minor detail though…" Xavier trails off as the other man's beast comes forward and my heart plummets as I realise what has happened.

Ali has grobbler blood in her system.

It shrieks and pins its eyes on me. Ali stands robotically; her body tries to resist the grobbler's silent command.

Her legs falter as she steps into a fighting stance, the one I'd shown her all too well. Her eye twitches and her mouth half opens.

The assistant puts his blade in her outstretched hand.

"Aim true," he whispers into her ear. She doesn't hesitate as she sends the blade flying towards me. Nardia's hand flies out before it can hit me. It breaks through the skin and she holds back from crying out. Zuriel and Cassidy step forward, snarling.

"You see, now that we have Ali everything is going to change. She will be the new face of our revolution and no one will know the true reason behind it. We will guide her into the light and use her in the way you chose not to. If you even try to follow us we will kill her without hesitation, or we'll make her kill you." he climbs back onto the grobbler. They don't need to shackle her; she'll be following them willingly by whatever hold the beasts have over her.

"We will be seeing you again, and your poor little Ali will not be the same creature you see now," Xavier says. The grobblers begin to screech; pacing impatiently. The world around me begins to spin as Ali's eyes focus on me one last time.

She turns away from us and begins to walk forward. Her movements are smooth; whatever fight she had left in her is gone.

They charge off into the forest and I fall to my knees. I don't hear what the others say as I lose sight of her, the one person who had made me feel human again. The girl who had shown me the light in my life of darkness.

They had taken the only thing that was holding me together, they had taken my Queen. I stare off in the direction they left, a defeated man.

I was not a vampire king.

Without my Queen, I was the King of Immortal Suffering.

Books by Shana J. Caldwell

Immortal Series

Immortal Awakening
Immortal Suffering
Immortal Reckoning
Behind the Immortals

Enchantment of Darkness

Shana J. Caldwell is an Australian self-published author, who is either knee deep in reading or crouched over her laptop with her trusty cat, Luna, as her writing companion.

Follow Shana on:

Connect with her online:

Facebook.com/shanajcaldwell/
Twitter.com/ShanaJCaldwell1
Instagram.com/shanajcaldwell
https://shanacaldwell03.wixsite.com/website

www.ingramcontent.com/pod-product-compliance
Lightning Source LLC
Chambersburg PA
CBHW020129120726
47903CB00007B/2170